Thank you so much for joining the tour, Shana! Hope you enjoy the book! :)

THE
SHAPE OF
TIME

R Caleja

P. S. Your Insta feed is so fun! I love the way you smoothly alternate color schemes! It's seriously cool!

RYMWORLD ARCANA BOOK ONE

THE SHAPE OF TIME

AMULET BOOKS • NEW YORK

Cataloging-in-Publication Data has been applied for and may be obtained from the Library of Congress.

ISBN 978-1-4197-5988-8

Text © 2023 Ryan Calejo
Interior illustrations © 2023 Julia Iredale
Book design by Chelsea Hunter

Printed and bound in U.S.A.
10 9 8 7 6 5 4 3 2 1

Amulet Books are available at special discounts when purchased in quantity for premiums and promotions as well as fundraising or educational use. Special editions can also be created to specification. For details, contact specialsales@abramsbooks.com or the address below.

ABRAMS The Art of Books
195 Broadway, New York, NY 10007
abramsbooks.com

To Maggie Lehrman, my wonderful editor,
for her wisdom, kindness, and endless enthusiasm

——————— ● ———————

ALL MY LIFE I've been obsessed with a world I never thought I'd find.

A place way out on the edge of everything, beyond the seas, beyond the sky. A phantom paradise haunting my sleepless dreams—the antidote to some great lie poisoning my mind.

Rymworld, Rymworld, Rymworld.

Even the wind seemed to whisper its name.

Rymworld.

CHAPTER ONE

---•---

THE HEART OF THE SCORPION

I guess I should start by telling you that this is a story of impossible things and impossible places. If you aren't willing to accept the impossible as possible—or even *plausible*—then you should probably stop reading this story, because you won't believe anything in it.

My name is Antares de la Vega. My parents named me after the brightest star in the Scorpius constellation, and no kid deserves to grow up with that kind of pressure.

I'm not saying it's the *only* reason for what's wrong with me, but it certainly didn't help any. See, I got a problem. I get these sort of . . . *panic attacks*. A pounding, pinching pressure in my temples; a slimy, sickly sweat breaking out over my hands and face.

And the next thing I know, I'm drowning in fear so intense it feels like I'm being swallowed by quicksand.

Once, it got so bad that I even blacked out and woke up floating twenty-two miles off the coast of Bal Harbour Beach, Florida, in some little fiberglass dinghy, sunburned, dehydrated, just barely clinging to an empty bottle of Mountain Dew—and my life.

I spent eight days at Mercy Hospital down in Bay Heights, getting better. My aunt took away my bike, my bus pass, my Metro-rail card, and basically forbade me from ever stepping foot on a boat again. It was probably the toughest two weeks of my life.

Anyway, the reason I'm bringing up my panic attacks is because they're part of my story. Not a huge part. But an important part.

The attacks come because I get scared.

And what scares me more than anything is not knowing.

Don't think I'm some kind of trivia geek or anything, because I'm not.

I don't have an unquenchable thirst to know every little fact about every little thing that's ever happened in the world.

I couldn't give an owl's hoot about who hit the most home runs in 1986 or the proper scientific classification for earthworms.

The only thing I want to know, *yearn* to know—burn with a gigantic and irresistible *need* to know!—is what's out there. On the other side of things. Wherever that other side might be . . .

My biggest wish, as far back as I can remember, was for the chance to explore some unexplored place.

It didn't matter where that place was. Only that it was out there, undiscovered, and that I'd discovered it.

Both my parents were professional cartographers, so that might have something to do with it. They traveled all over the world, surveying every hidden nook and every secret cranny this planet had to offer.

Maybe if my mom and dad were still around, they could take me with them. I could see the world and wouldn't feel so anxious anymore.

Maybe.

But it was just me and my aunt Celeste now.

A Coast Guard patrol boat rescued me that day out in the middle of the glittering sunbaked Atlantic. Twelve real-life coasties in navy blue aboard a sleek gunmetal-gray cutter. If it wasn't for them, I probably wouldn't be around right now.

It's funny—I remember my aunt being extremely relieved and the sailors being extremely confused.

"What were you doing on that floating sardine can?" they'd asked me. "How did you end up all the way out here?" they wanted to know.

So I told them the truth: "I don't remember."

Because I *didn't* remember climbing into that rusty, sorry excuse for a boat, and I *didn't* remember rowing out past the sparkling edge of Biscayne Bay, and I *definitely* didn't remember passing out with my arms wrapped tightly around the plastic belly of an empty soda bottle.

All I remembered was an overwhelming urge to reach the hazy horizon way off in the distance and discover what lay beyond.

My aunt never asked me any questions about that day. She knew why I was on the dinghy. My aunt knows all about my panic attacks.

She's known about them since they first started, way back when I was only eight years old. Six years ago now. But she swears it's perfectly normal.

"You'll grow out of it," she assures me in that sweet, sympathetic voice of hers. "As a matter of fact, I used to feel the *exact* same way when I was your age! Everyone in the family probably has."

Like the attacks were hereditary or something. Kind of like bad back acne, or our family's brownish-blond hair and heterochromia.

I'd found this really cool way of dealing with my anxiety, though. And it always worked, too. Actually, I take that back . . . It *almost* always worked.

My secret weapon? Paperbacks.

That's right—*books*.

If you've ever had asthma, you know just how important it is to have your inhaler handy. Well, books are my inhaler. Fantasy. Science fiction.

Action and Adventure. I love it all, and I always carry at least one book with me everywhere I go.

That way if—or more like *when*—an attack suddenly seizes me, and I can't breathe, can't think, can't move, I'll whip out a book and start reading.

You probably think I'm messing around, but I'm not.

Books are the only thing that saves me—the *one* thing that can quiet my panicking mind and breathe calm back into my life again.

My birth sign is Gemini. I was born on May 31 under the pale glow of a waxing moon.

I know this because my aunt is into all sorts of superstitions and stuff. At least once a month she sits down to read my palm, going on and on about how strong my fate line is and how deep and long my heart line looks and how beautifully and unbrokenly my life line passes between Venus and the Plain of Mars.

According to her, all this superstitious mumbo-jumbo (my words, not hers) points to a single, undisputable conclusion: that I was destined for an interesting life—fated to explore.

I was pretty good at math—best in my grade, actually—but even I couldn't make that add up. Honestly, for the longest time, I've felt like a goldfish. A lonely little goldfish trapped inside an invisible glass prison. I spent most of my days staring sadly out at a world I couldn't ever seem to reach.

I'd convinced myself that I had been born on the wrong side of the planet, in the wrong century, under the wrong star, at the wrong—*everything*.

Little did I know, I was right where the universe wanted me: a sitting duck in the crosshairs of Fate . . .

CHAPTER TWO

DO PLANETS GROW ON TREES?

1

Fate came for me on a Friday, a school day—and exactly seven days, five hours, and thirty-two seconds after my fourteenth birthday. You'd think some all-knowing, all-powerful intergalactic force would pick a nice sunny day to show up on your doorstep and ring the bell. But I guess stuff like meteorological reports don't rank too highly on its list of important things.

The weather was just awful—and I'm talking even by South Florida rainy-season standards. A raging tropical storm was slamming into the east coast of the "Sunshine State," driving a mini monsoon up from Islamorada to Palm Beach.

The moment I climbed off the school bus and heard the distant rumble of thunder and smelled the rain and saw the mass of dark clouds gathering in the faraway sky like an armada of puffy black battleships, I sensed disaster looming. And it wasn't a nice feeling.

Now, for the record, I'm not a paranoid guy. But all morning long—from the second I'd rolled out of bed—I felt as if I was walking some invisible tightrope. As if a single, tiny misstep would send me plummeting off the face of the earth—would send me . . . *where?* Where exactly did you end up if you fell off the face of the earth?

Space?

Somewhere between Atlas's shoulder blades?

I didn't have the slightest clue.

But I still remember sitting there in first period, maybe fifteen minutes before the opening bell, staring uneasily up at Mrs. Laura's hanging solar system display and telling myself to chill.

That it was just a stupid feeling.

And *especially* the whole falling off the face of the earth part, because a) gravity didn't work like that, and b) Earth wasn't flat. It didn't have edges. Or ends. Or any giant granite cliffs jutting out into outer space. It was, as a matter of fact, *round.*

I mean, just look at it . . .

I remember thinking all that while gazing up at the big blue-and-green plaster globe some third grader had probably globbed together as a Youth Fair project.

And I remember—like I remember my own name—the first time I ever met one of *them.*

You know how people say the strangest things come in threes?

Well, they're *right* . . .

"A peculiar thing, isn't it?"

Surprised, I looked up to see a tall, sharply dressed man in a black turtleneck and coat looming over me. He had dark eyes and dark skin and a thick, dark beard around a wide, white smile.

His hair was long and his nose was short and rather pointy, and he was looking down it at the little plaster Earth even though it hung above him.

"An odd, perfectly spherical hunk of rock floating in an ever-expanding universe, which itself possesses roughly the same dimensions as that of a *pancake*." His face scrunched up like he'd smelled something funky. "What's more, it looks to me to be about the same shape as that of an *orange*. Now, I know oranges grow on trees—but do planets . . . ?"

I'd honestly never been asked such a ridiculous-sounding question. *Ever.* Which I guess probably explained the silly, *huh-what-where?* look on my face as I glanced around the room to see if anyone else was listening to this guy. But it was just me and him in here. It was still early.

"Perhaps your most trustworthy instincts will tell you to disregard this fantasy as mere science fiction," he continued smoothly. "And although I assure you that many already have, such models are not *entirely* without their usefulness . . ."

He began quickly rearranging the planets, shifting them around on the skinny PVC hanger until he had them all aligned just so. "The rarest of mutual planetary occultations," he murmured with darkly glittering eyes. "Neptune, Pluto, and Mercury, accompanied by a retrograde Mars, the transit of Venus, and the lunar node, Dragon's Tail, in ascendant, approaching perigee. Simultaneously occurring, but which I cannot demonstrate: a Triple Jovian eclipse, created by the aligning of three Galilean moons—Europa, Callisto, and Io—above the nebulous crown of the great gas giant."

He pointed at Jupiter with an air of cool satisfaction and the tip of a perfectly manicured fingernail.

"Do you recognize this conjunction?" he asked coolly.

I really didn't, and I really didn't even know what to say, so I just sort of sat there, blinking dazedly up at him and wondering who the heck this dude was and what the heck I'd done to deserve an impromptu, early-morning lesson on the solar system.

Then, as if reading my mind, the tall beaky-faced man grinned down at me and said, "My name is Mr. Now, by the way." He gestured over his shoulder. "See?"

Up at the front of the classroom, below the clock and above the teacher's desk, I could see his name scrawled across the small white marker board in big green letters. So naturally I just figured he was a substitute or something.

"Oh. Uh, well, we haven't gotten to space yet," I said, dragging the class textbook out of my backpack. "We're still on oceans."

Outside, the storm was raging. Lightning flashed and sizzled and streaked, and the ceiling lights buzzed and flickered and dimmed. It looked like there was a Category Five hurricane brewing out there. Only had I known what was really going on, I would've *wished* there was . . .

As he peered out the rain-splatted window, Mr. Now began nervously rubbing his chin. A strange silver ring glinted on his pinky finger. Engraved in it was something like Earth, but halved, and with a small reddish, bluish, greenish gem where the core would be.

"Well, it just so happens," he said, turning back to the hanging model, "that *this* particular cosmic occurrence occurred last night, at precisely three mintocks to midnight, and will not occur again for another threescore millennia. It is known, in the more civilized parts of this world, as *the Tetrinox*. Did you happen to catch it?"

When I told him that I hadn't, that I'd probably been asleep (and "What's a mintock?"), he basically ignored me. Those dark, searching eyes of his never left the little plaster planets as he said, "Astronomy has long been a favorite subject of mine . . . I believe there is much we can learn by studying the cosmos . . . the stars. In fact, for thousands of years cultures all over this world have believed that every single one of our destinies are written *right* above our heads. That those radiant, gaseous orbs are the very handwriting of *the gods* . . ." He paused, his sharp, probing gaze flicking back to me. "What do *you* believe?"

"What do I believe about *what*? Stars being *the handwriting of the gods*?" I shrugged, trying not to look at him funny. "I think—stars are just . . . *stars*."

"Ah, well, if that is indeed the case, then pray tell how is it that even an amateur astrologist can reveal to you the most *interesting* things about yourself with only a few mundane pieces of information?"

There was something mysterious in his voice, the whisper of some great secret, and I couldn't help but feel a tickle of intrigue as I said, "You're talking about horoscopes and stuff?"

He was. And that's when he started asking me all sorts of random-sounding questions.

How old are you?

What's your birth sign?

What's your favorite color? (Blue, in case you're wondering.)

Then, without any warning, he pulled a fat green marker from inside his coat pocket and began sketching all over my desk like a maniac pre-schooler who'd just run out of sketching paper.

"Dude, that's permanent marker!" I shouted. "You're gonna get me in *trouble*!"

But the tall, strange man with the dark, strange eyes drew, and he drew and he drew, and his fist got all sweaty and cramped looking, and the marker's felt tip squeaked and scribbled and blurred as it flew across the glossy plywood.

By the time he was finished, my desk was covered with circles inside of circles inside of bizarre symbols and perfectly drawn triangles.

I actually recognized what he'd drawn, too. It was a skymap. An ancient astrological chart that has something to do with the planets and the angles between them on certain days and times. I knew that thanks to my aunt. She had entire books dedicated to the stuff.

But right then, I was just hoping I wasn't gonna get busted for vandalizing school property.

Finally, Mr. Now put away the marker. Another wide grin split his lips as he said, "It was a pleasure to meet you, Antares."

And before I could blink or think or even open my mouth to ask where he was going, or—more *importantly*—how the heck he knew my name, he slipped silently out of the room, out into the busy, noisy hall, and was gone.

At that point, I was pretty sure my day couldn't get any weirder.

I mean, it was only first period, but *c'mon* . . .

As it turned out, though, I'd thought wrong.

I'd thought *very* wrong.

CHAPTER THREE

•

MR. NOW, MR. MINUTES, AND MR. HOURSBACK

Mr. Minutes was somehow even weirder than Mr. Now, and at first, I'd thought they were the *same person*! They both had the same pointy nose, the same long, skinny legs, the same knowing stare, and the same dark-ish blonde hair. But if you looked closely—like, *really* closely—you'd notice the crow's feet around his eyes and the laugh lines around his mouth, and you'd see his hair was a little grayer, and his skin was a little lighter, and so were his eyes, and you'd realize that he was older than Mr. Now. Though it was hard to tell by exactly how much.

Mr. Minutes blew into my third period history class as if blown in on the storm, introducing himself with a small bow and a grand sweep of his hand while he squelched and squished, scattering a heavy trickle of rainwater all over the muddy linoleum floors.

His dripping-wet rain hat he tossed onto Mrs. Gomez's projector. His dripping-wet raincoat he flung carelessly over her computer. His flooded rubber boots he drained into the small trash can in the corner, and his bright pink umbrella he stuck in there, too.

Then, after giving us a quick weather update ("It's raining fishes and frogs, I tell you!"), he began rooting noisily around inside this huge leather doctor's bag that looked like something straight out of the Mary Poppins books.

His right hand had gone in first, followed by his head, but it was his left that came out holding what looked like a deck of glossy blue-and-red playing cards.

Glancing up at the clock, he said, "Since we still have a few mintocks before we begin, how about a little fun?" He held up the fancy cards. "Anyone know what these are?"

"Uno cards!" someone shouted.

"A Magic: The Gathering deck!" shouted someone else.

"Close," said Mr. Minutes with a cunning smile not at all unlike Mr. Now's. "It is, in fact, a deck of *tarot* cards . . ."

"Oh, I've heard of those!" said a girl sitting near the front—Evelyn, I think her name was. "They predict your future!"

Mr. Minutes, who had begun to shuffle the cards with surprisingly nimble fingers, was grinning as he answered. "The art of card divination has more to do with understanding the *current* path of one's life . . . The symbolism of the cards is important. Placement and arrangement are vital. But, I won't lie to you, under certain circumstances, yes, a skilled reader may very well be able to catch a glimpse into your ever-changing futures . . . And who knows," he said, turning his attention fully to me now, "it might just save your life. So, who would like to go first?"

Instantly every hand in the room except mine shot up. But—surprise, surprise—no one but me got called on.

"Uh, no, I don't wanna . . ." I protested as Mr. Minutes approached with quick, agile steps, the cards whispering between his talented fingers. And I was still shaking my head when he began to deal.

Three cards snapped down on my desk, picture side up.

Mr. Minutes frowned at the first, winced at the second, and straight-up *paled* at the third. The cards were, in the order they'd been dealt:

—an old weather-beaten compass (more brownish than gold), growing out of a nest of thorny red roses.

—a court jester (from medieval times) with hands for feet and feet for hands.

—and lastly, a bright, grinning, skeleton head. Something like a calaca.

It was probably only my imagination, but I could've sworn that each time a card struck my desk, a fresh crash of thunder rattled the windows and walls.

A heartbeat later, I heard Mr. Minutes breathe, "No . . ." and without any warning, without any hesitation, he quickly dealt two more cards, facedown this time.

And when he flipped these over, every single drop of blood in me *froze*.

Two more skull cards. These upside down and frowning, with masses of hissing snakes crawling out of their empty eye sockets.

I'm not gonna lie—they freaked me out. I mean, I *was* scared. Only not nearly as scared as I should have been . . .

I watched Mr. Minutes stagger back from my desk, white-faced and trembling, while the rest of the class crowded in, eager to get a closer look at the cards.

Voices murmured in my ears.

Heads butted in close to mine.

But a few steps away the strange teacher man who looked so much like the last strange teacher man was looking smaller and more terrified by the second. Which, by the way, was making *me* feel smaller and more terrified by the second!

"What is it?" I whispered anxiously. "What's wrong?"

"Oh, my dear boy," he answered in a low, shaky voice, "you . . . you've drawn the *Double Skulls*."

"Double Skulls? *So?*"

"*So?!*" he cried. "You have *DEATH* on your desk!"

Then came the hollow *smack!* of fifty or so hands clapping over about half as many mouths.

In the same moment, Mr. Minutes began frantically collecting his cards. And his handbag. And his bright pink umbrella. And hurried out of the class in the same sort of panicky rush as that famous white rabbit from Wonderland, as another angry sizzle lit up the sky through the row of windows above the bookshelves.

But at almost the *exact* instant Mr. Minutes went rushing out, another equally strange mister came marching in.

My first thought was, *Mr. Now!*

My second thought was, *No, it's Mr. Minutes again!*

But both were wrong. Sure, he might've looked more like Mr. Now than Mr. Minutes, and even more like Mr. Minutes than Mr. Now, but he was a few pounds too light to be the former, and a few years too old to be the latter.

And when he spoke, introducing himself as Mr. Hoursback, and taking his spot at the front of the class by the teacher's desk, I knew from his voice that he wasn't either.

"Greetings, students! I will be your substitute teacher for the day!"

"But our substitute just walked out!" someone in the back row pointed out.

"Did he now?" For a moment, Mr. Hoursback's face drooped into a befuddled frown. He honestly looked like some lost explorer from another world—what H. G. Wells's time traveler probably looked like when he wound up in the year 802701 A.D. "I thought that dapper gentleman did look *rather* familiar . . . In any event, the great clock in the sky marches on, and so must we!"

With eager hands, he rapidly rolled up the sleeve of his coat, and I saw that his entire left arm was covered with watches. Plastic ones, metal ones, shiny ones, dull ones—even what appeared to be a gold-plated pocket watch wrapped securely around the crook of his hairy arm.

For several seconds a classroom of gaping faces—mine included—stared silently at Mr. Hoursback while he stared silently at the many faces of his many watches; and for those few seconds Mr. Hoursback gave off the impression of being the world's first human grandfather clock—*tick . . . tick . . . tick . . . tick.*

"Ancient astronauts!" he cried suddenly. "Behold the hour!" Then he began to pace anxiously back and forth in front of the teacher's desk. "Time is already collapsing! Our window of opportunity shrinks by the mintick!"

He looked panickily around at the two dozen or so seriously confused students.

"In lieu of this, my dear children, I must forgo all further formalities and announce that I will immediately begin administering a surprise examination!"

Naturally, this wasn't a very popular idea:

"But no one warned us!"

"Mrs. Gomez never gives pop quizzes on Fridays!"

"You can't do this! You're not even our real teacher!"

"Silence—PLEASE!" roared Mr. Hoursback as another crack of thunder rattled the world. "The examination is to begin immediately. It will be administered one at a time—out loud—and if I hear any more complaints, I'll begin ejecting perpetrators from the premises!"

"Um, Mr. Hoursback, what's the pop quiz gonna be on?" asked someone behind me.

"Simple directional navigation," he replied with an almost cheery smile.

"But this is third period *history*!" someone else objected.

"Dear children! You must be willing to expand your minds *beyond* the limits of any given subject at any given time or you will find yourselves quite limited in *every* subject! Now, let us commence!"

Even before he spun to face me, I knew what was coming. But there wasn't a single thing I could do about it.

"YOU!" he snapped, whipping a long, thin finger at me like a fencing sword. "We'll begin with *you!*"

The next second he was looming over me, casting a Smaug-size shadow.

"Question number one! Which direction is that?" Now he was pointing forcefully toward the back of the room, at the wall above the row of cubbies.

I blinked. "*Huh?*"

"Answer instinctively!"

"I—*what are you talking about??*"

"The direction, please. Cardinal."

The weirdness of the question (not to mention its total *out-of-the-blueness*) had caught me completely off guard. But I managed, "That's—*east*."

I was pretty sure it was, too. I'd always been pretty good with directions.

Problem was, at the moment, my head was spinning so fast and my heart was beating so hard and my blood was hammering so loudly in my neck, my ears, my chest, that I wasn't even sure which way "up" was.

I guess I must've answered correctly, though, because he then followed up with a series of rapid-fire questions: "Which direction is the lunchroom?" and "How about the auditorium?" and "The PE field?"

North. Northeast. And south.

Those had been my answers. And I'd spat them out as quickly as I could, hoping—*really* crossing my fingers here—that it would be enough to make this watch-obsessed creepster leave me alone. To make him go pick on someone else.

But, of course, it wasn't. Instead, his hands shot out, quick as a snake, and he began picking through my hair like some hungry chimp on the hunt for the world's juiciest tick.

I'd just opened my mouth to shout "Dude, get away from me!" when—
BOOM!—a gigantic crash of thunder rocked the school, plunging the entire room into Stone Age darkness.

For several heartbeats, there was only the sound of rain beating furiously against the windows and the laughing, nervous screams of a dozen or so kids inside the room, and another dozen or so out in the halls.

Then, with an angry mechanical hum, the school's emergency generators kicked on and all the lights flickered back to life. But when I looked anxiously around again, I realized with a jolt of surprise that Mr. Hoursback was gone—that he'd completely vanished!

"I ALWAYS miss the cool stuff!" Mikey shouted, banging her fists against the flimsy tabletop.

The two of us were at lunch, sitting in our usual spot in the cafeteria by the broken soda machine and the tiny port-like window, Mikey complaining about not even having had a chance to see any of the three weirdos.

Outside, the storm hadn't let up at all, and from the howling of the wind and the pelting rain, and the way the clouds churned and boiled in the angry prune-colored sky, I had this awful feeling that either I was going to blow away or the entire *school* was. Fortunately, I had my buddy to distract me.

"It's like some family curse or something!" she grumbled. "Remember when Billy Baxter sprayed chunks in homeroom, but I missed it because I was home with a sprained ankle?"

"Billy spewing chunks all over the arts and crafts room wasn't *cool*," I couldn't help pointing out as I stabbed my spork into the hunk of mystery meat lying unappetizingly on my lunch tray. "It was probably the most disgusting thing that happened *all* year. And we dissected cow eyeballs in Mrs. Cooper's—you remember that?"

"No! See, that's MY POINT! I missed that, too! It's a curse, I tell you—a curse!"

Anyway, I gave her the CliffsNotes version of my morning "adventure," starting with the hanging solar system model and ending with Principal Lutz having our entire class give the men's descriptions to Ms. Gallardo, the school's art teacher, so she could draw up a composite sketch for the police.

By the time I was finished, Mikey was pretty much inconsolable.

"They sound so *fun!*" she said with a dejected sigh. "I really hope they come back . . ."

Meanwhile, I was squirming in my seat like a worm on a fishhook, anxiously watching the big clock on the wall and hoping with every bit of hopefulness in me that the short hand would hurry up already and swing around to three o'clock so I could get out of here before any of them actually *did* come back.

"Don't worry," I promised her, "if I see any of them again, I'll be sure to give them your phone number."

Mikey took a big bite of her apple. "And my gamertag, please!"

CHAPTER FOUR

—— • ——

OMEHAY EETSWAY OMEHAY

(1)

The PE field was totally flooded and the gutters were spitting up rainwater by the time the final bell rang.

It had been an awful day. Well, more *strange* than awful, and probably more surreal than anything else.

On the bright side, the Triplets of Weird didn't show up for any of my other classes—or anyone else's, for that matter. But I still couldn't get them out of my head—couldn't concentrate, couldn't shake the feeling that I was being watched or followed or maybe both.

According to Principal Lutz, though, there was no reason for concern. The police had conducted a thorough and rigorous sweep of the school, and the strangers were long gone.

"It was probably nothing more than a silly prank," she'd announced loudly over the school's PA system a few minutes before release. "Some social media personalities desperate for attention."

That was her theory.

Mikey, though, had a different theory altogether, and she told it to me when I found her by the bleachers near the row of waiting yellow buses after school.

"They're ALIENS, dude!" she practically shrieked.

"What? Who's an alien??"

"Antares, *seriously*? You're a math whiz and can't put two and two together? Those three fake teacher dudes, WHO ELSE?! I bet they were just recently sent down by Hivemind with the *sole* mission to track you down and abduct you! They won't stop until they bring you back to the mothership! Trust me, I've played all the video games!"

It was probably the first time ever I was glad that Mikey and I took different buses home.

Mikey's space alien abduction theory aside, I was pretty sure I'd never see any of those three weirdos again. Still, the entire bus ride home I kept expecting to see one (or at the very least someone who *looked* like them) lurking nearby. In a passing car. By a crosswalk sign. Waiting at the next stop.

The first thing I'd done before climbing on the bus was to double-check the driver.

Then—just to be *extra* safe—I'd gone one by one, double-checking the faces of every single kid before finally dropping, sweaty and a little dizzy, into a seat near the back.

But even all of that hadn't been enough to calm my nerves. Or slow my racing pulse.

Mr. Minutes had accidentally left one of his fancy tarot cards on my desk when he'd gone rushing out of the room—the Compass card. And thinking it was just too cool to trash, I'd secretly kept it.

Now, like five different times on the ride home, I dug an anxious hand into my pocket, feeling for it.

Twice, I actually brought the card all the way out just to prove to myself that I hadn't imagined the whole thing.

And each time I saw it and felt its smooth, glossy surface underneath my fingertips and could no longer deny what had happened, or pretend to myself that this was all some kind of bizarro-world nightmare, the same bunch of questions began tumbling through my brain like asteroids tumbling through outer space: *Who were those guys?*

Why had they kept showing up?

And why the heck did they look so much ALIKE?

Fortunately, by the time my stop finally came, my pulse had returned to normal—well, normal*ish*—and the fog of paranoia swirling around inside my head had begun to evaporate.

I started the short walk home, almost feeling good for the first time all day. And why shouldn't I? The worst of the storm hadn't quite blown this way yet, and a few spears of brilliant South Florida sunshine were still blasting holes in the cloud cover, warming my face and filling my heart with a sudden, cheery hopefulness.

I lived a short hop, skip, and a jump from Calle Ocho (aka Southwest Eighth Street), right in the heart of a funky Miami neighborhood known as Little Havana.

Little Havana is one of the oldest and most culturally rich spots in the entire state—basically ten square blocks of artistic murals, salsa music, palm trees, and the biggest Latin American street festivals and block parties you ever saw.

It was a pretty cool place to call home. A super cool place, as a matter of fact. Only . . . I can't say that I've ever exactly felt . . . *at home* here.

I mean, don't get me wrong. I loved South Florida. I loved the sunshine and the beaches, I loved the wildlife and the pristine public parks.

I loved the energy, the people—not to mention the dozens and dozens of juice bars serving up fresh sugarcane juice—aka guarapo—which happens to be my all-time favorite drink.

The Cuban bakeries were the bomb, too.

It's just that all my life I'd felt sort of . . . I don't know—*trapped.*

You know when you're exploring in a video game and reach one of those unseen walls? The kind that let you see past them but won't actually *let you* pass?

Well, that's what I felt like a lot of the time. Like I'd come to the edge of some man-made boundary I wasn't allowed to cross. No matter how badly I wanted to or how hard I might try.

That's probably where my panic attacks came from. That feeling of missing out. The feeling of being kept away from what was *really* out there—far from all the everyday places and beyond everywhere everyone already knew about.

Some people will probably think that's silly or whatever.

But it was the truth.

My hobbit hole was a little pink two-story town house a couple of minutes' walk from this awesome little burger joint humbly named El Rey de las Fritas.

When I came in, my aunt was standing at the kitchen counter flipping through a stack of today's mail.

Celeste—that's my aunt—has honey-colored skin (like me), one brown eye and one blue eye (also like me), and was about my height, almost six feet tall. But *un*like me, she was a Pisces, and that was a big deal to her.

The moment she spotted me, all the worry lines on her forehead instantly vanished and her mouth split into a relieved grin.

"Antares!" she whispered, quickly crossing the living room toward me. "You're home!"

"You sound shocked," I teased. Celeste *always* sounded shocked to see me. Like she thought that me making it home in one piece after a few hours at Glades Middle was a mini miracle or something. "Can't believe I survived another day of junior high, huh?"

Suddenly, the worry lines on her face were back for an encore. "Are you okay? How do you feel?"

"I feel *fine*, Aunt Celeste . . . Even better than I felt this morning, and I felt perfectly fine then, too!" Not exactly true, but I wasn't about to play a round of *tell-me-about-your-day* with my auntie dearest.

No joke, my tía had turned worrying about me into an art form. A way of life. Once she kept me locked inside for *three whole days* because she said Neptune was in retrograde and Jupiter was ascending.

I couldn't even begin to imagine how long she'd keep me cooped up under lock and key if I told her about the three amigos.

Worse, she was having one of her "extra suspicious days." The kind she usually has right before we're abruptly packing up moving boxes again and heading off to find another house in another neighborhood in another school district.

In fact, she'd *barely* let me leave the house this morning.

And that was only after reading and rereading my palm so many times I was starting to get friction burns on my skin from just the eye contact!

No, I'd tell her about Mr. Now, Mr. Minutes, and Mr. What's-His-Face some other time . . .

Next week, maybe. Or better yet, next *millennium*.

She was staring straight at me now, her bright eyes locked on mine. I'd always had this funny feeling my aunt could read minds. Only at the moment, the feeling didn't feel so funny. "Something happened today . . ." she whispered suspiciously. "*What?*"

And next thing I knew, her quick brown hands had snapped out, snatching one of mine.

"Oh, c'mon, Celeste . . . *Again*?? My palm hasn't changed any from this morning. *Trust me*."

Carefully tracing a line of my palm with her index finger, she said, "Variations in the creases of a palm can appear at any moment. And you don't look so great. You look . . . *strange*."

"I'm fourteen," I told her. "I'm sure I'll grow out of it." I offered her my most convincing *I'm-A-okay* smile. "Everything's good, tía. *Seriously*."

Celeste didn't seem to buy that, but what was she going to do? Read my palm for the billionth time?

"Listen, honey, I got to go. My break's almost over, but I'll be home early. We'll order a pizza or something."

My aunt worked at the nearby children's hospital as a nurses' assistant, and most of the time that meant late nights and pizza for dinner. Not that I was complaining about the pizza part.

She glanced quickly at her phone. "My gosh, look at the time! It really seems to be flying today, doesn't it?"

"That's what everyone keeps tellin' me . . ." I sighed, trying not to think back to third period and a certain watch-crazed "substitute," who was very likely a direct descendant of the Mad Hatter.

My aunt planted a loud peck smack in the middle of my forehead, started to turn away, then spun back around and said, "Oh, I almost forgot! I got you something!"

From her canvas shoulder bag she brought out an old leather-bound book and handed it to me. The title, scrawled in fancy cursive and glittering with tiny, rainbow-colored sparkles and gold foil, read *A Brief Metaphysical History of Mü.*

All of a sudden my jaw felt like it had detached itself from the rest of my face in shock. "Hold up," I said. "Isn't this one of your books?"

See, my aunt had this big old box of big old books which she never let me read—never even let me *flip* through. I'd always thought it was totally unfair of her, especially since she knew how much I loved books. But she'd never given in, and I'd tried pretty much everything—even heartstring-plucking strolls down Guilt Trip Lane.

"It is," she replied, beaming at me. "Happy belated birthday!"

"But . . . are you being serious right now?" I'm not kidding when I say that I've been trying to get my hands on one of these for as long as I can remember. Once, when I was around nine, I'd found the box where she kept them hidden and paged through as many as I could get my excited little hands on.

They were filled with stunning, elaborate maps that must've been hundreds of years old, because several of the continents were misplaced and there were countless drawings of islands I knew didn't exist. I'd always thought the books were super cool and figured they must've been super rare or super expensive, which is why she didn't want me messing with them.

"After you read it, we can talk. I . . . I think you're at that age now." The way she'd said that made it sound like she was trying to talk herself up into a conversation that would probably embarrass both of us—and suddenly, alarm bells were going off in my head.

I shot a panicked look at the title again. "Wait. This isn't a book on the, uh, *'birds and bees'* or anything, is it? 'Cause I really think that conversation should wait until I've *at least* had my first kiss, no?"

My aunt's head tipped back in a surprised burst of laughter. "No! ¡No te asustes! Nothing like that. Though now that you *mention* it . . . maybe we should have that talk pretty soon."

"No, definitely not!" I said. "Let's hold off on that. *Indefinitely.*"

"Bueno, okay. I gotta run. But you remember the rules, right?"

How could I forget? She'd been drilling them into me since I was, like, two. "Yeah, yeah . . . Don't open the door to anyone. Don't talk to any strangers, even through the door. Call *you* first and then the police

if I see anybody I don't know prowling around. Basically, trust no one."
My aunt's motto was "Es mejor prevenir que lamentar." In other words:
Better safe than sorry. But lately her paranoia was making me feel more
sorry than safe.

"Who's my brilliant boy, huh?"

"I'm not five anymore, Celeste . . . I think I can survive a couple of
hours by myself."

"Of course you can!" she happily agreed. "Because you follow the
rules. Love you! ¡Me voy!"

CHAPTER FIVE

SWORDS AND SPELLS

My shoes, socks, and T-shirt were still damp from all the rain (not to mention from my nervous sweating all day), so I went upstairs to change. Only I barely made it halfway into my room when my eyes caught on the photograph on my nightstand.

They always did that.

Almost always, anyway.

It was a picture of my dad. Antonio de la Vega. Laughing, squinting into the camera as the sun flashed in his eyes and winked brilliantly off the silver wing of a little single-engine airplane in the background—my dad looking so cool in a dark leather jacket with a pair of aviator sunglasses pushed up into his thick, wavy hair.

My aunt said that he must've been around eighteen or nineteen when she'd taken the picture. And I had stared at it more times than I'd ever own up to.

I knew it like I knew anything. I'd memorized every detail of his face, of the plane's smooth, silvery wings. Even every crack and crease in the photopaper.

It was the only picture—the only memory—I had of him. The only one I had of *either* of my parents. And that's because I'd never met them. Or at least I'd been too young to remember.

My dad was born in Mexico City and had Cuban heritage. My mom was part Indian, part Irish, and was born in Switzerland.

About thirteen years ago, their plane vanished somewhere off the southernmost tip of Argentina, near Antarctica. They'd been officially labeled as "missing." But I knew better. People didn't go missing for more than a decade and then magically reappear. Real life wasn't a fairy tale.

When I was little, though, I would sometimes sit up in bed all night waiting for one of them to finally come home. And when they didn't, I'd usually wrap my dad's photo around the back of this raggedy old teddy of mine, secure it with a rubber band, and then hug it until I fell asleep or stopped crying. I didn't cry so much anymore. Though I still missed my mom and him just as bad.

My aunt missed them, too. Especially my dad. I could tell by the way she talked about him sometimes. How she referred to him in the present tense. Like he was still around. *Somewhere*. Like he could walk in through the front door any second now.

We were both still waiting.

Exactly one hour later, I was sprawled out on the living room couch with my gaming headset on, in the middle of the second round of the online *Wizards of WarMage* tournament Mikey had randomly entered us in. Currently, we were squaring off against team Annihilator's Inc., who were pretty much living up to their name.

I'd been thundersmacked, soul-lashed, galactafried, infinity slashed, gigawhacked, icy doom'd, orc roasted, and mega death'd so many times it was starting to get old.

And Mikey was starting to get angry.

"OH COME ON, CAPTAIN ARITHMETIC! THIS ISN'T *A GAME*!" she roared at me (even though it obviously *was* a game). "LOOK UP AT THE SCOREBOARD AND DO THE MATH, BOY GENIUS! We're getting PWNED!"

The thing to know about Mikey is that she's mathophobic and loves video games, whereas I'm more or less neutral on video games and dream about math. Mostly geometry. (I'm not kidding.) Anyway, I knew that stuff like gamer rankings was a super big deal to her, so it wasn't like I was losing on purpose or something.

"I don't know what you want me to do!" I shouted back. "These peeps are REALLY good!"

I was respawned on the smoldering lava flats of the Deathly Woods. An instant later, a gigantic slime-green orc leapt out of the thick mass of enchanted pine trees and decapitated me for probably the hundredth time in the last sixty seconds.

I was actually kind of surprised the game was still bothering to reset my sorcerer avatar with a head.

"Hey, Mr. *HEADLESS HORSEMAN*!" Mikey exploded into my ear. "Can you try keeping your cranium attached to your shoulders for, like, FIVE SECONDS?! You're killing my ranking!"

"I'm trying, Mikey! I'm trying!"

"No, you're NOT! This is the worst I've EVER seen you play!"

She wasn't exaggerating, either. This probably *was* the worst I'd ever played.

For some reason, I couldn't seem to concentrate.

Maybe it was just the day I'd had. That was a definite possibility. Or maybe the weather was distracting me.

I mean, it was such a *strange* storm . . .

Outside, the whole sky had turned this odd shade of electric purple, and through the big bay window I could see dark clouds scuttling around like nervous crabs.

Farther away, under a misty slice of moon, red-tinged lightning broke constantly, sizzling from earth to sky and back again. I'd never seen a storm quite like it.

And it had been a *long* time since I'd even seen one this nasty. The last time was probably like two years ago, back when I was in summer camp.

All us campers had been on a scavenger hunt in this beautiful state park up near the Everglades, and the storm had pretty much rolled in right over Florida Bay and rolled right over the camp. The rain flooded the park and soaked the boardwalks and the bridges and turned the ground to mud, and ran down the trails, swelling up all the little rivers as well as the bay.

The worst part? Since we'd all been so spread out everywhere, almost fifty campers had gotten lost in the woods.

I was the only one who'd found my way back without the help of a counselor or a park ranger. And that was only because I'd always had a pretty good sense of direction, ever since I was little. Some kids, though, took hours to find. It had been a really scary storm.

But this one looked even scari—

"ANTARES!"

Mikey's voice snapped me out of my thoughts just in time for me to see my sorcerer avatar obliterated by a Screamer spell. Bits and pieces of grayish wizard cloak and brownish wizard staff went whizzing off to all four corners of the map. It wasn't pretty.

"YOU'VE GOTTA BE KIDDING!" Mikey erupted. "I MEAN, WHY DON'T YOU JUST DEFECT TO THEIR TEAM ALREADY?!"

I had just opened my mouth to say "my bad" (and for the *millionth* time now) when a bolt of crackling thunder ripped the sky overhead.

If I didn't know any better, I would've guessed that the race of giants Gulliver had run into on the island of Brobdingnag during his famous travels were setting off giant-size firecrackers right on top of my house.

A second later, there was a dull electric buzz, and suddenly all the lights in the house went out with a loud *pop!*

I sat up with a start, staring at the now pitch-dark rectangle of the TV. "Mikey, you there? Come in, Mikey?"

Nothing.

Man, she was going to go BALLISTIC on me . . .

No sooner had that cheerful thought crossed my mind than there was another buzzing sound, and all the lights snapped back on.

I tried again. "Mikey, can you hear me? Come in, Mikey!"

Still nada.

Fantastico . . .

If I remembered correctly, a disconnect from the game equaled an automatic loss. Not that it really mattered, because we had about as much chance of winning this round as the Wicked Witch of the East had of bench-pressing Dorothy's farmhouse. But still.

Just then, I was startled by a sudden knock at the door. I heard the handle jiggle, saw it wiggle, and figured it was probably my aunt. She'd probably forgotten her phone or something.

"Coming!" I shouted. But even before I could get up the door blew open, and in blew rain and wind and dripping-wet leaves—

And then my heart *stopped.*

Literally *stopped.*

Because sweeping in with the rain and the wind and the swirl of leaves was a man.

But not just any man . . .

It was Mr. Now!

CHAPTER SIX

—— • ——

STRANGER DANGER

"Antares!" he shouted, tracking muddy footprints all the way through the foyer as he hurried inside. "*Whiffsly now!* Everything's been prepared, but we have *minticks* at most!"

Instantly I jumped to my feet, knocking over my empty can of Pepsi. "Dude! What are you *doing*???"

"My apologies for the intrusion," he added quickly, "but time is now our enemy! We mustn't delay!"

"Man, you need to *LEAVE!*" I shouted. "Seriously! Get out or I'm gonna call the——"

Just then, another massive thunderclap absolutely *obliterated* the sky directly above the house. I stiffened—like *a corpse*—as it rattled through the windows and through the walls, shaking all the doors and making the lights flicker.

Mr. Now had stiffened, too. His dark eyes slid cautiously, fearfully, toward the ceiling as he whispered, "*They are coming . . .*"

Something about the way he'd said that and the anxious look on his face and in his eyes made my skin prickle with an itchy sort of fear.

"Wh—what are you talking about?" I breathed, backing away from this loony tune. "*Who* is??"

"What do you mean *who*??? Haven't you noticed the incoming THUNDER-HEAD?! Haven't you *smelt* THE LIGHTNING?! *They. Are. Coming.*" His tone was dark, dangerous—bordering on frantic. "The *Thunderwalkers* . . . *They're coming for you!*"

"The *who*?!"

"The crocs!"

"*Crocs??*"

"The crocodilians!"

"*Crocodilians???*"

"Please just pay attention! Do you remember the planetary alignment I showed you in class? The one I demonstrated, albeit *crudely*, with that ridiculous hanging model?"

"*Huh??*"

"The conjunction! The Tetrinox! Do you remember it or not?!"

"I—yeah, I guess!"

"Well, what I *didn't* tell you was that at the *exact moment* that sign was made manifest in the heavens, a stream of meteoroids *pierced* Earth's atmospheric covering, thus becoming a *meteor shower*, and came streaking and burning through the night sky at approximately one hundred and thirty-five thousand miles per hour—"

"*So??*"

"—and those stony-irons continued to streak, and they continued to burn until, due to the ravages of ablation (via vaporization), their cosmic mass was reduced to roughly that of a handful of *space pebbles*. And that handful of pebbles—now aptly classified as *meteorites*—made earth-fall *here*. After nearly *one hundred and sixty-two LIGHT-YEARS* of intergalactic travel! And it was *YOUR* roof, the uppermost covering of this *very* dwelling, where, at last, our brave celestial travelers *finally* found their rest!"

He was practically beaming at me by this point, but all I could do was stare dazedly back. Seriously, how do you respond to something like that?

"I see your thoughts are muddled," he whispered after a moment, "and for that, I can only blame myself."

Suddenly he spun away from me, mumbling to himself under his breath—

And that's when I saw my chance!

Reaching behind the sofa, I quickly snatched the book my aunt had gifted me off the side table. I hated that it had to be a book, and especially *this* book, but it was big and it was heavy and most importantly, it was *close*.

Mr. Now had a nice big head, too—*easy target*, I thought.

But right as I got ready to go all Babe Ruth on this stalker, he whispered, "Perhaps it would be best if I let your father explain . . ."

And those words were like a magic spell; I froze, mid-swing.

"*You know my father?*" I gasped.

Mr. Now gave a little shrug as he turned back to face me. "Probably better than anyone . . . We're all—well, *he's* waiting for you!" he said excitedly.

I slowly lowered my Whack-a-Tome. "He . . . *is?*"

The stranger eyed the book suspiciously for a moment. "Yes! He's been on a great quest, Antares . . . *A great quest!* He's been"—this part he whispered—"*searching! . . .*"

I blinked, shaking my head. "Searching for *what?*"

"The Star of Lôst, of course! And he believes he's finally found it! What's more, he wants *you* with him! Oh, how he's *missed* you, my boy . . ." Mr. Now whispered in a tender sort of way, and for several seconds I was too stunned to say anything.

"So—my mom and dad are . . . *okay?* I mean, they didn't die on the plane?"

His thick brows wriggled and furrowed in confusion. "What *plane?*"

"The one they vanished on."

Those caterpillar-like brows now shot halfway up his forehead. *"The one they vanished on?? Your father never vanished on any plane . . . But we will—well, he will explain everything. Now, let's 'it!"*

"*Wait.* How—how do I know anything you're saying is even true??"

"You can't! But such is life, isn't it? You have to trust people. That's the only way it works."

Exactly what a kidnapper would say, I thought—and, as if at that thought, Mr. Now's mouth turned down in a disappointed frown.

Then—

C
R
A
C
K
!

Another mighty thundercrack ripped the skies, and a flash of fresh fear shone in the stranger's dark eyes.

"You have only the next few moments to decide what course your life will take," he said ominously. "After that, the decision will be made for you."

Thunder rumbled again, and this time an arc of branched lightning lit up a pair of cloaked figures standing side by side in the middle of the street in front of my house.

They were tall—*very* tall (*Yao Ming* tall)—and very, very wide, wearing what looked like long yellow raincoats and black rubber boots.

It was hard to tell with all the rain and darkness, and the way the wind was lifting their collars and bending the brims of their broad black hats over their faces, but it looked like they were staring this way.

Mr. Now, no big surprise, had spotted them, too. *"Thunderwalkers . . ."* he murmured uneasily.

Moving quickly now, he hurried across the living room to the front door, then, whirling, looked straight at me and with a tremble in his voice that put a tremble in my bones, said, "Stay here. And if I am not back in ninety minticks—er, seconds—*run.*"

The instant he was out the door, I rushed over and locked it. I bolted it. I ran the little chain lock thingie and jammed the entryway table underneath the handle, and then slid the couch away from the TV and butted it squarely up against the legs of the table. Overkill? Probably. But I wasn't taking any more chances with this guy.

Swiping hair out of my face, I watched through the window as Mr. Now strode swiftly out into the rain-soaked air while thunder cracked and lightning crackled overhead, and met the two figures at the edge of my driveway.

I couldn't tell what they were talking about—or if they were talking at all—but every now and then, Mr. Now would shake his head and point, rather forcefully, toward my next-door neighbor's house, like, *You've got the wrong address, pal!*

I was still standing there, watching all this go down and wondering if there was even the *slightest* chance that this entire day wasn't part of some terrible, all-too-real hallucination, when a loud, shrill ringing had me jumping out of my skin!

Immediately my eyes swung toward the sound.

It was the phone.

The kitchen phone.

Somebody was calling.

Hoping—no, *praying!*—that it was my aunt, I ran over to snatch it out of its cradle with fumbling fingers. I don't know—I guess I felt like maybe hearing a familiar voice would make the world make sense again, would make all this weirdness just *stop*. It was stupid, yeah.

And it didn't matter anyway, because it wasn't my aunt. Sure, it might've been a woman's voice, but it wasn't any woman I knew.

"*They've found you*," she said.

That was it.

No hello.

No name.

No nothing.

And before I could come back with *huh*, or *what*, or even ask who the heck this *was*, I saw something terrible:

Out in the middle of my yard, in the middle of the raging thunderstorm, one of the figures in the yellow raincoats suddenly seized Mr. Now around the neck!

In the span of a heartbeat, it lifted him right off his feet as if he weighed nothing at all—then, as if he weighed even *less*, flung him toward my neighbor's house.

There was a crack of glass, a squeal of springs, and a car alarm began to blare.

It all happened so fast, and it was all so surreal, that at first I didn't feel any fear—not even shock. I simply stood there, *watching* it happen. Like it was happening in a *movie* or something.

Then our eyes met through the storm—the rain jacket dudes' and mine—and all the fear that I hadn't felt up to that point, and all the terror and shock and the mind-numbing horror of what I'd just witnessed, came slamming into me like a runaway freight train.

I staggered backward on wobbly legs, retreating without realizing it. And heard the voice on the other end of the line say, "Get down."

Too terrified to do anything but obey, I ducked behind the dining room table. The instant I did, a whipcrack of thunder—thunder like a *bomb!*— shook the house.

Lights flickered. The ceiling fan trembled. On the other side of the room the sliding glass door rattled noisily on its track, and through it, I saw a bolt of reddish-purplish lightning come zigzagging down out of the pitch-dark sky.

It struck the middle of the backyard, about a yard beyond the patio furniture. Except it didn't simply strike down; the bolt EXPLODED into the ground with the force of a supernovaing *sun*, rattling the roof, the floors, the house, and all the rest of the world.

Shielding my eyes with my free hand, I stared hard out at the bolt, expecting—any second now—for it to begin to dissolve. To disappear. To dissipate back into the atmosphere. (You know, the way lightning bolts *usually* do . . .)

Only this one *never* did.

This lightning bolt sort of just hung there, fully visible, like an electric scar in the dark.

And thanks to what happened next, I would never be able to look at a lightning bolt the same way ever again . . .

CHAPTER SEVEN

•

THUNDERWALKERS

(1)

Freaky shapes began to emerge from the impossible bolt—from *inside* it!
Like it was some kind of sizzling, electric zipper into another *dimension*.

Hardly believing my eyes, I watched through the rain-streaked glass
as first came something like fingers . . . then a hand, then a foot, and now
all the rest of it—an entire *somebody*!

The lightning-born figure slowly approached the sliding door. Tiny currents of electricity danced along its arms and legs as a huge greenish hand
reached out to try the handle.

Locked. My aunt always kept it locked. *And* barred. And I'd never been
so grateful for anything—*ever*.

A split second later, the figure vanished around the side of the house—
probably searching for another way in—and in my ear the mysterious
phone voice said, "Get to your bedroom. *Move!*"

I didn't think, just leapt to my feet, pounding straight upstairs with the
cordless phone still glued to my hand.

Oh my God, oh my God, oh my God . . .

Desperately I looked around my room for a place to hide. In the closet? Behind the dresser? Under my bed?

Sucky.

Suckier.

Suckiest.

"They're gonna FIND me!" I hissed, locking the door behind me in a panic.

But the voice's only reply was, "Climb out your window. You have forty seconds."

"What??"

"Head for the main road."

Head for the main—

But that was RIDICULOUS! Those guys were out there!

Only . . . maybe it wasn't *quite* as ridiculous as hiding under the bed.

A gust of stormy wind blew back my hair as I threw open the window with shaky hands. My eyes frantically scanned the little sliver of yard between my house and my neighbor's, and my heart almost leapt out of my chest as their cat (Missy Miss) came leaping (and screeching!) out of the bushes near the AC unit.

A burst of static in my ear: "The street signs will guide you. Go!"

"*Huh*??" The phone had begun to make that fuzzy, buzzing whine of a fading connection, and I could barely hear anything now. "HEY, HELLO?! I don't under—"

There came a jiggling, clicking sound, and my head snapped around.

I could see leaping shadows in the strip of light under the door.

My forty seconds were up.

CHAPTER EIGHT

NOT-SO-HIDDEN MESSAGES

The mystery lady hadn't been lying. The street signs really did guide me through the storm. Directions of all sorts—from flashing arrows to blinking messages—shone brightly behind the cages of the pedestrian signals and in the electric road signs and high in the traffic lights, pointing me south, always south, right through the heart of Little Havana.

LEFT ON SW 6TH STREET

RIGHT ON SW 15TH AVENUE

← (THIS WAY)

→ (THAT WAY)

RUN ↑

FASTER! ↑↑

I kept tripping over fallen branches and sliding on slippery sidewalks and stepping into puddles, and into potholes, and dents in people's yards, until I was soaked and sweaty and sucking wind so badly I pretty much hurt all over.

This area of Little Havana was a mix of neighborhoods and commercial buildings; and as I flew around the corner by Calle Ocho, an old Ford pickup suddenly jumped the curb to my left, nearly turning me into a human pancake. My hands banged painfully off the hood. A wave of steaming engine heat rolled over my face.

The driver, half hidden in the shadow, threw open the passenger-side door, shouting, "Antares, get in!"

And recognition slammed into me even harder than the pickup nearly had.

It was Mr. Hoursback.

No, Mr. Minutes!

I panicked.

I suddenly realized I was still holding the useless cordless phone and chucked it at the windshield. Then I ran.

Shops and cafes and people flashed by. In the distance, someone was shouting my name. And when I turned to look, I felt my eyes bug:

Standing at the corner in front of a small bodega and waving his hands frantically over his head to catch my attention was—I could hardly believe it—Mr. Hoursback!

Yeah, definitely him this time . . .

My brain felt like it was beginning to unravel. I mean, what the FRIJOLES was going on?!

As I raced in wild terror toward the busy intersection, my eyes ran up the upcoming traffic post and spied, in the pedestrian signal, the words:

KEEP RUNNING

THE TRIPLETS
ARE KIDNAPPERS!

All around me, streetlamps were snapping off in bunches and in rows, blacking out entire blocks, while the ones just up ahead seemed to glow brighter, hotter, as if illuminating a glittering yellow brick road for me to follow.

And so, like Dorothy, I did, flying down block after block. At the next intersection, the crosswalk box was flashing:

DOMINO PARK

FIND THE DOMINO GAME

Ignoring the angry shouts and honking horns, I darted across the three lanes of zooming traffic and didn't stop until I'd reached the middle of the little park named after South Florida's favorite tile-based tabletop game.

At its center was a large limestone table where five guys in colorful guayaberas were rebelling against mother nature and playing dominoes under a gigantic Marlins beach umbrella.

All five of them glanced up at me. Then all five of their phones rang. All five answered. And five mouths formed five little Os of shock.

And then all five held their phones out to me, saying, "It's . . . for *you*."

I snatched the closest one. "Hello??"

And the voice that answered made all the tiny hairs on the back of my neck instantly stand on end.

It was *her*!

"They're tracking you," she said.

"Tracking me?! How??"

"Pick up the radio. Pass it over your clothes."

"What???"

"Do it!"

On the table an old-school radio was blaring tunes from an even older song I vaguely recognized. Something by Celia Cruz, maybe.

Feeling like an idiot—and probably looking like one, too—I snatched it up and began passing it desperately over my body like it was some sort of AM/FM-enhanced metal detector.

I don't know what I expected to happen. Actually, I *did* know what I expected to happen, and that was *nothing*! Which, of course, left me completely unprepared for what *did* happen.

As I passed the radio over my pockets, the crusty old thing began to squeal like a terrified piglet.

"Empty them!" ordered the lady.

"But I don't have anything IN them!" I snapped, digging Mr. Minutes's glossy tarot card out of my right pocket. "Just one of my Teeny Traveler's edition books and this stupid thing!"

"Tear the card in half!" commanded the voice, and so I did (ridiculous as that was), and—¡Dios mio!—inside the sturdy, laminated paper I discovered some sort of tiny . . . *microchip*?

The world began to seesaw around me.

This was too much.

"They're coming," said the mystery voice.

She wasn't lying, either. Three more of those huge dudes in the yellow raincoats—Thunderwalkers—were stalking toward me from the opposite end of the park.

And as if that wasn't bad enough, I saw Mr. Minutes's pickup pull into a parking space on the east side while Mr. Hoursback was closing in by foot from the west.

In other words, there were *one, two, three, four, five* of them and exactly *one* of me. You didn't need to be a math whiz to calculate that the odds weren't exactly in my favor.

"They brought more than I had anticipated," said the lady, obviously annoyed, and I heard myself gulp. "They must know."

"Know WHAT??"

She ignored the question. "Listen to me very carefully, Antares . . . What will happen next you will not like, and I cannot stop. But if you wish to live, remember this: when they capture you, *lie—lie about everything!*"

And suddenly the line went dead.

Suddenly I was alone.

And just as suddenly they were all coming for me.

Without thinking, I took off, bumbling and stumbling into an unsteady run. Up ahead, another Thunderwalker emerged from between a knot of shadowy buildings like something that haunted the pages of a Stephen King horror novel.

My breath caught, and I darted into a narrow street—only to spot yet *another* one!

Whirling, I kept running. Flinging myself down one street after another, unable to shake the feeling that I was being surrounded—*herded*, even!

And I had no clue just how right I was until I'd shot into a dark, empty alleyway and felt movement around me and sniffed the lightning smell and heard the hollow sound of feet pounding on metal and realized, too late, that those were *my* feet, and that the alley wasn't empty at all.

There was something in here.

Something like a giant metal shipping container.

And I'd already run halfway in!

Even as I spun, a large, squarish door slammed noisily shut behind me, swallowing my entire world in darkness.

CHAPTER NINE

ELECTRIC TORNADOS AND OTHER UNPLEASANTRIES

With a jolt of brain-frying panic, I began pounding on the metal door and the metal walls and the metal ceiling, shouting, "HELP! SOMEBODY HELP! ¡AYUDAME!"

Then, from all around me (from *everywhere*, it sounded like!) came the wet, sizzling snap of electricity. And next thing I knew, the container was completely saturated with electrical energy. I mean *saturated*. It snapped and crackled, and crackled and snapped, leaping from wall to wall and arcing across the ceiling like an electric snake, peeling rust and leaving dark charred marks in the corners. Then the container began to spin. And spin. And spin. And suddenly it felt as if I'd been caught in the middle of a massive electric tornado!

And when you're caught in one of those, there's really only one thing to do . . .

"Heeeeeeeeeelp! Somebody Heeeeeelp!

Heeeeeeeelp meeeeeeeeeeeeeeeeeeeee!

Soooooommmeboooooooooodddddyyyyyyy!

Hhhhheeeeeeeeeeeeeeeelppppppppp!

Hhhhhhhhhhhhhhhhhhhhhhhheee

eeeeeeeeeeeeeeeeeeeeeeee

eeeeeeeeeeeeeeeeeeeeeeeee

eeeeeeeeeeeeeeeee

eeeeeeeeeeeeeeeeeee

eeeeeeeeeeeeee

eeeeeeeee

eeeeee

eeeelllllll

llllllllllllll

lllllll

lllll

pppp

ppp

p!"

Just when I couldn't take it anymore, just when I was sure I was gonna pass out from the panic and fear and the sickening way the container seemed to be, at the same time, rising and falling, and falling and rising, the world went totally, completely, absolutely *still*. And quiet, too. The only sound—the *only* one—was the wheeze of my rapid, shallow breaths.

But the quiet didn't last.

A fraction of a second later, the front of the container dropped open with a hollow *bang!* and my mouth dropped open with a hollow gasp.

Maybe a dozen Thunderwalkers were gathered around the opening like a gang of granite gargoyles. Gigantic. Stone-faced. Fresh rainwater ran in rivulets down their sleek yellow rain jackets, and in streams down their sleek rubber boots.

And in that awful moment, two things became very clear to me: one, there was no getting away from these guys. *None*. And two, they weren't even *human* . . .

CHAPTER TEN

•

LIONS AND TIGERS AND CROCS, OH MY!

(1)

Sure, they might've *looked* humanish. They all had eyes and ears and noses. They had heads and faces, arms and legs. They were bipedal, so they moved like humans. They wore pants and boots and jackets and gloves, so they dressed like humans. But once you got past all that surfacy stuff—once you *really* looked at them—you started to wonder how come you hadn't seen it sooner.

First off, they were all *waaay* too big. Easily over seven feet tall and wide as refrigerators. Their legs were like tree trunks. Their hands like catcher's mitts with jagged, talon-like claws for fingernails. Then there was their skin. It was all molted and scaly in places, especially around the sides of their necks. And it had a sickly greenish tint to it.

But the deadest giveaway of all was *their eyes* . . . Those terrible eyes, so beady and unblinking, with black vertical slits for pupils.

Croc eyes, I thought numbly. Those were the eyes of CROCODILE MEN! That ridiculous urban legend!

"*This really is a nightmare . . .*" I breathed.

Only deep down, I knew it wasn't.

You couldn't feel fear like this in a dream.

I was wide awake, and that was the most terrifying part of all.

The instant one of those lizard-things dragged me, kicking and screaming, out of the big shipping container, I felt my entire body tense up.

This time, though, it wasn't out of terror. It was out of shock. The shock that we weren't in Miami anymore—that we might not even have been in *Florida* anymore!

Somehow, someway, we'd ended up in the middle of a remote, tropical island. Except this wasn't your typical tropical island. What I mean is, usually on an island, you can see ocean all around you, for miles. Well, not on this island. On *this* island all you could see was *storm . . .*

Planet-size clouds fringed with lightning churned and boiled maybe twenty miles offshore. The wind howled. Thunder rolled. Sweeping bands of rain lashed down in angry torrents. In fact, the entire island appeared to be surrounded by the eyewall of a massive hurricane! A roaring, raging, roiling storm so dark and dense that it choked the sky.

And it didn't seem to be moving, either. Like, *at all*. The storm was just sitting there, right off the beach, as if trying to decide when and where to make landfall.

I had time to think, *What the—?*

Then those reptile things were shoving me sideways and when I looked up, I saw the scariest thing yet . . .

CHAPTER ELEVEN

THE TERRIBLE TOWER OF TERRORS

It was a castle. No, a *fortress*. Like something straight out of Bram Stoker's *Dracula*! It loomed, impossibly tall, beyond a high barbed-wire fence, clearly visible only in the flicks and flashes of red-tinged lightning. Way, way up high, up near the very sharpest point of the thing, huge black birds (bigger and blacker than any birds I'd *ever* seen!) swooped and screeched like something terrible.

It definitely didn't look like the type of place you wanted to visit in the middle of a thunderstorm.

Unfortunately, my scaly tour guides were insisting.

The lobby was vast and dark, and a forest of bare bulbs dangled from the ceiling on cords, flickering like fireflies caught in a spiderweb. An antique cage elevator took us up maybe a hundred floors and opened onto a large chamber shrouded in shadows.

A moment later, the rough, scaly hands of some crocman thrusted me out of the elevator and into the heavy silence of the room.

And a moment after that, I nearly jumped out of my sneakers as a voice spoke up from the shadows.

"Chances are you're feeling a bit like a sparrow caught in a hurricane," it said coolly. "Torn away from a familiar nest, blown halfway across the world to a mysterious land with no idea where you are or how it is that you came to arrive here. Ironically, like that little bird, a naturally occurring weather phenomenon is responsible for your sudden and miraculous voyage. However, in your case, there were also *guiding hands at play* . . ." Bright silver eyes peered back at me from the darkness on the other side of the room. Then the man whom those eyes belonged to added, "I understand your apprehension—I do. I'm sure there is a raging wildfire of questions blazing through your mind at this very moment. Unfortunately, this is not the time nor the place to quench them. Even as we speak, the sands of time slip out from beneath our feet. I'm sure you can sense this as well."

The only thing I sensed right then was fear. My *own* fear. I literally couldn't stop shaking. But I knew from my favorite books that the times when you're the most scared are the times you need to be the most brave. Just ask Mr. Frodo.

"What . . . what are you talking about . . . ?" I whispered.

"We believe that a great evil has turned its eye upon you."

"A great evil?"

"Yes. A warlord known only as the Mystic. For what purpose it now seeks to contact you, we cannot say. For how long it has had this desire, there is no way to ascertain. But there exists a direct and *powerful* correlation between the amount of information you can provide *us* and the amount of protection we will be able to provide *you*. Do you understand what I am saying?"

"I—I don't know anyone called the Mystic," I said. Then, with the mysterious lady's warning still ringing in my ears (*lie—lie about every-thing!*), I quickly added, "And, uh, no one's tried to contact me . . ."

Sure, this guy didn't really seem like the type of person you should lie to. But he also didn't seem like the type you should be too honest with, either.

And standing in this strange little room inside this huge, strange place, it just felt like the right thing to do.

There were several seconds of dreadful silence during which the only sound was the hissing rattle of a croc thing's breathing.

When the man spoke again, his voice was even colder. Flatter. "Well, perhaps someone did and you did not realize it. Have you run into any *unusual* people in the past few hours?"

Ha! That was practically the *only* sort of people I'd run into. And that wasn't even counting him or the reptile-freaks.

"Not . . . any more than usual, but I'm from Miami," I said, trying to make a funny. No one laughed.

I heard myself gulp. The sound was awfully loud in that cramped lit-tle room.

"At the risk of stating the very obvious," continued the man with unsettling calmness, "if you lie to me, things will not go well for you . . ."

"I'm not lying. I—I'm *not*."

The strange silver eyes dropped to something shaped vaguely like a notebook—a folder, maybe. "Is your name Antares De la Vega?"

"No," I lied.

"How old are you?"

"—I'm fifteen," I lied again.

"You've recently had a birthday, no?"

"No." *Another lie.* "Not recently at all, actually. Like ten months ago. I'm almost *sixteen* now." *Lie, lie, lie.*

Another silence. Longer this time.

A bead of sweat formed at my temple and ran hotly down the side of my cheek. I wiped it away with shaky hands.

At last, from deep in the shadows, the figure said, "I think I see the problem . . ."

I blinked, surprised. "You do?"

"Yes. Apparently, what we have is a case of mistaken identity."

"*Mistaken identity?*" I blurted out. Then, catching myself: "I mean, *yeah*. That's exactly what it is! Mistaken identity. I'm not who you think I am."

"We've obviously caused you a great deal of stress today," the man went on as if I hadn't said anything, "and for that I sincerely apologize. But there is no longer anything to fear. Someone will escort you home now . . ."

"You—you're letting me go?"

The silvery eyes were steady on me. "Why wouldn't I?"

"No, exactly. What I mean is, thanks. *Thank you!*"

"You're quite welcome," he replied politely. Then he signaled to the croc things, and the door to the little room creaked open, and the lizards began filing out.

I gotta admit, at that moment, all I felt was relief. Total, heart-swelling relief! But I would soon learn the consequences for telling lies . . .

One of the crocodilians led me back to the elevator. We rode it down maybe fifty floors, and all the while I thought I could hear the muffled, terrified sounds of dozens and dozens of kids screaming or crying in the distance, on the different levels. I took deep, shaky breaths, telling myself that it was all just my imagination. And by the time the elevator finally stopped and the cage rattled noisily open, I'd almost convinced myself it was true.

The hall stretching out before us was dim and dimming as we went. At the opposite end we came to what might've been the silhouette of a doorway.

The reptilian, who—like most reptiles—probably had very good night vision, stepped aside, motioning me through with a clawed hand. I went in but couldn't see a thing.

Now a light flickered on, and as its pale glow spread, foot by foot, through the space, I saw, bit by bit, that it wasn't an exit but another room.

And not much of a room, either. Small and sort of squarish with no one and hardly anything in it. I didn't understand. Then:

"Welcome home," the lizardman hissed into my ear. And just like that, every single cell in my body turned to *ice*.

It was a horrifying thing to hear. But not as horrifying as the vicious smile in that low, rattlesnake-like voice, and not *nearly* as horrifying as the hollow clang of a heavy steel door slamming shut behind me.

I whirled, panic rising in my throat like a wave, and began kicking and banging on the cold, hard metal as I shouted, "Wait! Hey! Hey, *wait up*! HEY!"

For a moment my thoughts ran

away

on

me,

cycling

through

fear and terror

and spiraling off

on tangents

and wild visions of escape until I looked around and saw the thick concrete walls and smelled the cold stale air and felt the crushing weight of absolute silence beginning to settle over me—over the entire room—and realized, with a fresh tidal wave of panic, that I was alone.

That the crocodile things were gone.

And that they'd trapped me.

Again.

4

The room they'd stuck me in was too small to walk around in and too cold to just stand there, so I climbed onto the little cot in the corner and wrapped myself in the scratchy sheets and sat there and shivered and waited.

But for the longest time nothing happened. (Which was almost a relief, because at least that meant nothing *bad* was happening.)

Sitting there in the silent chilliness, I thought about my aunt. Wondered what she'd done when she got home. What she'd told the police when she called to report a break-in and her missing nephew. I wondered if they'd be able to track me down somehow.

Only I didn't really see how, because the truth was, I didn't even have the slightest clue where I was.

I kept telling myself this was all just a nightmare. A horrible, surreal, all-too-*real* nightmare where monsters in yellow rain jackets came leaping out of lightning bolts to kidnap kids and lock them away in some terrible tower on a lost and forgotten island—an island surrounded by hurricane.

But the worst part about this nightmare? Like the scariest of *all* nightmares, I couldn't seem to wake up.

5

The seconds stretched to m i n u t e s
    And the minutes to h   o   u   r   s
    And the hours stretched o

                        n

                                    a

                        n

                        d

o

n

until soon entire days were slipping by. Then a week. Then two weeks. Then a whole month. And then I lost track.

I was drowning in loneliness, being suffocated by the isolation and the fear and all the thoughts of not-knowing.

I mean, *Why was I here?*

Who were these people?

When were they going to let me go?

And what in the world had made them think that I knew something?

The thought of living the rest of my life as a prisoner and the fear of what might come next pretty much annihilated my appetite.

I hardly touched the bowls of tasteless greenish stew that were slid in through a slot in the door three times a day. Hardly drank the water from the little fountain by the sink.

All I really did was sit there and shiver and wait.

One day, a life-size robot—this incredible Jetsons-looking thing with tracks for feet and skinny metal pincers for hands—whirred quietly into my room to empty the hamper in the corner. Only by that point I was in such a state of despair that I refused to believe my eyes until it was too late, and the robot was gone and the door had closed again.

That was it, I thought miserably, lying there on the cot. *My one chance to escape. Probably my ONLY chance to escape!*

"You'll be stuck here forever," I told myself.

And I believed it, too.

Thankfully, I was wrong.

CHAPTER TWELVE

A MIDSUMMER NIGHT'S SURPRISE

It was probably a little after midnight. The room was freezing cold, and I was sort of floating in that hazy place between awake and dreaming, when all of a sudden, a small scratching, tapping sound caught my attention.

Scratch, scratch. Tap, tap. Tap-tap-tap!

It wasn't in the walls, exactly—and it wasn't in my head, either (at least I *hoped* it wasn't)—but it was close.

My bleary eyes strained to see through the darkness. And that's when I saw it! There—*right* there!—in the center of the room, one of the floor tiles had begun to quiver.

The only light in here (a strip of something in the ceiling) had dimmed way down. It always did that around the time I started feeling sleepy. But even in the dark I'd caught the tiny movement.

I stared with slowly widening eyes. The tile was bouncing and bobbing, it was wiggling and jiggling and wriggling.

It's the world's tiniest earthquake! I thought dazedly.

And then, without warning, the entire square of tile pried itself free and picked itself up and placed itself gently, lightly, and oh-so-*quietly* down on top of its neighbor.

And from out of that hole—or was it some kind of tunnel?—came the most random bunch of "things" *ever.*

First, something like a shovel. Next, something like a pick. Next, something like a mechanical spider with something like a thousand miniature headlights in the center of its round steel face. And finally, something that looked very much exactly like a *chipmunk!*

The ridiculous duo scrambled out of the hole in a puff of crumbly cement. Their tiny dusty tracks seemed to chase them as they skittered about all four corners of the room, racing speedily along the walls and under the few pieces of furniture.

For a crazy second I thought I was witnessing the greatest (and quite possibly *the first*) interspecies—er, inter*something* prison break of all time.

But then a pair of pigtails appeared out of the very same hole!

Well, not pigtails all on their own. These pigtails (like most pigtails) happened to be attached to a head, and that head happened to be attached to a girl, and that girl just so happened to be wiggling herself, ever so quietly, out of the dark tunnel and into my life.

She was about my age, wearing a wrinkly, ratty onesie that once probably looked a lot like the neatly pressed one hanging by my sink.

But the freakiest part? She wasn't alone. From out of the same hole came another somebody: a man, tall and basically shirtless, with wild white hair and a wilder whiter beard.

He was skinnier than the girl (who was pretty skinny), dustier than the robot (whose squat, steel body was pretty much covered with cement dust), and almost as hairy-chested as the chipmunk (who was more or less hairy all over).

From underneath the cover of my bedsheets I watched as they moved busily about the room, measuring the smooth white walls, inspecting the cinderblocks, counting the paces from the door to their hole, from the sink to the door, from one end of the room to the other, until I was dizzy and confused and more than a little annoyed. I mean, who in the heck were these people??

Whoever they are, I thought, they look SERIOUSLY ticked off.

And they sounded it, too . . .

"No! It's another room," the girl was saying in a harsh whisper. "How can it be ANOTHER room??"

"Ancient astronauts!" cried the old man. "I simply do not understand! My calculations were perfect!"

"Obviously not perfect enough!" huffed the girl, throwing her hands up in frustration.

"Well, no, obviously . . . But how could I have been so off???" The man's wild gaze flew around the dark. "I've charted this course for YEARS! I've mapped out every floor, every hallway, every corridor. But to be perfectly honest, I do not have the vaguest notion of what this enclosure even is!"

Finally, I just couldn't take it anymore. Sitting suddenly upright, I said, "This enclosure happens to be MY ROOM!"

And since neither one of them had seen me yet, they both jumped and shrieked and nearly knocked heads in surprise.

The girl, who was holding a short metal rod, suddenly whipped it toward me like she thought it was King Arthur's mighty Excalibur or something.

"Identify yourself!" she demanded.

"What?? You—you identify yourself!" I demanded right back.

She rattled "Excalibur" threateningly. "In case you haven't noticed, I'm the one holding a weapon . . ."

And yeah, I guess she sort of had a point there. "I—I'm Antares. Antares De la Vega."

A flicker of something flashed across the man's dusty face. Was it . . . *recognition*? A spark of memory? I couldn't tell. But then his eyes crossed and his mouth dropped open and he let out this HUGE stinky belch, and I realized it must've just been gas . . .

"Well, *Antares*," snapped the girl, "you frightened us!" The way she said it you would've thought I'd violated some *sacred* law punishable by death.

And now, as she came over to get a closer look at me, I got my first up-close look at her. Her hair was long and dark and purplish, and her eyes were the color of turning leaves: violet, brownish, bordering on magenta, with flecks of gold. She could've been from anywhere in the world—Asia, Latin America, Africa, Europe—and she was, like, *seriously* pretty. Well, at least once you got past all the smudgy, gritty, grayish dust coating her hands, face, and neck.

"I frightened *YOU* . . . ?" I snapped. "You're kidding, right?"

"It seems," said the old man with a relieved sigh, "that we have frightened *each other* . . ."

Then he slunk silently over to the door and, after digging around in his raggedy pockets, brought out a very large (and equally raggedy) rectangle of paper, which he held loosely between his dust-covered fingers. It looked something like a map, only stitched together from many different pieces of paper, sort of like a big paper quilt.

Anyway, since he seemed like the less dangerous of the two, I decided to join him.

"What is that?" I whispered, peering over his shoulder.

"*This*," he proudly announced, "is Blueprint X! It's taken me quite some time to compile. But through a potent combination of physical reconnaissance, logical inference, sub-sonar infrared, remote viewing, and, of course, a fair bit of guesswork, I've managed to map out this *entire* facility!"

I felt my head beginning to spin. ¿Que tontería es esto? "This makes no sense . . ."

"My thoughts exactly!" He raised his "map." "See, we were supposed to end up *here*. But we must've taken a wrong turn *here*. Or perhaps several wrong turns *here, here, here*—and maybe even *here* as well—and wound up somewhere in this general vicinity . . ."

His bony finger traced a quick circle over a section of that quilt-like map that looked suspiciously like a used napkin, and I started to feel even dizzier. "My head feels like it's spinning circles around the room . . ."

"Precisely my sentiments as well! All my life I've prided myself on my *innate* ability to chart and follow a course. On my sense of direction. But in the end, look where it's gotten me—three hundred meters off course and a minimum of *three weeks!*" His wide, wild eyes flew around the room again. "But what's *really* twisting my neurons is this room . . . I was COMPLETELY unaware of its existence! Which can only mean one thing: it must have been built very recently. That is to say, sometime in the last *twenty years*."

"You've been stuck in this place for *TWENTY YEARS???*" I burst out.

"Of course not!" he snapped, which—to be completely honest—calmed me down a little. At least until he added: "Twenty years is merely how long I've been trying to *escape!*"

"You—you're joking, right?" That really wasn't something I could handle hearing at the moment. "I mean, that was a silly joke, *right??*"

But the strange skinny dude with the strange cruddy map didn't answer. He was just sort of gazing blankly off into space. A picture-perfect *the lights are on but no one's home* gaze, too.

"HELLO . . . ?" I practically shouted in his face.

Nothing.

Not even a blink.

But considering how he'd probably spent the last twenty-plus years, I decided to cut him some slack and went over to see what Queen Arthur of the Underground Table was up to.

I found her investigating a dark little corner of my room, tapping her stick lightly against the base of the wall.

My only guess—my only hope—was that she was trying to find a way out of this place.

"I don't suppose I could . . . help?" I asked, coming up beside her.

"No, I don't suppose so. Now *skrat!*" And she went on tap, tap, tapping.

This was too much! It really was.

"Who the heck are you people?!" I hissed.

This time, though, Little Miss Attitude didn't even bother answering; she just shoved me away with the pointy end of her left elbow. So I went back over to the scraggly bearded dude, who seemed to be more or less back at the controls again.

I was just about to ask "Is she okay?" when a big, dusty, dirty hand that smelled oddly of Swiss cheese clamped tightly over my mouth.

"*Hush!*" he whispered, pressing one ear flat against the door of my room. "For we must always be on guard for the *night watchmen!*"

From the other side of the room, the girl rasped, "*Think I've found water . . .*"

I turned and saw that her stick seemed to have come suddenly alive in her hand, clicking rapidly against the bottommost blocks of the wall.

Tap, tap, tap-tap-tap-tap!

The man's large gray eyes suddenly lit up his craggy face. "Ah, most excellent!"

"Mmf mmfmmf??" I said. Then, prying his filthy hand off my mouth: "Why is she looking for *water?* In a WALL??"

"Because she isn't!" he replied cheerily. "Not exactly. She's looking for *pipes* through which, at some point in recent history, water has *flowed.*"

"Okay, so why is she looking for pipes?"

"Well, she's not . . ."

"*Huh??*"

"She's looking for spaces between the walls. *Cavities.* The pipes are merely an indication of their presence."

"But how is she supposed to find pipes or water or whatever with a stick?"

"Ah, I see you are unfamiliar with the ancient and majestic technique of *dowsing*! It's actually more mystic art than technique. But dowsing has been used for centuries by detectives and amateur treasure hunters alike. And Magdavellía, not so surprisingly, has quite the talent for it."

Right, I thought grimly. *Just as I suspected: they're both cuckoo for Cocoa Puffs!*

"But pipes this close to a west-facing wall—well, that's WONDERFUL news!" exclaimed the man.

"Actually, that's the east-facing wall. West is *that* way." I pointed toward the little oval sink, and Magdavellía (or whatever-her-face) sighed and rolled a pair of violet eyes.

"*East,*" she replied sharply, "more likely than not, is *that* way." Pointing impatiently toward the door with her stick.

"Uh, that's actually *south*. And just so you know, I'm pretty good with directions . . ."

Dust-covered Santa, meanwhile, had brought out something like a ruler and was, by the looks of it, making measurements on his map. Suddenly his large, ovoid-shaped head snapped straight up like a Pop-Tart popping out of a toaster and he cried, "*Ancient astronauts!*"

"What is it?" whispered the girl.

"He's right! That way IS west! Which explains why we were thrown so far off course! See, in attempting to calculate the cardinals, I must've fouled up my geometry, thus interpreting east as west and west as south and—well, the result of my error is fairly obvious . . ."

Huddling together, they began whispering harshly back and forth, and as they did, a tiny sound caught my attention: something like a soft, plasticky clicking out in the hall.

Pressing my ear to the cold steel of the door, I said, "What is that?"

"Oh, that's nothing," Mr. Map Man replied distractedly. "Merely a night watchman moving about on this floor . . ." Then, catching himself: "A NIGHT WATCHMAN IS MOVING ON THIS FLOOR!" He whirled on his heels, nearly flying out of his filthy socks. "Magdavellía, whiffsly, back into the tunnels!"

"Hey, where're you going??" I whispered, chasing after them even while the chipmunk and spiderbot scuttled into the hole in the floor, taking most of the tools with them.

"As do all things in the end," said the man, "back to whence we came."

"Can I come?"

"'fraid not."

"But I gotta get outta here!"

"And while I share your enthusiasm for escape, as you can see, we have yet to find a way out. But if we do, you will be the first to know! Well, most likely the third or fourth. But certainly top five!"

"But, uh, how can I contact you?"

"You can't."

"Then how will I know when you've found a way out??"

"You won't." His soot-covered face grinned down at me. "But my intuition is telling me that we are bound to meet again!"

As he started down the hole I called out, "Wait!" And he paused, looking curiously back up at me through the dark.

"Yes?" he whispered.

"Wha—what's your name? I never got your name . . ."

Now the old man's face fell with a sort of shameful look. "I have no name," he admitted. "Names are for free men. But you can call me Zamangar, which in the Ôlden Spёek means 'Forgotten One.' For that I truly am. And you, for the time being, must also forget that I exist!"

Then, returning the tile to its rightful slot, he disappeared beneath it, and the next moment all four strangers were gone.

CHAPTER THIRTEEN

---•---

A MEETING IN THE WALLS

It was easily the most bizarre encounter of my life. Which, considering the fact that I'd recently met walking, talking crocodile people, was really saying something. The good news, at least: I'd finally found my ticket out of this place! Now I just had to wait for them to figure it out, then come back and get me.

So that's exactly what I did. I watched and I waited. I ate and I waited. I slept and I waited. I woke up and ate some more and slept some more and waited some more, and woke up again and waited and waited and waited, but the tile never shook, never moved, never even quivered, and I just sat there, all alone. All by myself. *Waiting.*

And as the seconds and minutes and hours continued to slip sluggishly by, I started to think that they'd never show up. That maybe they'd never *shown up* in the first place. That maybe I had hallucinated the whole thing.

A few times I even lifted the tile out of the floor with the edge of a toothbrush I'd found just to prove to myself that there was actually a tunnel down there. And there was. Every single time.

But it was always a mega relief to see.

It also begged the question: If they *had* come (which they obviously had), and if they *were* real (which they obviously were), then why hadn't they come *back*?

Had they forgotten about me?

Had they *escaped* without me?

Had they been caught or gotten lost—or *worse*?

I had no idea.

But the more I thought about it the more nervous I got, and the more nervous I got the more that familiar panicky pressure began pounding in my hands, my temples.

My panic attacks were back.

Well, sort of.

This panic wasn't so much a fear of missing out, but a fear of what might've happened—what might've gone wrong. A fear of being all alone again when I'd just found other people! (*Four* other people, if you wanted to count the chipmunk and robot, which I, for one, definitely did.)

At any rate, I only knew of one way to deal with my panic attacks. And I just can't describe the *tsunami* of relief that came crashing over me when my anxious fingers dug into my shorts pocket and felt the familiar, rectangular shape of my Teeny Traveler's *Around the World in Eighty Days*!

I'd read maybe half a chapter when inspiration hit me. The book was all about adventure—all about making YOUR OWN adventures. But here I was, too scared to even leave this room!

No. I refused to sit by like some helpless prisoner—even if I *was* a prisoner. It was time to take matters into my own hands.

And since every tunnel I'd ever heard of worked in both directions (meaning, if they could come see *me*, I could just as easily go see *them*), I decided it was time to get some answers.

The hole underneath the tile was crumbly and dark and just about tight enough to make a badger feel claustrophobic. But the moment I'd dropped through, the whole place suddenly opened up, and I found myself standing in the middle of a long, rocky, low-ceilinged tunnel, which sort of reminded me of an old mineshaft.

I started walking, slowly at first, without the slightest clue where I was going. The tunnel bent, and it turned, and it branched off endlessly, and I tried to stay on the main path so I wouldn't get lost, but that was way easier said than done.

It all looked the same to me. The same rocky walls. The same glittery stone. The same rusty, busted pipes running along the ceilings.

"Zamangar . . . ?" I whispered, and listened to my voice echo on ahead of me forever.

It smelled down here.

It was wet down here.

It was dusty and dirty and dank down here.

"Spider robot thingy . . . ?" I tried.

Silence.

"Chipmunk?"

"Mean girl with the stick?"

"Anyone?"

"Anyone at all . . . ?"

Just when it was beginning to look like I should probably turn around—like maybe this *hadn't* been such a bright idea, after all—a hand with all its fingers spread reached out of the shadows and clapped roughly over my mouth!

"HAVE YOU LOST YOUR MIND??" hissed a dangerously angry voice dangerously close to my left earlobe. "YOU'RE GOING TO RUIN YEARS—NO, *DECADES* OF METICULOUS PLANNING AND UNCOMMON DEDICATION WITH YOUR SIMPLEMINDED *BUFFOONERY*! AND NOT ONLY THAT, YOU'RE GOING TO GET US *HANGED*! AND QUITE POSSIBLY *QUARTERED*!"

It was the mean girl with the stick. Magdavellía.

I recognized her by—well, her *meanness*.

"I—*wait*. Is that still, like, *a thing* . . . ? Quartering people?"

"What do you want?!" she spat.

I turned to stare at her through the darkness. Those bright strange eyes were narrowed in annoyance. "No—nothing . . . I've just been waiting for you people, you know?" It sounded desperately uncool. But whatever. It was the truth.

"No, I *don't* know! Why were you waiting for us??"

And suddenly I was the one getting ticked off. "Because I wanna get out of here, that's WHY! I mean, I—I don't know who kidnapped me, or *why*, when they're planning on letting me go—*IF* they're planning on letting me go—or even where in the *purple FREAK* I am right now!" I paused, trying to catch my breath. "Seriously, where are we??"

"Take a look around you, brainiac. Where does it look like?"

"I dunno . . . some kind of *tunnel*?"

"I didn't mean look around *right now*! I meant look around your *cell*. Your *prison* cell . . . You know, the one with the *six-inch-thick steel door* that hardly ever opens?"

I gaped. "This is *a prison*?!"

"It's not *just* a prison. It's the most high-security prison in the world. This is Bermythica."

"*Bermythica?*" I'd honestly never heard of it. But you'd think from the way Magdavellía was staring at me that it was as famous as Alice's trip to Wonderland.

"Yes, Bermythica. The legendary *Hurricane* Prison? Located in the most remote, most *dangerous* stretch of the Bermuda Triangle?"

"Wait. Are you saying we're in the middle of the BERMUDA FREAKIN' TRIANGLE right now?!"

She gave me a funny look. "Did you hit your head on the way down? Of course we are! Where else would Bermythica be??"

The Bermuda Triangle.

THE Bermuda Triangle . . .

I mean, it was *easily* one of the scariest, most mysterious places in the ENTIRE world! I couldn't think of another spot anywhere on the planet where so many people, or ships, or airplanes had straight-up disappeared with so little known about their disappearances, or so few clues left behind.

If possible, I was now even more terrified of this place . . .

"Wh—why do they call it the Hurricane Prison?" I asked in a shaky voice, hardly knowing what to ask.

Magdavellía looked at me like I was a few peanuts short of a Snickers bar. "Because it's surrounded by *ten tons of raging hurricane . . .*"

But who—who in their right mind would build a prison in the middle of the Bermuda Triangle?!

Suddenly dizzy, I slumped weakly back against the husk of a rusted-out pipe, trying to ventilate my panicking brain. "Listen, I just gotta get out of here, okay?"

"Said by probably every prisoner *ever.*"

"But I don't belong in prison! I didn't *do* anything!"

"*Also* said by every prisoner ever . . ."

"Look, just let me help. ¿Más ven cuatro ojos que dos, right? Four is always better than two."

"Not always. Think broken bones." She gave me a real meaningful look, but I wasn't too good at taking hints. "Besides," she said, "I don't trust you."

"Why not??"

"Because you. Are. A. PRISONER! For all I know you could be a *thief*. Or a bloodthirsty *murderer*!"

"Newsflash, kiddo, *you're* a prisoner, too! For all I know YOU could be the bloodthirsty thief murderer person!"

"*Lower your voice!* . . . Are you"—she was shaking her head now, sort of the way people do when they're grasping at mental straws—"from one of the great families of Mü?"

"What? No, I'm from the great family of De la Vega!"

"Your accent. There's something's *unusual* about you . . ."

"Yeah, well, you're not so 'usual' yourself, little miss high and mighty."

Just then a low, twangy vibrating stirred the stale air of the tunnel, echoing around us.

It sounded like a plucked guitar string.

"*SHHHHH!*" Magdavellía snapped (even though I hadn't said anything) and clapped a hand tightly over my mouth (even though I hadn't opened it).

She was staring at something. In the shadows.

Then I saw what: *wires*. About half a dozen or so thin, silvery ones zig-zagging over the stony walls and between the rusty pipes.

That's what was making the sound.

"I have to get back!" she whisper-shouted.

"Why? What's going on?"

"A guard is moving on the floor below us. My floor!"

"How do you know??"

"Because that's what the wires are for! It's our early detection system. Do you know the way back to your cell?"

"I think so."

"Follow the top wire if you get lost. Now go!"

And suddenly I saw my opportunity.

I said, "How good are you about keeping promises? Not very good, I suspect?"

Her eyes flashed angrily. "I've never broken a sworn oath in MY LIFE!"

"Oh, good. In that case, I'll go once you promise to let me help you escape."

"What? NO! Now, go!"

"You gotta promise me first."

"How DARE you disobey a direct order?!"

A direct order? Man, this girl definitely had an attitude problem.

"'Cause I'm daring like that," I replied coolly. "Now promise."

"No!"

"Please?"

"NO!"

"Oh, c'mon—it's not THAT big a deal!"

"You're going to ruin EVERYTHING!" she growled, stomping her feet in frustration.

"Just promise, and I'm gone!"

"You are sooo INFURIATING! And ANNOYING!"

"Me in a nutshell. So is that a promise?"

Magdavellía had that boiling, unsteady look of a teakettle that was about to blow its top. "Yes, FINE! It's a promise! NOW GO!"

And this time, I was more than happy to obey.

CHAPTER FOURTEEN

TUNNELCRAFT

By the time I made it back to my room, I was smiling so hard it hurt. I guess it was just nice to know that I wasn't alone, and that they were still here, still searching for a way out, and that I could find them if I ever really needed to.

Anyway, the second I got back, I climbed onto my cot and gazed cheerfully up at the smooth cement ceiling and started fantasizing about our upcoming great escape.

I pictured us tunneling between the floors like a gang of jailbreaking moles. I imagined us slipping out of the prison under the cover of night, stealing some sleek black speedboat, and launching out, heading toward the Keys or South Florida or heck, even the Bahamas.

Man, I couldn't wait to get outta this place! To *do* something!

Fortunately, it wasn't long before I got my wish.

Barely an hour had passed before the lights dimmed and those awful giant birds stopped screeching and the loose tile in the middle of my cell picked itself up and slid itself aside again, and from up out of the hole emerged two familiar figures—first a smaller, then a bigger.

I sat up, grinning at them from under a teepee of bedsheets. "Don't you two ever knock?"

"Good evening, Antares!" whispered Zamangar with a smile, brushing himself off as the chipmunk and spiderbot scampered past his dirty feet. "And my sincerest apologies for disturbing you at this late hour! But it seems as though fate has once again crossed our paths. See, according to my blueprints, the fastest way out of this prison is through *that* wall beside your bed. And because time is always of the essence, *particularly* when one is trying to escape from a location where the powers at be prefer you *not* escape, I must regrettably ask, would you mind terribly if we hacked through it?"

My grin widened. It was the best news I'd heard in forever. "Not even a little. Mi cell es tu cell."

Those two had this tunneling thing down to a science. An *art*. They didn't simply use brute force to bash and hack their way through the hardened cement walls.

No, they used their *brains* more than anything. In fact, they'd even come up with a method of *softening* the cement. According to Zamangar, colonies of nonaggressive, semi-venomous spiders lived inside the ancient, out-of-order pipes that ran between the walls, and by expertly extracting that almost deadly neurotoxin and mixing it with two tablespoons of powerful cleaning solution (which their chipmunk had stolen from the prison's laundry room) and one tablespoon of regular old table salt (which their chipmunk had stolen from the prison's kitchen), they'd been able to formulate an acidic, semi-corrosive, and borderline stable serum that they kept in a sort of squirt bottle and applied liberally to the cement just before they began their bashing. When life gives you lemons, you make lemonade. In their case, they'd made the kind of lemonade that chews through cement.

As crude as their handmade tools might've looked, they were surprisingly effective, and in really no time at all, Magdavellía had hacked out the grout lines around a square of exactly four cinderblocks at the base of my wall.

On the other side, we discovered a dusty, dirty, narrow little room about the size of a kitchen pantry.

"An old storage closet," whispered Zamangar, "long since sealed and built around. We might be closer to the outer wall than I had initially suspected!"

Magdavellía turned toward me. "You mentioned wanting to help, yes?" And then, handing me a pick: "So help."

The routine of the prison was as reliable and precise as clockwork. First were the meals: the nasty, snot-like stew that was supposed to be super good for you according to Zamangar was served three times a day—at eight o'clock in the morning, twelve in the afternoon, and eight o'clock at night, respectively.

Second were the head counts: a guard checked in on me once every day—always right before lunch—and always very sneakily through a slot high in the door.

And third, the room service: that life-size Jetsons robot that I'd seen a while back popped in every couple of weeks to freshen up the place. (On its most recent visit, I realized that there was a guard—of the human variety, not lizard—standing watch just outside the door while Rosey did its thing.)

Anyway, what all that basically meant was that we could spend the majority of the day however we chose and, surprise, surprise, we chose to spend it in the walls, tunneling.

Early the next morning we were back at it. We chipped and chiseled and hacked and hammered, tunneling deeper and deeper, as quickly (and as quietly) as humanly possible, until we'd dug our way out of that first cavity and into a second. It was hard work. *Very* hard work. And pretty soon my entire body was aching and we all needed to catch a breather.

"*Oh, Antares!*" sighed Zamangar, dropping heavily onto the floor beside me. "How fortunate we are to have your pair of strong hands at our disposal . . . Each and every one of my old bones graciously salutes you!"

I had to laugh at that, even as tired as I was (and as much as it hurt to laugh).

"May I ask—and hopefully this doesn't offend you—but what *heinous* crime did you commit to have earned yourself a stay at this *lovely* establishment?"

I almost laughed at that, too. *Almost.* "Nothing," I said. "I didn't do anything."

"Now, now, don't be shy . . . You are in the company of fellow *law-breakers.* We've all committed transgressions, or at the very least have been *accused* of such . . . Ah"—a mischievous twinkle flashed in his gray eyes—"perhaps therein lies the dilemma, and so I rephrase: not what crimes have you committed, but rather of what crimes have you been unjustly *accused?*"

"I'm serious. Nothing. Like I told Magdavellía, I was kidnapped."

"Yes, she mentioned that to me, thus stirring my curiosity. But I must say, it would be most *unlike* the Society to detain someone without cause. Certainly, *some* accusation must have been leveled against you . . ."

"I—I don't even know what 'the Society' *is*," I admitted.

A confused look came over his face. "Your accent is difficult to place. Are you from the eastern coast of the Maltrads, perhaps?"

"Nah, just the east coast of Florida. I was born in Miami."

"Oh, I see. And how long have you lived in Rymworld?"

"I . . . don't know what you're talking about."

"What don't you know?"

"I don't know what Rymworld is."

That stopped him. "How could you not know Rymworld . . . ? Or are you simply saying that you have yet to visit?"

"I'm saying I've never even heard of it."

"But surely your parents must have at least mentioned it, no?"

"I never met my parents. My aunt raised me. And if she ever mentioned it, I must've been distracted reading a book or something."

All of a sudden, Magdavellía, who had been sitting across from us, petting her eight-legged robot like it was some kind of *house cat*, leapt to her feet like her pants had caught fire.

"He's a spherer!" she shouted, flinging an accusing finger at me. "An *inworlder!*"

I flung a finger right back (no idea why). "An *in-what-er???*"

"*Ancient astronauts!*" cried Zamangar. "But . . . but why in *the Rym* would the Society kidnap a child from inworld?!"

(Even the chipmunk, perched on Z's shoulder, shook his brown furry head like the idea was unthinkable.)

"I *told* you I heard voices!" Magdavellía said hotly. "*Children's* voices . . . He's not the only one!"

"What's *inworld?*" I asked, looking between them.

"Further proof that the Society has been corrupted!" said Magdavellía, totally ignoring me. "Totally and UTTERLY corrupted!"

"Uh, excuse me," I tried again. "What are you people talking about . . . ?"

But again they ignored me—

"The Society has *not been corrupted*, Magdavellía . . ." groaned Zamangar.

And again—

"We have the evidence!" she snapped. "He's sitting right *there!*"

And yet again—

"He is *not* evidence, Magdavellía! We don't know why the Society decided to imprison him. In fact, we don't know anything about him at all!"

Until I just couldn't take it anymore—

"HEY!" I shouted.

And finally—*finally*—they both seemed to remember that I was still sitting here.

"What are you two talking about? And what the heck is *the Society*??"

When it became pretty obvious that neither one was going to answer me, I turned to Magdavellía and said, "Hello?"

But she only sighed. "It would be . . . difficult to explain these things to an inworlder."

"Well, I have no idea what an inworlder is," I said, "but I'd really, really appreciate if one of you would try."

"Telling you anything more will only further endanger you," explained Zamangar. "There is certain knowledge in this world that carries with it great risks. In plain English, the more you know, the less safe you will be . . ."

"Forget *safe*. I wanna know who kidnapped me! Who the freak are these people?!"

Silence from the peanut gallery again. At last Zamangar said, "There are penalties for divulging such information to—well, inworlders . . . But seeing as a more severe punishment is already being leveled upon me, I suppose there isn't much harm in it now, is there?" He hesitated for a moment, as if gathering his thoughts. "I'm sure you've heard of certain organizations such as the Illuminati and the various Hermetic Orders of antiquity—the secret societies of your world. Well, these are nothing more than branches of a very wide, very *ancient* tree, the root and the trunk being *the Society*. The Society is, strictly speaking, what you might call an occult. But you must rid your mind of any dirtiness associated with the word and understand it in its simplest terms: They are the keepers of the secret knowledge."

I shook my head. "What *secret knowledge* . . . ?"

"All knowledge either too terrible or too dangerous for open dissemination. However, the *primary* secret they are charged with keeping is the secret of Rymworld itself."

"And what's a Rymworld?"

"Perhaps a visual aid . . ." Zamangar picked up a sharp bit of concrete from the dusty ground and sketched a sort of misshapen rectangle on the nearest wall. Next he began to fill it in with shapes I vaguely recognized as the six continents.

"Allow this to represent planet Earth . . ." he said, and I couldn't help making a funny face. I mean, a rectangle was just such a silly shape to choose.

"Um, if that's supposed to be Earth, don't you think you should've drawn something a teensy bit closer to a circle?"

"Exactly what a spherer would say . . ." Magdavellía grumbled.

"Actually, that's probably the last shape I would have drawn," Zamangar replied matter-of-factly.

Which confused me. So I said, "What? Why?"

"Because Earth," he answered, "is, in fact, *flat!*"

CHAPTER FIFTEEN

·

BEYOND THE ICE

I could feel a goofy smile spreading across my face as I stared up at him, waiting for the punchline. But he only stared back, poker faced. And suddenly I wasn't so sure one was coming.

"Inworld, or 'the world,' as you know it," began Zamangar, indicating the continents as he spoke, "North America, South America, Eurasia, Oceania, Africa, and Antarctica, lie here at the center, surrounded by a great boundary of ice, known, rather appropriately, as the Great Ice Wall . . . This icy boundary stretches all the way around, linking what you know as the Arctic and Antarctic, and forming a perfect ring. The kingdoms that exist beyond the wall are the various realms and territories known, in totality, as Rymworld."

He paused, giving me a second to absorb that. "The Society's complete name is *the Flat Earth Society*. They were created as a final, desperate attempt to keep our two worlds separate. To keep inworlders from finding their way out into the kingdoms beyond the Ice Ring."

"But—what's the big deal with keeping inworlders out?"

"Ah, well, see, many, *many* thousands of years ago, those born inside the ice discovered those born outside it. They were driven out to the sea and toward the edges of the map by lore and legends of highly advanced civilizations existing on the very rim of this world. And neither distance nor lack of technology was discouragement enough, for the spirit of exploration beats like thunder in the souls of all living things, and soon they discovered them: kingdoms and principalities small in number but great in knowledge, wisdom, technology; and so two worlds very different from one another in thinking, in temperament, and not least of all in resources, met like colliding planets, and nearly all life on Earth came to ruin.

"It was in the aftermath of this tragedy, known as the Hundred Sunsets' War, that the Flat Earth Society was formed. They were charged with the task of rewriting human history and erasing Rymworld from the knowledge of the inworlders so as to ensure another such tragedy would never occur. A truce was struck with the leaders of the inworlders, and the Society's first step to ensure the safety of this world was one of immense elegance: the concept of a spherical Earth. This myth was perpetuated throughout inworld in order that no man, woman, or child would ever be tempted to seek out the places said to exist off the edges of the map, because there were in fact no edges at all, and any searching would ultimately and *inescapably* lead you right back to the place where you started."

He drew a circle in the air with his finger and his lips pressed together and smiled humorlessly. "The essence of futility. And of course, as part of this truce the kings and queens of Rymworld gave much technology and wealth to those inside the ice wall and those inside gave the Society members positions of great power in their various governments to ensure that the past could indeed be rewritten and thus all contact between our worlds forever severed. The rest, as they say, is history."

"But that's—*bananas!*" I whispered.

"No, no . . . Contrary to popular belief, the seeding and consumption of tropical fruits was only a *minor* point of contention in the war. It was simply a case of self-preservation. For war is the only contest in which the winner becomes the greatest loser of all."

"But, no—hold up," I said. "The Earth isn't flat, though. I know it isn't . . ."

A sly grin spread slowly across Zamangar's thickly bearded face. "Is that so? And how may I ask did you come to this most resolute of conclusions?"

"Because I just know, okay? I'm not stupid. I've seen the pictures."

His grin widened. "Is it a habit of inworlders to believe everything you see in pictures?"

"Uh, no. But I know the whole flat Earth thing isn't real. It's make-believe. Made up. I mean, it's impossible . . ."

"Let us consider impossible for a moment. Let us consider make-believe. Let us consider how it was that you came to arrive here . . . Certainly not by any standard means of travel—no, not at all."

I felt the hairs on the back of my neck stand on end. "How—how did you know that?"

"Because there's only one way to reach this place—save for a crash landing or shipwreck, of course. Some would call it thunderporting, a novel process of time-space manipulation. Others might call it teleportation. Still others might call it science fiction. And yet still others might even go as far as to call it impossible . . ." His gray eyes sharpened on mine. "In effect, you were kidnapped by creatures widely thought of as imaginary, transported through time-space via a means considered impossible to arrive on an island that doesn't exist on any map. A place most would think of as make-believe . . ." He knocked lightly on a hunk of cinderblock behind him. "Seems real enough to me, wouldn't you agree?"

I realized I was shaking my head, trying to deny the truth of words whose truth was pretty much undeniable. Heck, I'd seen all that . . . I'd lived it!

And besides, why would he make all of that up? Why lie to me? What would be the point?

"There would be no point," answered Zamangar. "And I *wouldn't* lie to you."

A chill colder than an ice cube ran down my spine at his reply—a reply that just so happened to be a direct answer to my . . . *my thoughts.*

My voice was barely a whisper as I asked, "Did you . . . *just read my mind?*"

"I would say yes, but something tells me that telepathy is also on your list of *impossible* things." I could hear the hint of playful humor in his voice. It was actually sort of annoying, to be perfectly honest. "As I said, knowledge too frightening or dangerous for open dissemination." His face darkened. "You shouldn't ask frightening questions unless you are prepared for frightening answers."

Then, after several moments where the only sound was the chitter of his chipmunk in his pocket and the click and purr of Magdavellía's robot on her lap, Zamangar sighed and said, "But alas, it is time we return to our cells."

"Wait," I said. My brain felt like it was bursting with questions, and I was half afraid it might actually burst if I didn't get at least one more out. "So what exactly lies beyond the Great Ice Wall?"

And now a gleam of something like excitement sparkled in the old sage's wise eyes as he turned back to his sketch. "Ah, well, beyond the Great Ring lie wonders beyond your *wildest* imaginations . . . And your *deepest* fears!"

CHAPTER SIXTEEN

THE FINGER OF FATE

When I was younger, I'd use the phrase "mind blown" for pretty much anything. Any time I read a cool new book. Or watched a cool new movie. Or even saw a random hilarious cat video online. Only I'd never really experienced the power of something truly, legitimately, *genuinely* mind-blowing until *that* talk, in *that* tunnel, above and beneath and between who-knows-what and who-knows-where.

I felt like a goldfish again. Just like I had so many times in the past. Except this time I felt like a little goldfish that had spent all of its tiny little life living inside a tiny fish tank inside a tiny pet shop inside some tiny town and now, all of a sudden, someone had come along with one of those little green nets and scooped me up and carried me off to the nearest pier and dumped me, fins first, into the great big ocean.

If everything Zamangar had told me was true (and I had no reason to doubt him), then this world was a much, *much* different place than I had assumed. Which was *unbelievably* cool. But also kinda terrifying.

Truth was, I'd always thought there was more to the world. At least

I'd always hoped there was. Had always wished there was. But *this?* Never could I have I imagined *this* . . .

Still, that night I dreamed of mermaids and bigfoots. Of mist-covered islands surrounded by giant sea serpents, and forests so old and wise that the trees still spoke.

And the following morning I pestered Magdavellía nonstop with questions about Rymworld, most of which she brushed off in her usual *don't-bother-me-with-such-nonsense* kind of way, the rest of which she flat-out ignored while she chipped and chiseled and hacked.

To say the girl was antisocial (or at least anti-*me*) would've been the understatement of the millennium.

Anyway, later that afternoon, during our first break, Zamangar and me got to talking again. But this time it wasn't Rymworld he wanted to discuss. It was my part of the world. Inworld. And more specifically, *me.*

He was more than a little curious about how I'd wound up here, and since he was curious and I didn't have anything better to do, I told him everything. Starting with Mr. Now, Mr. Minutes, and Mr. Hoursback, all the way to when those lizard-things in the yellow rain jackets kidnapped me.

Zamangar listened attentively, nodding his head occasionally. When I was through telling my twisted little tale he said, "The weather machines the Society designed, in effect, terraform the area prior to thunderporting. Once a powerful enough storm has been generated, they then harness its electrical energy to tear holes in the fabric of space-time, thus creating narrow evanescent tunnels (not too unlike the one we are currently digging) across vast distances. It is based off ancient alien technology."

"That's pretty awesome," I had to admit. (I was just happy that I hadn't hallucinated that part.)

Magdavellía slid a curious sideways look at Zamangar. "What do you make of his story?"

"I cannot pretend to understand all," he answered thoughtfully, "but at least some things are now becoming clear."

"What things?"

"The most obvious: There were three different groups after Antares that day. Each working either to help or to snare him. The crocmen, clearly working to snare. The three strangers, likely a team, and likely attempting to help him evade the crocmen, but also to ensnare him themselves. The mysterious caller, very obviously working against the three men, but *also* very obviously working against the crocodilians and thus the Society."

"Quite the tangled web to weave around a simple inworlder," said Magdavellía.

"Exactly," I agreed quickly. "Well, except for the simple part . . ."

Zamangar turned to me. "Now, this man who came into your home—Mr. Now—what exactly did he say to you?"

I shrugged, trying to recall. "No, nothing. Just what I told you. He's the one who warned me about the Thunderwalkers, and he said he knew my father. Oh, and that he was going to take me to see him. He said my dad was searching for something or had found it and wanted me with him. Something like that. But that's when he went outside and got attacked by the croc freaks."

"*Most interesting . . .*" Z's thick white brows pressed together in deep thought for a moment. "And let me ask you this: Did he happen to mention what your father was after, or what he'd found?"

"The, uh, the *Star of Lôst* or something," I said, remembering. And you would've thought I'd set off a bomb right there in the tunnel!

Magdavellía gasped, her pick tumbling out of her hand to clatter nosily to the ground while her robot gave several nervous beeps and Zamangar's entire face instantly turned deathly pale. In his pocket, the chipmunk appeared to collapse in a dead faint.

"*What did you just say?*" Z breathed.

"What? The Star of Lôst? Pretty sure that's what he said . . ."

Zamangar's voice trembled as he whispered, "Are you absolutely *positive* those were his words?"

"Pretty positive, yeah." And when they both only gaped, "Why? What's the big deal?"

"The *big deal*," snapped Magdavellía, "is that only someone born in Rymworld could possibly know about the Star. In fact, *most* born in Rymworld don't even know about it."

"So . . . you're saying my dad was born in *Rymworld?*"

"Born in or intimately acquainted with its deepest secrets," explained Zamangar. "But let us focus on what we know: a father whom you've never met has discovered or is on the verge of discovering the most sought-after object this world has ever known. He attempts to contact you out of the blue, but is thwarted by the Society, who instead kidnaps and secretly transports you to the most secure prison on the face of this planet. For what purpose? Protection? *Leverage*, perhaps? This is all very curious . . . very curious, *indeed*."

Only I wasn't sure that *curious* was the right word. More like *disturbing*. Or maybe even *highly illegal*.

"Antares, there's no way you could have known this," continued Zamangar, "but that artifact you spoke of, the Star of Lôst, is the very object I've spent my *entire life* searching for! The very object Magdavellía herself had been trying to locate before she got locked in here. And is in no uncertain terms the very reason the two of us—no, in point of fact, the very reason *all three* of us now find ourselves imprisoned on Bermythica!"

I stared at him, half in shock, half in wonder. "But—what is *it* . . . ?"

"It's like a compass," Magdavellía explained, scooping her robot up onto her lap.

"Wait. You're saying we're all locked up in a secret prison in the middle of the Bermuda Triangle because of some stupid *compass?*" Talk about tragic. And with a capital *T*.

"Oh, no, that artifact is so much more than a simple tool of navigation," said Zamangar. "Neither was it forged by human hands, nor has there ever been another like it. But even so, it is merely a means; the end is *power*."

"What do you mean?"

"See, there is said to exist, on the very edge of the world, an island called EverLôst. And within its vast and uncharted jungles there stands a temple—or so the legends claim. And within this ancient temple is said to exist the four treasures of creation: the Wellspring of Knowledge, the Fount of Youth, the Throne of Earthly Power, and, of course, the Cavern of Limitless Wealth . . . Understand, these are the very things sought by all human beings since the beginning of time. And anyone brave enough to enter the temple may take full possession of its treasures. The only obstacle, of course, is the labyrinth that lies deep in its dark heart. A twisted, impenetrable maze, which cannot be navigated with any common instrument of navigation. And so, an instrument worthy of the treasures is required: *the Star of Lôst*. That compass is the only instrument on this planet capable of determining magnetic north inside the boundaries of the temple, and without which no other bearings can be determined nor the labyrinth within penetrated." He leaned contentedly back, shaking his head and smiling softly as if recalling some secret joke. Zamangar's chipmunk, who seemed to be okay again, was standing attentively in his pocket, watching the old sage as he spoke. "It is simply *breathtaking* to watch the finger of fate intervene in the affairs of lowly stardust . . ."

"What are you talking about?" I asked.

"Antares, understand, it was fate—no, *destiny* that has brought you to us, or rather us to *you!* I do not believe in chance, and I see no reason in coincidence, but I can tell you with absolute certainty that mathematical probability alone is not *nearly* enough to account for our tunneling into your cell that night. No, we were *meant* to find each other—meant to *help* each other!" His fingers, dusty and bony but still strong and full of life, firmly gripped my shoulders. "See, we are not the only Star hunters in this world . . . Another also seeks it. A menace. A *monster!*"

And that's when he mentioned a name I hadn't heard since I'd first arrived on Bermythica: *the Mystic.*

"Some say that the terror never sleeps, always searching like the wind. Others believe it is a wraith, a living curse sent from another realm. Whatever the truth may be, we must pray that this Mystic never acquires the Star nor the treasures hidden deep within the heart of the temple, for this world would quickly be plunged into darkness."

The first shivers of real fear now slithered through me. That didn't sound good. Like, at all. "And you . . . you think my dad is trying to stop the Mystic or whatever?"

"I do. In fact, many are. Magdavellía and myself included. Even the Society."

"Hold up. You're telling me that the Society is actually on *our side*? If that's true, why'd they imprison her? Or even *you?*!"

"Mine is a more complicated case. But she was brought here for her own protection."

"That is *your* belief," Magdavellía said crossly.

"Ah, yes, of course. Magdavellía is of the belief that the Mystic has infiltrated the Flat Earth Society and now wields them to its own wicked ends. And though I wouldn't put that completely out of the realm of possibility, at the moment, I choose to believe otherwise." His bright eyes sharpened on mine. "Antares, your father is after the Star. *We* are after the Star. Together we can liberate ourselves from this place, and *together* we can finally discover what for so long so many believed undiscoverable! And in so doing, perhaps even save this world from the *cruelest* of fates! That is, of course, if you would like to join our little company . . ."

Did this guy have any clue who he was talking to? I'd spent my entire *LIFE* dreaming about something like this! It was my first real chance to have an adventure. My first real chance to explore a world I could only have *dreamed* of! Not to mention it was my ticket out of this place and maybe the only legit shot I'd ever get of finding my dad. Who could say no to that? "Yeah—*of course*! I'm in! I'm a million percent in!"

Magdavellía, though—surprise, surprise—didn't seem too psyched about the idea.

"No," she said sharply. "He's a sphere. An inworlder. He doesn't understand . . . *anything*! He'll only endanger us. And himself."

"So we teach him!" said Zamangar. "We train him."

"What can we teach an inworlder??"

"As much as he can absorb. And we'll continue teaching him along the way! Every day. Until he is as knowledgeable and skilled as any Rymworlder."

"Liberating him from this place is one thing. But anything more would be a foolish mistake. You, more than most, understand that the fate of the Rym now hangs in the balance; and I do not want it hanging on the skill, nor the intelligence, and especially not the wiles of some inworlder. We do not need his help. We can find the Star. *Alone*. Just like we planned."

Z sighed and I saw frustration etch deep lines in his weathered face. "Plans *change*, Magdavellía . . . Where has searching alone gotten you? Where has it gotten *me*, for that matter? We both wound up in here, and fairly desperate, might I add—that is, until we found each other . . . And now we have found yet another. One more ally," he said, gently taking her hand in both of his. "Don't you see, my dear? His destiny is aligned with ours, if only for a moment. Why should we tempt fate by rejecting its ready help?" He smiled at her. It was a tender look. "A friend is the most valuable treasure one can find in this great big world. And the bigger you realize it is, the more value you'll place on friendship."

There was a long silence, during which Magdavellía didn't say anything. Wouldn't even look at me.

Finally, I turned to Zamangar. "So you're going to teach me? Train me, or whatever?"

"Yes, we will help you expand your consciousness, thus freeing your mind from the shackles that have bound you from your childhood. But first, you must forget everything you think you know and embrace the reality of what *is*."

"And what reality is that?"

"The reality that you know nothing of this world you live in—not the *slightest* thing!"

CHAPTER SEVENTEEN

—— • ——

THE PERPLEXING PEDAGOGICS
OF ZAMANGAR

(1)

My training was to begin immediately. For the next several weeks, Z showed up in my room a few minutes before we began tunneling and tried to teach me how, through "sheer willpower" and "the irresistible force of thought," to move physical objects through a mostly physical space. He started me off with a rock, and when I told him that I was pretty sure I couldn't do that, he said that I should stare at that rock with "all my concentrated will" until I was confident that I could because belief was the foundation of all force.

Anyway, it wasn't too long before I realized that psychokinesis wasn't a strong suit of mine. And it wasn't long after that I came to the firm conclusion that if mother nature had really wanted rocks to fly, she would've given them a nice big pair of feathery wings.

One night, out of the blue, Zamangar asked me to guess his favorite color. Basically to read his mind (i.e., telepathy). I guessed pink, and to my total shock—*and* Magdavellía's—I was right! Then, a couple of days later, he asked me to guess the chipmunk's favorite time of day and I guessed morning (it was just what I sensed in the moment), and once again he said I was right!

Magdavellía, of course, didn't buy it. And I'm not gonna lie—I wasn't so sure he wasn't just lying to try to build up my confidence or whatever.

But the more time passed, the more *psychic*-y I began to feel. Then, about two weeks into my training, I had my first *almost* breakthrough.

Zamangar had asked me to read his mind again. This time to guess what number he was thinking of. So I focused all my mental energy into the shape of a hand (just like he'd taught me) and then reached up and out with it (just like he'd taught me)—and for a moment it felt as though I was peering into the vast universe of his consciousness!

In my mind's eye, all I saw were numbers:

$$\left({}_{35}58{}_{31}\,{}_{11}9{}_2\,7\,655{}_3\,341{}_{88}1 \right)$$

Numbers, numbers everywhere, but not an integer to square!

But there, *right* there—right in the middle of all that numerical chaos—was one number in particular: it was bigger than all the others and pulsing like something *alive.*

Seven, seven—the number is seven!

And so I opened my mouth to say it, to *scream* it—

But what came out instead was, **"GREEN!"**

Magdavellía and Zamangar both turned to stare at me.

The old man's lips curved up into a big grin.

Magdavellía's bent down into a small frown.

"I think he's getting worse . . ." she said.

And after a total embarrassment like *that,* it was hard not to agree.

But later, when I spoke to Zamangar about it, he just laughed and said, "No, no, no! You're not getting worse at all! You're improving by leaps and laps!"

"But I guessed *green* . . . You told me to guess a number, and I said GREEN!"

"Ah, yes, but what you do not yet understand," he whispered in that low, wise voice of his, "is that numbers have shapes, and they have smells, and they have colors as well!" His eyes, dark and knowing, shone in the soft candlelight of the tunnel. "This world is *far* grander than most give it credit for, Antares. In fact, the only limitations in this unlimited world are those of our own limited imaginations, our own limited dreams, and our own limited hearts with their limited compassion."

Zamangar wasn't the only one teaching me stuff, though. For instance, Mags—yeah, I'd started calling Magdavellía "Mags" occasionally, and mostly just because it seemed to annoy her—anyway, she blew my mind by showing that there was a shower in my room (hidden in the wall next to the sink), which I could open up by pressing the small blue button above the faucet, and which, after sniffing me once down in the tunnels, she strongly suggested I make use of.

Also, she enlightened me (her words) to the fact that Zamangar's chipmunk, whose name was Cheepee, was actually a Nuertinee, a species of hyper-intelligent rodents native to the Rym, and that her bot's name was Deus Ex (it was some kind of personal protector bot that the Society couldn't legally separate her from) and that its name was some kind of joke, but she refused to explain it—which, I'd discovered, was typical Mags. She even refused to answer most of my questions about Rymworld, sort of brushing them off like they weren't even worth her time.

Occasionally, though, she'd let a tasty little morsel slip, accidentally mentioning something about rainbowgem mines or impenetrable sky fortresses, and once she even spoke of a legendary frozen forest where—from what I'd gathered—the first Yeti clan supposedly originated from.

Anyway, as the days passed, my training became more and more complicated and less and less sensical. And when I wasn't learning about clairaudience (the ability to receive thoughts and messages from another realm) or clairgustance (the ability to taste the essence of a substance through the ethereal realm), I was learning about claircognizance (the ability to receive intuitive signals), or I was digging, or hacking away at cement, or crawling through tight claustrophobic spaces with a pick clenched tightly between my teeth, or learning how to raise a metaphysical shield around my brain to hide my thoughts.

But let me tell you—this stuff was harder than it sounded, and it had all sounded pretty impossible. At least it had to me.

A few times I almost gave up on the whole thing. I just didn't feel like I was strong enough, mentally or physically. Then one morning, after another long (and pretty embarrassing) session of telekinesis, Z said to me, "True strength isn't best measured by success, but by one's willingness to fail."

It was the first time I'd heard that. And I guess it sort of hit home.

At any rate, Zamangar promised that my skills would continue to improve, and that soon I would see the point in all this seemingly pointless training.

Little did I know that only a couple of days later he would be proven right. Because only a couple of days later, it was all that pointless training that would save a life.

CHAPTER EIGHTEEN

REAL MAGIC

It was a little past midnight and the three of us were still in the walls, digging. Well, Magdavellía and Zamangar were digging. I was practicing one of Z's mind relaxation techniques (one where you retreat deep into your subconscious) when suddenly something caught my attention.

Movement.

Overhead.

A huge gray hunk of concrete was tumbling through the air. Tumbling right for Magdavellía!

My heart stopped.

My brain stopped.

But somehow the rest of me leapt into action!

Diving forward, I tackled her around the waist and we both went down hard on our sides. As my head smacked painfully off the cement I heard Mags hiss, "*What's WRONG with you?!*"

I could barely answer, my pulse was racing so fast. "*The thing*—it was about to hit you!"

"What *THING*???"

"That piece of *wall*!" I shouted, pointing at the spot on the floor where it had landed, except—

It *hadn't*.

It wasn't there. It wasn't in the air, it wasn't *anywhere*!

Zamangar rushed over. "Are you both all right?" he said breathlessly.

Magdavellía nodded, but all I could do was shake my head, because I didn't know if I *was* all right.

"Claustrophobia," Magdavellía snapped angrily as she pushed to her feet. "It's getting to him. He can't—"

A low whistling sound drew my eyes up as a huge hunk of concrete came tumbling down through the dusty air.

A split second later, it smashed to the ground exactly where Magdavellía had been standing, leaving a deep dent in the floor—which, had I not channeled my inner linebacker, would've been left in *her head*.

For a moment, no one said anything.

Magdavellía was speechless.

Zamangar was speechless.

I was speechless. I mean, that was the *exact* same hunk of concrete I thought I'd just "seen," only I *hadn't*, but yet somehow I *had*! It was wild!

Finally I managed, "*Whoa*."

"You're a *WONDER*!" Zamangar said as we made our way through the tunnels later that night—er, morning. "I've never seen anyone take to the mystic arts so quicksumly! Granted, little children perhaps, with those sponge-like brains of theirs. And of course, I speak only of those little ones who have been steeped in the Old Ways from birth. But someone who just *four weeks* ago believed that the Earth was *ROUND*??? It's mindbafoggling!"

Back in my cell, Z decided that he and Magdavellía would rest here for a bit. Their rooms were still kinda far and he needed to do a little meditation to relax his lower back muscles, which were tightening up on him. He also wanted Magdavellía to check me out. Make sure I hadn't hit my head too hard during our little tumble. So the two of us sat down on the edge of my cot, watching the old sage bend and twist and re-twist himself until his lower half more or less resembled a hairy, cement-covered pretzel.

"Where did you hit yourself?" Magdavellía asked me.

"Oh, uh, right here . . ." I rubbed the aching spot on the back of my head. "I can feel the bump."

"And I can see it."

"Is it bad?"

"Well, it's . . . oh."

"Oh? I don't like ohs. Is that a good oh or a bad oh?"

"Relax, little Nostradamus . . . I was simply admiring the breath and texture of your follicles."

"Of my what?"

"It's basic scalpology. The art of divining a person's character and future from their hair."

"That's really a thing?"

"Uh-huh . . . You'd be amazed how much you can learn about someone by what's growing out of their head."

Ha. I guess that made sense. Kind of. "So . . . what can you tell about my hair?"

"That you could use a haircut."

"Oh, that's hilarious . . ." I said dryly. "Seriously, though, can you divine anything?"

"I should say, I'm not a Seer or anything. But let's have a look . . ."

Her nimble fingers began picking methodically through my hair, starting at one temple and ending at the other. Then, after a few quiet seconds, she said, "You have very broad follicle structures . . . Similar to a donkey's."

"Is that—bad?"

"Typically, it forespeaks of danger. A destiny of walking perilous paths."

Yeah, I probably could've told you that myself.

"Your roots are also quite wide. Like a camel or a horse. And the strand coiliness is reminiscent of that of a goat."

"What's with all the barnyard animal references?" I said, and I thought I heard her choke back a laugh.

"Well, it is *your* hair . . ."

Couldn't argue with her there. "Let me guess, that means I'll probably be kidnapped and held in an island prison in the middle of the Bermuda Triangle at some point."

"Actually, it's typically a sign of great happiness in your future."

"Great happiness?"

"Yes. And often to do with a loved one."

That got my attention. "Wait. You think it means I'm really gonna find my dad?" Just the thought—the mere *possibility*—sent a thrill rushing through me!

"Not . . . *exactly*." Her fingers pressed and they poked and they prodded, and my scalp got all tingly and hot. "In fact, judging by the texture and growth pattern, it doesn't feel like familial love at all. It actually feels more like—*romantic* love . . ."

"*Romantic love?*"

The words echoed in my ears (and in the quiet of my cell) like a struck gong.

Suddenly, we were both sitting very still. Magdavellía's hands retreated immediately to her lap like we were playing the hand slap game, and now I didn't have the slightest clue what to do with mine.

I was about to ask if they played any sports in Rymworld—the awkward silence was *killing* me—when this loud grunting, gruffing, grumbling sound interrupted my thoughts.

At first, I had no idea what it was. But then I realized where, or rather *who*, it was coming from:

Zamangar!

The dude had totally dozed off.

But the funny part? He was still in that funky yoga pose with his legs all twisted up above his head. Even funnier—his chipmunk was doing the exact same pose on Z's head!

Magdavellía and I turned to look at each other. Silent. Serious. Then we both just burst out laughing. It was *waaay* too funny not to.

"That must be some *deep* meditating," I whispered, and probably shouldn't have because it only made us laugh louder. Harder.

Once she'd gotten herself under control, Mags said, "Sounds like he might be out for a sunset. Perhaps *two*."

I grinned. "Is that what a day is called in Rymworld? A sunset?"

She nodded.

"How come?"

"Because we always name things by their most beautiful part."

That's pretty cool, I thought. "By the way, how . . . *old* are you?"

"Five thousand, one hundred and thirty-two sunsets."

Wow, counting by days could make anyone sound *ancient.* "So, like— fourteen years old, then?"

"If you set this so-called year to equal 365 sunsets, then yes."

"—And where are you from exactly? In Rymworld, I mean."

"No place," she whispered.

"*No place?* Is *No Place* nice this time of year?"

A smile tugged on the corners of her lips. She looked nice when she smiled—friendly, almost. "No place *you've* ever heard of . . . And yes, it's *very* nice."

"You miss it?"

Silence.

Then she said, "You never really know how much you miss home until you can't go back." Which, I guess, was her way of saying yes.

"What about your parents? Do they know you're here?"

"My parents are . . . *gone.*"

I waited for her to say more, but she didn't. And I could see she didn't want to talk about it, so I didn't push.

Another silence.

"Do you remember *your* parents?" Magdavellía asked after a few moments.

I shook my head. "Never met them. I have, like, one picture of my dad. Never even seen my mom. I live with my aunt. She's great." And suddenly, I was missing Celeste like crazy.

"Maybe it's for the best," Magdavellía whispered. I thought I could hear tears in her voice. "Maybe this way you won't miss them as much."

"Maybe," I said. Though I wasn't sure it worked that way.

A few minutes later, there was a scramble of movement in the corner (followed by a loud yelp of surprise), and I looked around to see Zamangar springing to his feet.

"*Ancient astronauts!*" he cried. "Did you two doze off??"

"Uh, that was all *you,*" I pointed out.

"No time for blamecaking! Magdavellía, *whiffsly,* we're late!"

Next moment, all four of them had dropped into the hole in the middle of my room.

But just before replacing the tile, Magdavellía looked up and through the dark at me and her eyes smiled as she said, "By the way, did I ever thank you for saving my life?"

Which was sort of a funny question. And I was pretty sure she hadn't, so I grinned and shook my head.

"Remind me to." She grinned back.

Then she was gone.

CHAPTER NINETEEN

THE FORGOTTEN TRAVELER

"Never in my entire life have I seen anyone smile so hard while hacking through a block of hardened, recalcified concrete," Zamangar remarked early the next afternoon when it was only the three of us (me, him, and Cheepee) in the tunnels. Magdavellía and Deus hadn't shown up yet; there had been an unexpected roaming patrol on her floor a few minutes before lunch, and Z wanted her to wait a bit to make sure nothing else unusual happened. "Care to share the reason?" he said, turning to grin at me as I tried—and totally *failed*—to wipe the silly smirk off my face.

"Guess I'm just happy we're getting out of here soon," was what I told him, though it wasn't the truth. Or at least not all of it. Truth was I'd been smiling pretty much since the moment I'd woken up. And I really wasn't even sure why. All I knew was that every time I thought of Magdavellía, I found myself smiling even wider.

"Ah, well, if that is the occasion then allow me join you," Zamangar said cheerily. "After all, that should give me more reason to smile than most."

I couldn't help but laugh. That was actually pretty funny. But also kinda sad. Taking another whack at the wall, I said, "I don't think you ever told me how you ended up here . . ."

"Ah, well, that was courtesy of Kermicus Vae VII, Royal Consiglie-rato to the Chief Inquisitor of the Lonely Isles. His official title was that of *Guardian of the Law*, which I've always found rather ironic considering how easy he found it to trample upon the very thing he'd been sworn to uphold."

"But why'd he lock you up in Bermythica?"

"Because he thought I was lying to him."

"About what?"

"My whereabouts. Where I'd come from. What I'd been doing . . ."

"Were you?"

"Was I what? Lying? No—on the contrary, I spoke *only* the truth."

"And what was the truth?"

"The truth was, and still *is*, that I don't remember a great deal about my past. It is as if my memories have been fragmented, shattered like glass upon the altar of forgetfulness."

"You mean you don't remember—*anything?*"

Zamangar's gaze turned distant. "I remember . . . waking. Many, many sunsets ago. Lying in a field of white lilies, without any knowledge of who I was, where I was, or how I'd ended up in that field. My only possession— my only light—was a single goal burning like a supernova in my mind: I had to find the Star of Lôst. I *had* to. So naturally, I endeavored to do just that, seeking it with single-minded obsession as if finding this artifact of myth would somehow complete me. As if it would somehow bend reality back into shape and make the world make sense again." His eyes grew dim. "I feel as though I've been searching for it for a *hundred* lifetimes . . ."

"But Kermicus didn't believe that," I said.

"No, unfortunately, he did not. And because he died only a short time after having me secretly imprisoned, I never got the chance to change his mind."

"Wait. You're saying that you're in here because someone secretly imprisoned you, didn't tell anyone, and then *died*??" ¡Orale! That was a tough break!

"That is the general gist of my plight . . . By the way, did you know that I am considered the most dangerous prisoner in all of Rymworld?"

"You're kidding."

"I wish I was. Because the charges against me were never revealed, the guards have taken it upon themselves to bestow upon me all manner of high crimes and misdeeds. I believe I am up to 1,396 executionable offenses."

"That's . . . almost funny."

"Quite. Though the joke has lost a bit of its humor over the past few decades," Zamangar said dryly. "—This wall must be pure limestone . . ." He looked around like he was missing something. "Now where in the world is my—"

But Cheepee was already dragging over a squirt bottle of that anti-wall venom.

Zamangar grinned at his hyperintelligent little helper. "Ah, yes! Many thanks, my friend."

And as he reached up to squirt some on the wall, the raggedy sleeve of his raggedy top pulled back and I caught a glimpse of a small tattoo inked into the pale skin of his left wrist. This cool triple triangle thingy with what might've been an all-seeing eye in the section where all three triangles intersected.

Before I could ask him about it, footsteps echoed in the tunnel and we both turned to see Magdavellía step into a pool of orangey candlelight.

Only . . . she looked *way* cleaner than usual. Her hair was nicely combed, and her prison-issue jumpsuit looked pretty fresh. But her hands, knees, and face were already covered with a fresh layer of cement dust. You just couldn't avoid the stuff down here.

"Ah, Magdavellía! Come to relieve the weary, have you? My old bones are so *very* appreciative . . ." Zamangar paused, frowning. "Where's your pick?"

"My *pick?*" Magdavellía blinked. Then, looking pretty embarrassed (and very pretty): "I must've forgotten it in my room . . ."

"Uh, well, I could, uh, help you—*find it* . . ." someone chimed in. (It was probably me.) I mean it *was* the gentlemanly thing to do, right?

And now Magdavellía—for the first time in *all* the time I'd known her—sort of blushed. "Yes . . . *yes,* that would be—*helpful.*"

Zamangar, meanwhile, was eyeing us like a quick-eyed teacher who'd just busted a secret note-passing ring. And standing on his knee, so was Cheepee.

"I could also make sure . . . that you get back . . . safely and stuff," I added (no idea why).

"Exactly," agreed Mags. "That would make me feel . . . *safe.*"

Zamangar's bushy brows arched. His suspicious look was slowly morphing into a sly half-grin, which he was now doing his best to hide.

"Yes, why don't you help her, Antares . . ." he said as he raised his makeshift pick to begin hacking at the wall again. "But please do be brief. We still have a prison to escape."

The older tunnels—the ones Magdavellía and Zamangar had dug out before I'd arrived—were really something. They reminded me of a secret underground lair, something a superhero might have, with all the nooks for sitting and hiding things, the piles of supplies, and the seemingly endless rows of makeshift tools hanging from a seemingly endless row of makeshift pegs.

"Watch this," whispered Magdavellía, and I watched her press the palm of her hand flat against a plank of rotten wood that ran up and along the tunnel wall.

All of a sudden, the plank seemed to burst apart as thousands of tiny, glowing insects came swarming out on translucent wings.

"How'd you do that??" I gasped as one hovered, flickering, right between my eyes.

"I simply asked them to come out," Mags said matter-of-factly. "Glomites, like many insects, are hive-minded, so they're easy to communicate with."

The girl could talk to bugs. Now *that* was awesome.

As we continued down the tunnel, Magdavellía and I couldn't stop laughing as we let the glomites land on the tips of our fingers, and on the tips of our noses, and blew them, buzzing and twinkling, off the tips of each other's hair.

For a while there, I almost forgot we were stuck in some terrifying island prison in the middle of the most terrifying stretch of ocean in the entire world.

I guess the old saying was true after all: no hay mal que por bien no venga. There really wasn't any bad from which something good couldn't come.

CHAPTER TWENTY

—•—

PYTHAGORAS' RIDDLE

The entrance to Magdavellía's room was through a loose tile in the gap underneath her cot, which Deus was kind enough to remove for us as it led the way in.

Crawling into her room was like crawling into the pages of some huge concrete book. Every inch of the walls was covered with writing, and every bit of the writing was that loopy, fancy lettering you typically see in calligraphy books or very important historical documents.

Words were everywhere. They scuttled up the walls. They flew across the ceilings. In places, they scuttled back *down* the walls, spilling onto the floors in long, inky smears.

I could see headings and page numbers, strange symbols and little doodles, and even great big blocks of text (like in an encyclopedia)—and I found myself turning in slow circles, trying to take it all in.

"What do you think?" whispered Mags.

"What . . . *is* it?"

"My parents' journal. Every single word they wrote over their decade-long search for the Star."

"Your parents were after the Star, too?"

"They died trying to find it. Trying to beat the Mystic to it."

"I—I'm *sorry*."

"Don't be. They were happy to risk their lives to save this world. Which is why I'm happy to risk mine." Her voice was strong, steady, but I could tell there were tears joined to those words. And since I didn't want to see her cry, I sort of changed the subject.

Running my fingertips along the jumbles of strange letters, I said, "So these are *clues* . . . ?"

"Clues. Bits of information. Really anything they thought could help."

"But why did you . . . decide to turn it into *wallpaper?*"

"Because I didn't want to risk forgetting something. The Society confiscated the journal when they arrested me."

"Hold up. You did all this by *memory??*"

She nodded. "A strain of hereditarian hyperthymesia runs through my family."

"Huh?"

"It's a form of photostatic memory. I can remember most things I see. Doesn't mean I can't ever forget—I *can*. But my memory is fairly strong."

"I'll say." My eyes traced the flow of the words up one wall and down another, around the little sink, and then up onto the ceiling where the writing looked the lightest and freshest. "Is that where the journal ends?"

"Yes. That is where my parents' quest for the Star ended and where mine began."

Up above her cot was a large, bizarre-looking triangle with smaller, even more bizarre-looking symbols drawn along its sides.

The symbols were sketched within and without: streaking comets and shooting stars, bright full moons, swirling nebulas, and in the midst of it all, a great tree bearing planets instead of fruit.

"What is that?" I asked, squinting up at the rad design.

"One of the oldest secret marks of the oldest secret society in all the world."

"What does it say?"

"*All is number.*"

The words sparked a memory. I'd heard that before. "Who said that?"

"He is known in inworld as the first mathematician. But some simply call him Pythagoras."

"Ah, right . . . He of the triangle fame."

That got a smile out of her. "My parents, like most who've studied Star lore, believe that the Pythagoreans were the most erudite Rymworldian cult when it came to knowledge of the Star. At one point they possessed nearly all its sacred texts."

"But the Pythagoreans are from *my* part of the world—I mean, inworld."

"Pythagoras was born in Trïgôs, in Rymworld, not Greece. But yes, he and his followers also rose to fame within the Great Ice Ring after they were expelled from Rymworld for some of their more . . . *radical* beliefs."

Whoa. Who would've thought? "So, that triangle is supposed to be, *what?* Another clue?"

"I think so. It's the last one my parents ever wrote in their journal, only it's not like the others."

"How do you mean?"

"I don't believe it's something my parents found. I believe it's something they *made.* Something they left for *me* to find."

"What makes you think that?"

"See the small cursive *D* in the top left-hand corner? It's how my mother and me marked all the letters we passed back and forth since I was little."

Like a mark of authenticity, I guess. Pretty cool. "So—have you been able to figure it out or whatever?"

"No. But it's not uncommon to see this ancient mark in books and monuments throughout Rymworld. It usually means there's a secret hidden in the midst."

Interesting. Okay. So there was a secret hidden in here. *Somewhere.* Somewhere in this "journal."

But . . . *where?*

My eyes carefully scanned the intricately drawn symbols and words— and slowly, and mostly by chance, I realized that a few of the page numbers had been circled, five of them to be exact—6, 10, 21, 36, 55.

"Why did you circle those?" I asked, pointing.

"Excuse me?"

"Those page numbers. Why did you circle them?"

Magdavellía shook her head. "I didn't. That's how they were in the journal. I simply transcribed it as it was. Why?"

"Those are *triangular numbers* . . ." I said as it dawned on me. "It's missing some in between—15, 28, 45. But yeah, I'm pretty sure they're all triangular numbers."

"*That's right* . . ." she murmured. "How could I have missed that?"

"Maybe those numbers are the secret hidden in the journal. Maybe they're a combination to something."

"What? 6, 10, 21, 36, 55—"

She got that far, and not another word before the weirdest thing happened: Deus Ex, who had been sitting patiently at her feet, began buzzing and glowing like an angry glomite.

Suddenly, a hatch on the underside of the spiderbot's bloated steel body slid silently open, and it got up and sort of clambered sideways like a hen climbing off a nest. And like a hen, the bot had left behind an egg. Or at least what *looked* like an egg.

"Um, what just happened?" I whispered to Magdavellía, who was staring with golf-ball-size eyes down at Deus, looking about as shocked as I felt.

"I think you may have just uncovered the secret . . ."

"Deus Ex has storage capabilities," she explained. "I used to keep trinkets inside of her when I was little. But . . . *this*"—she picked "the egg" slowly up off the ground with careful fingers—"this I've never seen before."

Up close, I could now see that it was more lead-colored than white, and more ball-shaped than egg-shaped. In fact, it looked almost like a tennis ball, except that it had twelve sides, twelve flat faces, which technically made it a—

"A *dodecahedron*," Magdavellía whispered, turning it slowly in the overhead light.

And that's exactly what it was. A dodecahedron! A three-dimensional shape with twelve plane faces.

I'd just opened my mouth to say, "So what do you think it *is*?" when a sudden, violent shudder went through the floors and through the walls and up the soles of our feet.

Magdavellía froze.

I froze.

Then, just as quickly as it had started up, the shuddering stopped.

¡Santo cielo! "What the heck was that??" I rasped.

"An earthquake?"

"You think?"

"What else?"

We stood there for several seconds, blinking uneasily in the silence.

"Good thing we weren't down in the tunnels," I whispered, thinking of all the pieces of rusty pipe and loose hunks of cinderblock that had probably been rattled loose by a tremor that strong.

"Very good thing," agreed Mags, and that's when we realized it— realized it at the *exact same time*—

"ZAMANGAR!"

Fortunately—thankfully!—our fears never materialized. Z was totally fine, and we found him wiggling his way into my room through the hole in the base of the wall just as we came wiggling our way up through the hole in the middle of the floor.

"There was an earthquake!" Magdavellía shouted. "Did you feel it?"

"I felt it," Zamangar replied. "But that was no earthquake. It was an *explosion*! Bermythica is *UNDER ATTACK!*"

CHAPTER TWENTY-ONE

THE SIEGE OF BERMYTHICA

"But who in *the Rym* would attempt to besiege Bermythica??" shouted Magdavellía, just as a low metallic hum vibrated through the air.

We all turned.

They both paled.

"The early detection strings!" Mags shouted, turning to Zamangar. "Your floor!"

Z's cell was the farthest from mine, and when we finally made it, sweaty and sucking wind, he very carefully jiggled a stone loose from the base of the wall and then very, *very* quietly slid it aside, opening first a crack, then a sliver, then a slit.

We stood in a row, peering anxiously into his cell.

And as we watched, a maintenance bot came rumbling through the open door, beeping, buzzing, and scrubbing the floors with its myriad of soapy brushes.

"It's early . . ." Mags whispered. "That almost never happens."

And, I noticed, there wasn't a guard standing watch at the door, which absolutely *never* happens.

Right then a squad of soldiers in full battle gear went pounding down the hall, shouting and barking orders. In the distance I heard a series of resounding **BOOM!**s that sounded an awful lot like cannon fire.

Magdavellía looked straight-up shocked. "Bermythica really *is* under attack!"

"Undoubtedly!" agreed Zamangar, pushing the stone in the wall completely aside, "and in every crisis, an opportunity! Whiffsly, children, this way!"

Without wasting a mintick, we followed Z into his room and then into the large plastic hamper in the corner, burying ourselves beneath a pile of dirty sheets, while Mags hissed, *"This isn't going to work!"* and Cheepee screeched something that sounded suspiciously like *"Bad idea! Bad, bad, very bad!"*

Which was exactly what I was thinking, too.

But the next moment we were moving, the maintenance bot dragging us steadily toward the door between its strong metal pincers and then dumping us, headfirst, into the big laundry basket parked out in the hall.

Then we were moving again, rolling rapidly along while distant shouts and the jingle of heavy armor sounded all around us, coming from everywhere.

Zamangar's head poked cautiously out of a pile of dirty socks to look around; in that same instant I heard someone yell, "Prisoner! In the laundry basket!"

Magdavellía's bot began buzzing uneasily. I couldn't blame it.

The next second, a crackle like a bolt of lightning sizzled by just overhead, and Z instantly ducked back down, shouting, "My apologies, children, but it seems that we have been discovered!"

And now I could hear the pounding feet of soldiers closing in from every direction. ¡Madre mía!

A heartbeat later, our "getaway" basket shuddered as we slammed into something—a wall, maybe.

Magdavellía cried, "WHAT WAS THAT??"

But no sooner had those panicked words come flying out of her mouth than the rear of the basket began to rise jerkily off the ground.

And before any of us even knew what was happening (at least before I knew what was happening), the basket tipped all the way forward, and I caught a glimpse of a square section of wall sliding open, and a deep, dark chute beyond.

We tumbled down a steep steel chute so fast and in such a tangle of arms and legs and laundry that I could hardly see or even scream!

Below us, another hatch slid open, and we dropped onto a mountain of rumpled sheets and pillowcases, standard-issue gray shorts and standard-issue gray shirts.

"We've made it into the laundry!" cheered Zamangar, picking someone's dirty underwear off his head. "And alive! This is wondificent!"

But even more "wondificent," the laundry room just so happened to have a large vent to the outside—basically a way to let all the hot air out. And while this vent might've been pretty much impossible for any of us "larger" inmates to open, it was a slice of carrot cake for a certain dynamic duo. At Z's instruction, Cheepee scampered into the vent to undo some inner anti-tamper mechanism while the Swiss Army knife of personal protection bots extended a kind of electric hex-wrench from within its spider-like body and undid the fifty or so complex-looking security screws holding the vent in place in about five seconds.

In no time at all, the five of us were rappelling down the outer east-facing wall of the legendary tower prison, using a similar technique to the one developed long ago by another prisoner by the name of Rapunzel. Only instead of about seventy feet of braided golden hair, we were employing roughly seven hundred gold-colored dirty bedsheets, tied end to end, to climb our way down to ground level.

The instant our feet touched the solid earth, we ducked stealthily into the marshy, mushy tangle of black mangroves, which grew wild around almost the entire island.

Behind us, lightning bolt after lightning bolt slashed viciously across the sky, lighting up the world in the most violent shades of blue. I turned, expecting to see a raging storm rolling in off the opposite coast. But what I saw instead was even scarier.

It looked like a war zone. A futuristic laser beam shootout right out of *The War of the Worlds*!

On one side you had team Bermythica—the prison guards and rain-jacket-wearing crocmen. That bunch of jerks was taking cover behind tank-like hover-jeeps or poking their heads out of high windows while unleashing volleys of screaming red laser beams.

On the other side you had the "away" team—battalions of freaky-looking peeps in long, dark robes and dark hoods, dark iron masks and dark iron boots. Their blaster thingies, which looked pretty similar to those of the prison guards, produced slightly longer, slightly more purplish beams that instantly liquefied any carbon-based life-form unfortunate enough to find itself in their sizzling path. Kidnapping crocs included.

I could hear shouts and screams and the ear-busting echo of explosions; every now and then a fresh lightning bolt would come zigzagging down from the sky, and from inside it another iron-masked soldier— sometimes two, sometimes three, sometimes four—would leap out to join the others. *Thunderporting . . .* I remembered. *They were invading through the skies!*

I gaped. "Who the heck are those guys??"

"Enemies!" replied Zamangar. "The Mystic's foot soldiers!"

A moment later, a giant black shadow passed briefly over the mangroves, and I crouched instinctively, swinging my eyes skyward. High above everything, those enormous black birds had begun to swoop and screech like nightmarish winged ghouls.

I heard someone gulp. Chances are it was me.

"How are we getting off this island?" Magdavellía asked anxiously.

"The same way we all got here." Zamangar's long, pale finger pointed east.

Maybe three hundred yards away, I caught a glimpse of a bizarre machine—something straight out of an H. G. Wells novel. It looked like a Frankensteined cross between Tesla's famous coils and a ginormous bug zapper, sending these great sizzling bolts screaming into the black sky, tearing holes in the cloud cover.

"Is that the Thunderporter?" I asked, and Z gave a fast nod.

"You *do* know how to operate that thing, yes?" said Mags. "Because I've heard some fairly *gruesome* stories about people being *thundersnatted* . . ."

"Have no fear, my child! I have spent the last *fifteen years* carefully observing every action of the operators from my stony perch. Memorizing every button, every lever, every *switch*! If there is a soul on this island qualified to operate that machine, I tell you, it is me!"

Only we never got to find out how much of an expert he really was because just as he said that the roar and buzz of a powerful turbine engine filled the air. An instant later, a massive jet-black hovercraft came careening around the far side of the prison and plowed straight into the Thunderporter with the force of a runaway freight train.

There was a small explosion—near the Thunderporter's control console—then a much bigger one—in its shallow pit—and the next moment, the three of us were suddenly lifted off our feet on the wings of a ginormous greenish-orange shockwave and flung backward into the marsh.

We landed in a tangle of limbs and mangrove roots, and when I could finally feel my face again, I croaked, "Hope you spent a few years studying a *different* way outta this place, 'cause option A seems to have blown up in our faces. *Literally*."

Zamangar's left eyelid had begun twitching spastically. I don't think he had been mentally prepared to see something like that happen.

Magdavellía's robot, which had now attached herself to her upper arm like a vambrace, had begun to beep uneasily. Magdavellía glanced down at the bot, then swiped her hair out of her face, looking desperately around. I knew exactly what she was thinking, because I was thinking the exact same thing: *There HAD to be another way off this island!*

"Deus Ex is right!" she said suddenly, nodding toward the south side of the island, where I could just make out the outline of some huge square building, black against the thunderlit sky. "We can take one of the planes!"

Zamangar, still looking dazed with shock, began shaking his head in disbelief. *"A plane,* Magdavellía?! The skies surrounding Bermythica are LIVING DEATH! They're saturated with super gravity waves, electronic fog, random rips in time-space. And lest we forget, even if we somehow survived all that—which, mind you, is EXCEEDINGLY unlikely—we'd still be flying through roughly ten tons of *RAGING HURRICANE!* . . . It's a *fool's* hope!"

"Maybe," said Mags, "but it's our *only* hope."

CHAPTER TWENTY-TWO

THE GREAT ESCAPE

The depot—also known in these parts as the Cemetery, according to Z—was located at the marshy southwest tip of the island, next door to the armory. The bad news: both the armory and the attached barracks were crawling with Society soldiers. The good news: they were sort of distracted at the moment, and the mangroves were dark and thick and the swampy, murky water was deep, giving us plenty of cover along the way. We managed to slip in through a busted window without being spotted, and not five minutes later had found our ticket out of this place—a little seaplane with a doo-doo brown nose and single, not-so-shiny propeller—among the huge graveyard of wrecked airplanes and shipwrecked ships.

There was only one problem . . .

"How are we supposed to start the thing?" I said, even as one of Deus's spindly metallic legs sort of reconfigured itself into the shape of a key and hacked the ignition.

Well, that works, I thought.

Only it didn't.

The engine wouldn't turn over.

"Perhaps the battery cables are loose!" shouted Mags.

In the next instant, Zamangar and I were out of the cockpit and popping the hood. I knew enough about boat engines to quickly locate the battery and enough about batteries to tell that this one was properly connected but also ancient and crusty and probably long-since *dead*.

I'd just gotten the bright idea to go snatch a fresh one from another (i.e., *a not-so-crusty-looking*) plane when a voice said—or rather *hissed*, "Move not, die not."

Zamangar turned. We *both* turned. And slowly, very, very slowly, peered up into the leathery, lime-green faces of two crocodile men. Two crocodilians!

In each of their clawed hands was something like a crackling, electric sword.

And naturally those swords were pointed at *us*.

Fantastico. Now I could officially cross being held at swordpoint by Captain Hook's least favorite species of reptiles off my bucket list.

On the other side of the grimy windshield of the little seaplane, I could see Magdavellía in the cockpit watching this scene unfold with wide, fearful eyes; in that same moment, I felt—no, I *heard* (only not with my ears):

Do not panic, Antares.

I will handle them.

And then (and with a wave of emotion that I felt in the very deepest part of me):

Go on, my son! Find the Star. Find your father. Save this world!

And take good care of my little Cheepee.

It was Zamangar. He'd spoken directly into my mind! And suddenly, I understood *his mind*! He was going to sacrifice himself for us. His freedom for ours.

Without thinking—without even caring what might happen to me, or to our escape plans, or to *anything* else!—I opened my mouth to shout, "No—Z, *don't!*"

But it was too late.

Because right then Cheepee, who'd been chirping menacingly at the pair of bipedal crocs, sprang out of the old man's pocket as if flung out of a slingshot.

He landed on the wrist of the nearest croc freak, and a mouthful of tiny razor-sharp chipmunk teeth bit down. *Hard.*

The reptilian let out a ghastly hiss of pain and surprise just as Zamanga threw himself at the other one, tackling it around the scaly waist.

The crocodilian Cheepee had clamped down and swung its electric sword twice (and I was pretty sure at me) as I turned to run. And clearly those swords weren't just for slicing—they could apparently shoot blasts of energy, too, because that's exactly what happened!

The first one went screaming past my cheek in a sizzling blue blur, making all the little hairs around my ear instantly stand on end.

But the second was a direct hit. Only *probably* not at all how Mr. Tall, Mean, and Scaly had intended.

That blast hit smack in the middle of the plane's little engine, sizzling first into the metal framing, then into the wires, and finally into the dead battery, giving her the ole Frankenstein *zap of life!*

A heartbeat later, the plane's big aluminum propeller spun, sputtered, popped, then sped into a screaming silver blur, which blew my hair back from my face and nearly blew the rest of me away, too.

Translation: the stupid croc had basically given us a jump start!

"GET IN!" Magdavellía shouted, flinging open the pilot-side door.

"Coming!" I shouted back.

Only I barely made it two steps before another sizzling crack ripped the air of the mechanical graveyard and a sizzling purplish bolt struck me square on the chest!

The massive electrical charge knocked me clear off my feet, and I went sliding in a wild tailspin for maybe ten yards before I finally came to a not-so-soft stop with the not-so-gentle help of a gigantic rusted ship anchor. (In other words, it *hurt*.)

For a dreadful moment, I was too terrified to look. I knew exactly where that bolt had hit me and that was roughly a *nanometer*—if that—above my heart!

I sat up in a panic, yanking down the collar of my shirt, expecting to see a huge smoking crater blown right through the middle of me.

But the only smoking crater—and not much of a crater at that, barely the diameter of a golf ball—was in the breast pocket of my prison-issue top.

My skin was fine.

My heart was fine.

Everything seemed perfectly, one-hundred-percent fine.

But how could the blast not have hur—

My *Teeny Traveler's* Around the World in 80 Days!

I'd put it in my pocket, and yes—there it was! Well, at least what was left of it . . .

My fumbling fingers dug it out and I saw that about 432 of the 453 pages had been instantly incinerated, and what was left of those pages were singed black and smoking.

But it had saved me! It had absorbed the blast!

I always knew a book would save my life . . .

"ANTARES! ARE YOU ALL RIGHT?!" I heard Mags cry from inside the cockpit.

"Uh, I think so!"

"Then stop wasting time and get in!"

Good thing I listened, too, because not a split second after I dove in through her open door, reptile brain over here unleashed another string of blasts, which pinged and whined off the nose of the little plane as Magdavellía pointed it at him and put the pedal to the metal—or, in this case, *the throttle.*

Just before Mags shut us into the cockpit, Cheepee—easily my favorite rodent of *all time* now (sorry, Mickey)—leapt nimbly into the cockpit, skittering up my side.

"Hold on!" shouted Mags.

I tried to rattle the passenger-side door open, but the stupid thing wouldn't budge. "WHAT ABOUT ZAMANGAR??" I screamed. "We can't leave him!"

"He's made his choice."

"But we CAN'T!"

"Do not even *THINK* about rejecting this kindness!" Magdavellía snapped, and already I could see bright tears forming in the corners of her violet eyes. "For that will be a *FAR* greater insult to him than any prison cell!"

Cheepee, now standing on the rusty doorframe, furry little face pressed against the dusty glass, was staring sadly back at Zamangar with tiny, tear-filled eyes. Somehow, he understood.

For several awful seconds, we both watched with sinking hearts as Z did everything physically possible to distract the croc soldiers, wrestling with one, grabbing at the other's legs, trench coat, electric sword. But it clearly wasn't a struggle he was going to win.

The plane lurched forward, rusty, wonky tires squealing. One moment we were rolling out through the side doors of the depot, and the next the nose lifted and the cockpit shuddered and the wing flaps caught wind and the-little-plane-that-could surged up, up, up, carrying us—almost sort of bravely—into the black and boiling sky.

I could hardly believe it. But—

"We're flying!" I screamed with a rush of exhilaration. Then, with an equally powerful rush of sadness, I thought: *Goodbye, old friend . . .*

And felt a single tear tumble coldly down my cheek.

"Strap in," ordered Magdavellía. She sounded nervous. Anxious. And then I saw why:

Up ahead, the ten tons of raging, roaring hurricane that surrounded this secret island in the middle of the Bermuda Triangle churned and boiled like something very much alive and very, *very* angry.

Lightning crackled. Thunder boomed. Huge black clouds bumped up against us on all sides while rain lashed the windshield like liquid whips, making it impossible to see anything.

Suddenly this didn't seem like such a great idea.

"Keep an eye out for black holes," said Magdavellía tightly.

I gaped. "For *WHAT?*"

"Black holes. Slivers of space-time where gravity is so strong that light cannot even escape. They've been known to spontaneously form within the boundaries of the Bermuda Triangle."

Was she kidding right now? "Please tell me that you're jok—"

Just then, something came streaking through the thunderclouds and the rain and struck the windshield with almost enough force to shatter it.

Magdavellía and I both screamed, jumping back in our seats as claws like sharpened daggers suddenly appeared through the pounding hail, scrabbling lightly across the glass.

Thunder shook the air, and in the flash and sizzle of a lightning bolt, I saw arguably the scariest thing I had *ever* seen.

Through the cockpit windshield, a single cold-blooded eye—predatory and prehistoric—glared menacingly at us from an equally cold-blooded and ridiculously *elongated* face.

A pterodactyl . . . I thought numbly. *¡Dios mío! That's what those giant black birds were! The ones always swooping and screeching around Bermythica!*

"You hit a freakin' DINOSAUR!" I screeched.

"Pterodactyls *aren't* dinosaurs!" Mags shot back. "They're winged reptiles that *happened* to have lived in the same epoch. Now, get it off!"

"*What?!* HOW???"

"With your MIND!"

Ah, telepathy. Right!

Closing my eyes, I visualized a huge "mental hand," just like Z had taught me, and then, just like he'd taught me, reached out and into the pterodactyl's mind.

All at once the creature's wild, prehistoric consciousness crashed over mine like a dark tidal wave, and all I saw/felt/heard/knew was:

kill . . .

kill . . .

FEED . . .

kill . . .

feed

Feed

KILL . . .

KILL!

It was all rage. So dark and restless and hungry—always hungry. And suddenly, I wanted *out!*

Wrenching my eyes open, I flopped back against the seat with cold sweat streaking down my face and hot fear pumping through my veins.

"What happened?" shouted Mags.

And all I could say (or more like *whimper*) was, "Please don't make me go back in there . . ."

"Oh, *Rym's edge!*" she snapped, and then she wrenched the yoke and the plane's left wing abruptly dipped, sending the thirty-thousand-year-old reptile that was NOT a dinosaur twirling off into the clouds.

"Geez . . ." I could feel my heart pounding painfully in my ears, my fingertips, my toes. Where had that thing even *come* from? "Please just don't hit anything else on the Extinct Species List, okay?"

Branched lightning crackled overhead, momentarily turning the world spaceship white. In that instant, I caught a glimpse of the dark sky ahead—a churning, angry world filled with giant birds diving in and out of the churning, angry clouds.

No, not birds, I thought with a fresh surge of fear. *More pterodactyls!*

Cheepee, who'd taken cover in my pocket, now popped his teeny, dome-shaped head out, uttered a loud chitter of shock, and quickly ducked back in. I couldn't blame him. I was looking for my own giant pocket to jump into.

"They're coming for us," Magdavellía breathed, her knuckles white on the trembling yoke.

"What? *Why?!* Because you hit their friend??"

"No, you moron! Because that's what they've been *bred* to do! No one enters the island uninvited, and nothing and absolutely *no one* leaves. They are the Guardians of Bermythica . . ."

All of a sudden, the entire cockpit shuddered as something enormous slammed into us.

My blood froze. An absolutely GIGANTIC pterodactyl had landed on the not-so-massive wing of our little seaplane.

Then came another *thump.*

And another.

And it didn't take a genius to figure out that there were at least *three more* winged, killer reptiles now riding shotgun with us!

But the worst part? From the screeching, shrieking sound of tearing metal, it was fairly obvious that they'd decided to rip our little sea plane to pieces.

"DO SOMETHING!" I cried, making sure my seat belt was tight (not that it would've helped any).

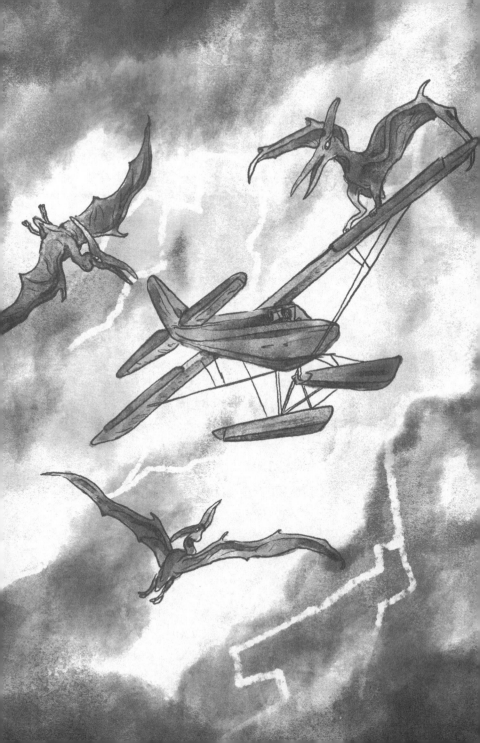

And it was right at that moment, right as those panicky, horrified words flew out of my panicky, horrified mouth that a bolt of bloodred lightning burst out of the thick mass of boiling clouds dead ahead.

It streaked like an electric bullet through the sky and rain and hail as if thrown by Zeus himself, and slammed directly into the nose of the little plane. Except it didn't simply slam into it. The bolt DETONATED into it!

The plane shuddered on half-eaten wings. Caterpillars of electricity leapt up all over the control panel, hissing and popping, sending up bursts of angry sparks.

I felt the buzzing tingle of high voltage and smelled the stink of singed steel, and then I heard, from all around me, from everywhere, a chorus of awful prehistoric shrieks as the gang of aluminum-chomping monsters were instantly zapped to a golden crisp!

As we watched in total OMG shock, they went tumbling through the sky like smoldering scaly stones, plunging in the dark clouds below. And then they were gone.

Which was, well, *awesome*.

Unfortunately, it wasn't the only side effect of being struck by roughly ten gigawatts of freshly brewed sizzle . . .

CHAPTER TWENTY-THREE

•

OUTTA THIS WORLD

Suddenly every single electrical component inside the plane's cockpit went *kaput*. Meters reset. Needles fell limp. The plane's heading indicator began to spin and spin and spin, and Magdavellía's wide, terrified eyes found my wider, even more terrified ones.

A moment later, the seaplane's once-dead engine battery once again died.

I had time to say, "Well, that can't be good . . ."

And then we began to fall—arcing

through

the

sky

like

a

silent

dart

as

the storm

raged

and thunder

rattled

the world.

At that point, there was only one thing left to do, and we did it in perfect synchronized harmony (Cheepee included):

"AAAAAAAAAAAAAAAAAAAAAAAAAAAHHHHHHHHHHHHHHHHH HHHHHHH!"

And as we plummeted, so did the temperature.

Rain turned to rocks. Spiderwebs of frost began to form along the edges of the windows, creeping and crackling across the glass until we couldn't see outside anymore.

And even though my eyes were already half-shut with panic, they were still open enough for me to see something huge and black and seemingly bottomless rushing up toward us as we went plunging down toward it— *The sea*, I thought in a daze of panic. *It has to be the sea!*

I guesstimated we had a very short time left to live.

Somewhere in the back of my mind, I wondered if my aunt could give us a more accurate projection by studying our life lines. I figured she probably could. Not that it would matter any.

At this speed we wouldn't feel the impact that killed us, or even live long enough to see the cockpit flood with freezing water.

I was expecting a sudden stop, followed by a very long, very *permanent* nap.

But the instant we crashed into the blackness, it felt as if we were *swallowed* by it. The cockpit went pitch-dark, and the world seemed to bend and ripple like waves breaking at the seashore.

Then, after what felt like forever (even though it was probably only nine or ten seconds), everything seemed to brighten back up again, bit by bit—

And, all at once, things sort of . . . *stopped.*

The plane stopped.

The propeller stopped.

Everything just *stopped.*

And what I noticed next was what *wasn't* there.

There was no more lightning.

No more thunder.

No more storm.

My eyes blinked slowly, almost sleepily, as an old No. 2 pencil drifted lazily past my nose. I watched it twirl silently through the air, spinning so slowly and so softly that it seemed to weigh nothing at all.

And as I stared at it with rapidly growing wonder, I realized that all the other random junk I'd seen lying around on the floor of the cockpit was also floating! A toothpick, a bubble gum wrapper, an empty can of Materva, some pastelito crumbles—

Even *Magdavellía* was floating!

And—*whoa*—so was I!

What. The heck. Was going on . . . ?

Mags cleared her throat. "If I told you that we were free-floating some fifty or so miles above the last vestiges of the thermosphere, would you panic?"

Hmm. Good question.

"Guess that depends on whether it was actually true or not," I admitted.

Then came silence. A strange, silky sort of silence. A silence that seemed to grow louder and louder in its complete and utter lack of sound, and felt something like this:

$$\text{s I L E }\mathbf{N}\mathbf{C}\mathbf{E}$$

"Am I going to regret looking out the window?" I asked, already regretting the question.

"Guess that depends on what you're hoping to see," was Magdavellía's cheeky reply.

The sharp straps of my seat belt dug painfully into my shoulder as I leaned forward to peer through a tiny gap in the layer of dirty gray window-frost.

And what I saw was incredible. Only at first, my brain totally rejected it. Because at first, it was just too much. Too *huge*! The infinite night lit only by the blue-white sparkle of an equally infinite number of stars. But in the end, there was no denying it.

I knew what I was looking at.

And that was space.

Boundless, beautiful *space*!

"We're okay, we're *fine* . . ." Magdavellía insisted. "The pressure of the hurricane must've hermetically sealed the doors."

"Maybe the word *fine* means something different where you're from," I said dryly.

"—Any chance *you* can fly us back down to Earth somehow?"

"No."

"Any chance we won't die of asphyxiation, radiation, or I dunno, *freeze to death* inside the next five minutes?"

"No."

Well, at least she was being honest. "Really nice view, though . . ."

Before I could say anything else, or blink again, or even begin to wonder how in the refried frijoles we'd found ourselves floating in the middle of outer *FREAKIN'* space (though I was pretty sure I knew, and I was pretty sure it had something to do with those spontaneously forming black holes), I spotted an absolutely ginormous rock.

What, in technical terms, I believe would be referred to as an asteroid.

Yeah.

A *LEGIT* asteroid.

The thing was utterly massive, probably as big as a small planet.

And, of course, it was barreling straight toward us . . .

Now, I wasn't a rocket scientist or anything, but judging by its dimensions (and ours) and its relative speed (and our total lack of speed), I just couldn't imagine a scenario where this was going to work out for us in any pleasant sort of way.

So I screamed, "WATCH OUT!"

And Mags screamed, "OH, I'M WATCHING, JUST NOT SURE WHAT YOU WANT ME TO DO ABOUT THE GET-OUT-OF-THE-WAY PART!"

And that's when the strangest thing happened: the asteroid began to break up. No, not *break* up. More like *OPEN* up!

Like a hatch.

Or a loading bay.

Or a giant, hungry asteroid-mouth!

Wait—did asteroids even HAVE mouths . . . ?

CHAPTER TWENTY-FOUR

ABADACUS THE ABDUCTOR

After spending the last who-knows-how-long trapped in a tower prison in the middle of the Bermuda Triangle and more recently having escaped the aforementioned prison with the help of the Isaac Newton of chipmunks and an eight-legged wonder robot named Deus Ex, I was pretty sure my life couldn't possibly get any weirder. I was wrong.

I barely had time to process the fact that our little single-engine seabird had just been swallowed up by what was apparently some kind of alien ship disguised as a giant space rock (and that we were now *inside* the belly of said space rock ship) when the doors, both passenger side and pilot, were ripped completely off their hinges. Then hands—or at least something *like* hands: three-fingered and spindly, with skin that was a little too smooth and a lot too blue—yanked us roughly out of the cockpit and had us stumbling and tripping over ourselves as they shoved us, just as roughly, down a dark, rocky-looking tunnel. In all my fear and shock—not to mention with how *dim* this whole place was—I hadn't been able to get a look at the thing that had grabbed me. But I *did* manage to get a pretty good look at the one that had grabbed Magdavellía. The "being" (if that was even the right word) was around six feet tall, blue as a blueberry, slim as a salamander, and strong as an ox. It had incredibly long arms and legs, and its head (guessing here) kinda resembled a strawberry, both in shape and with all the little black specks—seeds in the strawberries' case, and eyes (again, guessing) in this thing's case.

A second later, we emerged from the darkness of the tunnel into the brightness of a huge, wide-open room where dozens and dozens of—well, I guess, *more beings* sat in rows inside of dozens and dozens of podlike workstations. They poked at invisible buttons with antenna-shaped fingers and gazed attentively up at screens that were sort of there, sort of not (holograms, maybe?) with about a hundred different styles of eyes.

Thirty yards away, on the opposite side of the room, an entire curving wall—what a *Star Trek* fan might call a "viewscreen" or "viewport"—gave us a completely unobstructed, crystal-clear (and pretty freakin' *incredible*) view of outer space.

I even caught a glimpse of a little yellowish slice of Earth's moon at the bottom left-hand corner. Just a glimpse, though, because those two outer-space *idiots* that had grabbed us were still pushing and shoving. And they didn't *stop* pushing and shoving until we'd reached the center of the room, where some kind of something-or-other sat on a huge, twisted throne of steel-like something.

If someone stuck the Incredible Hulk's arms onto Jabba the Hutt's torso and then mechanically attached Iron Man's titanium alloy legs onto that gigantic mess you'd basically get this abomination.

Something like a great giant face either glared or glowered—or maybe even *grinned* (I couldn't be sure)—down at us.

Slowly, slowly, it began to dawn on me that we were now standing in a room full of extraterrestrial life-forms. *Aliens.* And I couldn't believe that all this time, after all the years of UFO sightings and people being laughed at for claiming to have been beamed up onto flying saucers or having met little green spacemen at the local truck stop, that things like this—that real-life *aliens!*—actually existed, and that *I* was now getting my very own up-close encounter of the *weird* kind!

The giant extraterrestrial's puckered lips flapped apart, and I heard (precisely): "Hhhhhmmerpomphhhhhh. Ahermmmmmmphhhhhhhhh. Gerberrckeermmmmmmmmphmm."

I shook my head, somewhere between giggles and throat-choking panic, and whispered, "What'd it say?"

Magdavellía shrugged. "How should I know? I don't speak Yargaanish. But I will . . ."

"What do you mean, *you* will? Are you planning on learning some *incomprehensible* alien language in the next *ten seconds*??"

"No, you sphere-brain—"

No sooner had she said that than one of the strawberry-headed dudes stuck a hand between us like it was offering us breath mints. In the center of its bluish palm were a pair of teeny black bugs. Fleas, maybe. Definitely not bite-size candy.

Mags pinched one, and I watched her press it to the base of her skull, just below her purple hair.

"What are you doing??" I hissed.

"It's a Talk-talk Tick."

"A *what*??"

"They were first discovered more than 300,000 sunsets ago on the planet Ęetchnskratch. They're universal linguists."

"*Universal linguists?*"

"Language is a superficial construct," she explained. "True communication occurs on an emotional, rhythmic level. These insects instinctually understand that rhythm and can pass the translated messages directly into your posterior temporal lobe. How did you figure dogs from all over the world can understand their masters regardless of language?"

"Why? Because they have *ticks*?!"

Sighing, she pinched the other bug and pressed it, very gently, into the soft skin of the back of my neck. I didn't even get a chance to object before a flash of pain made my lips pull back in a hard wince, and I realized that the stupid thing had bit me!

"Leave it," Magdavellía said as I reached back to flick the nasty little sucker. "It's connecting to your neural pathways . . ."

I could feel it "connecting," too, and it was all I could do not to squirm or scream or try to *squash* the sucker.

"If I get space cooties, I'm comin' after *you*."

The giant alien, meanwhile, had been watching us with a sharklike grin. Once again it opened its impossibly wide mouth, and this time I heard, "Ggggaggaaaammmeeerr haaaaaperrrra jjjaaabbbergerarara . . ."

It didn't shut up, either. It kept babbling on and on and suddenly, like magic or Google Translate, I was able to make out the occasional word:

"Sand gargling grout saggling tart taggling gar gaggling . . ."

And then something like sentences:

"Reds 'n' flutes 'n' bendy boots with branching, brackety broods and chutes . . ."

And finally the thing almost started making sense:

"A most wondrous, plunderous occasion, fiz is!" it exclaimed. Its voice was a deep, belching growl, like the sound of soapy water being sucked down a half-clogged drain. "I cannot tell you how many yecades I've spent lurking near backroads and smusty towns collecting terrestrial test subjects for my extraterrestrial research, and never—no, not *once!*—have two such exemplary, bicempetary, and foruntucous specimens sought ME out!"

Snorts of alien laughter drifted over from the nearby pods. Or what I *guessed* was laughter . . .

Then the biggest, ugliest thing in the room (maybe even the universe?) primmed itself up in its throne and, with the nose-melting belch of someone who hadn't brushed their teeth since they'd last passed Jupiter, it exhaled: "Out of curiosity, do either of you rymlings happen to know who I am?"

Resisting the urge to scratch the back of my neck—or puke—I said, "Should we? Who are you?"

"He's Abadacus the Abductor," whispered Magdavellía tightly.

"*Abadacus the Abductor? Why do they call him Abadacus the Abductor?*"

Mags stared at me like I was a couple of eggs short of an omelet. "Because he has this nasty little habit of *abducting* people, Antares . . . He's a Yargaan. They're believed to be the first scientists in the entire universe. They pioneered the fields of anatomy, biology, cosmology, taxonomy, autecology, physiology, anthropology, cytology, bacteriology, and, of course, aromatherapy. And naturally, in order to investigate such a vast number of fields, you require test subjects. *Many* test subjects. Hence why they're usually found traveling the galaxies in search of new species to abduct and, well, *dissect . . .*"

"*Dissect?!*" I was really hoping I'd misheard that. Maybe she'd said Dieseckt. Well, no, unfortunately . . . 'cause that wasn't a real word.

"I mussum say," gurgled Abadacus, peering excitedly down at us, "I take your arrivals as a most fortuitous omen! You see, recently, with our orbiting in such close nextimity to Earth, some of the more carnivorous elements of my crew have begun to complain about the lack of, shall we say, *carnivorous offerings* on board our vessel . . . Of course, we are well stocked for our expedition, but when there's an entire planet of warm-bodied and readily munchgestible organisms floating less than fifty miles away, even heliumgenized jelly snacks—as delicious as they are—begin to lose their appeal. Additionally, and also due to our nextimity to your *extraordinary* planet, I find many of my deepest scientific urges once again rekindled. Now, pay close attention to this part because it concerns you. See, I believe that the two of you provide me with the *perfect* solution to one of these difficult dilemmas. However, in the spirit of Yargaanian hospitality, I leave the choice as to which dilemma you'd like to remedy solely up to *you.*"

"Option one: you turn around and kindly follow my auxiliaries down to the feeder, where you will be emulsified, liquified, synthesized, and finally slushified into a hardy, nutritious soup for me and my crew. Or option two: you happily offer yourselves as my very *first* voluntary test subjects!"

"So far I'm looking forward to hearing option number three," I admitted.

"There is no option three!" the Abductor in Chief replied gleefully. "Now, before you make your monumental decisions, please note that due to a certain piece of lawcode ratified in the epoch *one un-toch niń*, a foul and backward ruling which I nevertheless wear as a crown of high honor, I was thus forboden from visiting Earth in any capacity save for that of trigalactic trade. Which means that my scientific endeavors have, consequently, and rather unfortuitously, been put on hold. And since I, being a Yargaan from the outer branches of the Triangulum galaxy, am both genetically and superfeticionally predisposed to be among the most inquisitive of life-forms, with a thirst for knowledge that exceeds even the most erudite inclinations of the Hiveminds of the Wester Cerebrus, this has been a most *cruel* punishment indeed . . . In plain Yargaanish, and in short, I would like both of you to know that by selecting *option two* you will be making a very old Yargaan very, *very* happy."

Oh, yeah. Sure. That was my number one goal in life. To make some ancient hunk of space sludge very, very happy . . .

Even though something told me that I really didn't want to know, sheer morbid curiosity had me asking, "And what exactly does being one of your 'test subjects' involve . . . *exactly?*"

Abadacus beamed like he'd been hoping for that question. "Me and my talented team of anatomical researchers will perform a battery of diagnostic and exploratory procedures with a dazzling array of prongs, pokers, probes, and electrodes. In short, you will experience a wide variety of very peculiar, very extraterrestrial tests on your very terrestrial bodies. Tests which will hopefully reveal a great deal about the many *nuances* of your species."

"Sounds dreadful," I said. I was pretty sure I'd never heard anything so horrifying in my entire life. "I think I'll take the blender."

"I don't blame you," replied the alien with a cruel smile. "Many of those tests can be *particularly* excruciating . . ."

You could tell the freak was enjoying watching us squirm. Magdavellía, however, had apparently heard enough.

"Silence, outlander!" she snapped with the sort of spiciness in her tone that I was pretty sure would earn us a one-way ticket to the Blender O' Death.

Immediately the entire control room hushed like a pre-K class at naptime, and about a hundred sets of extraterrestrial eyes swiveled in our direction.

I'm not gonna lie—it was pretty terrifying. Though obviously not to Magdavellía, because she didn't stop shouting.

"Yargaan, I *demand* that you put this ship into orbit and return us to terra firma et immeldaté!"

Deus Ex, still wrapped around her arm like a vambrace, gave several uneasy beeps, but Magdavellía stroked her a couple of times as if telling it to relax.

Abadacus, meanwhile, looked shocked out of his socks. Well, at least as shocked as something as huge and vicious-looking as the galactically renowned kidnapper/dissector can look. "And what, might I inquire, gives you the confidence to make such a *bold* request . . . ?" he purred.

"The knowledge that you cannot touch us, or in any way contribute to our bodily harm," replied Magdavellía haughtily.

"And what, if I may again inquire, undergirds your confidence thus?"

"Over a half dozen terrestrial laws trustfully signed and vigilantly enforced by all parties under the threat of war and/or trigalactic sanctions."

The monstrous alien's translucent lips curved into a malicious grin. "Oh, little Rymling, you'd be surprised how *easily* I find it to violate terrestrial law when sailing so far above terrestrial *rule*."

I gulped. Yeah, not exactly what I was hoping to hear . . .

"And as if such treaties still frighten me!" scoffed Abadacus. "Soon the Rym will *succumb*. A power your earthly mind can hardly comprehend grows in the weakness and infinite complacency of the Terrarealms. Your governments will topple, your kings and queens will bow before their new ruler. And I, for one, am *most* excited! My extraordinary intuition tells me that this new order will be far more receptive to my *particular* brand of science . . ."

Magdavellía shot the giggling waste of intergalactic space a glare that would've fried bacon. Then her gaze snapped toward a sort of humanish-looking lady sitting at a nearby station. A mess of colorful seashells hung loosely on cords around her neck, and I thought I could see, behind the popped collar of her shaggy, coral-textured jacket, something like scaly pink gills beneath her scaly pink ears.

"Soldier, I demand your attention!" Magdavellía shouted, and slowly, slowly (and rather annoyedly), the woman—er, thing—I mean, *person*—swung slitted eyes around to her. "You were in the Agarthian army, were you not? You bear the secret mark of the Roial Court. How can you sit idly by while this *space scum* arrogantly boasts against the Terrarealms?"

"I dun't have the slightest clue what yer yambling about, young miss," answered the scaly lady, lifting her jacket collar to conceal a strange, tear-drop-shaped tattoo at the base of her neck, "so why dun't you do us all a favor and volunteer yerself to the gross domestic fattening."

Abadacus was now glowering down at Miss Seashells with the sort of angry look a mama chicken might give a naughty chicklet. "Does this rymling speak true, Navigator . . . ? Were you in a past life a *foot soldier* of the Rym?"

The Navigator lady's thick, seaweedy hair swept her shoulders as she shook her head, saying, "She's very obviously confused me fer someone else, your Majoris. I'm guessing it's a result of the oxygen deprivation she suffered while floatin' around in the vacuum of space . . ." Her wide green eyes narrowed on Mags in thinly veiled annoyance.

"If you are lying to me, Navigator," replied Abadacus with a false sweetness, "rest assured that my crew isn't particular on whose carne they are given to feast."

Meanwhile Aqua Girl looked like she'd just been asked to eat a fish stick. "Abad, when have I ever lied to you, eh?"

And now a confused look came over the giant alien's blubbery face. "Surely you must mean metaphorically?"

Just then, from the other side of the room, another one of those strawberry-headed things shouted, "The asterrock field is now inbound, your Majoris!"

"See??" snapped Navigator, pointing a long, webbed finger up at her holographic display. "Here come the asterrocks. Just like I promised. And we're in *perfect* position! Look at those thermastraphic readings . . . They indicate that there're enough rare Rym minerals just in the outer belt alone to let us spend the rest of our lives lying out on some Lemurian *beach!*"

Abadacus's impossibly huge, impossibly deep-set eyes fixed on her. "I have never trusted you, Navigator. And my most reliable instincts have always warned me that this endeavor of yours would end in disaster. On the other hand, I can't help but admire your unceasing *greed* . . ."

The fishy-looking gal returned Abad's fierce, excited grin. Guess she'd taken that as a great compliment.

Suddenly, something small and pretty hard pinged off the center of the viewscreen. Alarms began to wail, and the tracks of bright white lights embedded in the rocky ceiling now flashed in alternating shades of yellow, red, and quasar blue.

Abadacus belched, "Prepare the nets!" Then, with the kind of vicious, evil, hungry-eyed grin that only a vicious, evil, hungry-eyed space thug can muster: "And take these rymlings away! We'll discuss *dessert* later . . ."

The same two aliens that had shoved us into the main control area now shoved us down a dim, dank hallway and into an even dimmer, danker place that was more closet than room, and more cubbyhole than closet. The moment the doors hissed closed, Magdavellía plunked herself nonchalantly down in the middle of the floor, legs crossed, like she was getting ready for a picnic on Mars or something.

"Uh, what are you doing?" I said, throwing up my hands in a burst of impatience.

"Thinking."

"Thinking? We don't have time for *thinking*. We need to be ESCAPING!" I started scrambling around the room, sliding things outta the way and peeking behind the shelves for air ducts, vents—*anything*!

And when I didn't find any, I got mad, and when I got mad, I directed that anger at the only carbon-based life-form close enough for me to direct it *at*. (And hint: it wasn't Cheepee, who'd been playing possum in my pocket pretty much from the second he'd sniffed alien air.)

"Hey, since you're obviously not interested in helping me find a way back to *Earth*, why don't you tell the class what's on your mind?"

"The dodecahedron orb we found inside Deus."

"What about it??"

"Don't you understand *anything*?!" she snapped. "Time now stands as a foe. If we don't find the Star before the Mystic, chances are there won't *be* an Earth worth returning to. And the fact that my parents hid *that* orb inside of *my* protector bot very clearly tells me something: that they wanted *me* to find it. And if they wanted me to find it, it's because they wanted me to finish their quest, and if they wanted me to finish their quest, it's because they were *close*. Which is probably why the Myst—why that *monster* murdered them . . . And why I must make all haste in discovering the orb's secret."

And while she might've been right about that, she was also missing the big picture.

"I hate to point out the obvious, but unless we find a way off this flying rock and back onto the bigger one we both call home, none of that stuff you said is gonna matter."

"I *also* hate to point out the obvious, but you do realize that even if we happen to locate a vent or crawl-duct and somehow manage to find our way back to the bayport and back to our little seaplane—without, of course, being seen or captured or roundly *slushified*—even if we managed all that, you do realize that we'd still be trapped *in the middle of outer space.*"

I blinked. That was a good point. A terrifying point, but pretty much irrefutable. I could feel panic rising in my throat again like bad gas station nachos and happened to glance over my shoulder—

And froze.

I gaped, I gasped, I goggled. I stared and struggled to breathe. I looked but struggled to see.

And that was because through the small squarish window on the opposite side of the room and maybe forty or so miles off the starboard side of the alien asteroid ship, my eyes had locked on the most incredible sight yet . . .

CHAPTER TWENTY-FIVE

---•---

THE BLUE PLANET

Earth!

There it was, like a T-shirt without a hook or a painting without a wall, hanging on nothing and doing nothing at all except for sustaining life as we knew it.

It had great MOUNTAINs.

It had little hills.

It had e   it had c
d   o
g   r
e   n
s   e
                     r
                     s

And it was, against all logic, all reason, against everything I'd ever seen in a photograph or read in a book—undoubtedly, unquestionably, unmistakably *flat*.

Quite flat, in fact.

Flat as a coin.

Flat as a frisbee.

Flat as the top of a pie or the bottom of a shoe.

It was JUST like Zamangar had said . . .

"It's . . . *incredible,*" I breathed. "—I mean, you really should see this."

"I've seen it. It's breathiful," Magdavellía agreed.

Breathiful. Huh. Breathtaking and beautiful, maybe? Either way, it was one of the most spectac—

Right then, a hollow BOOM! echoed through the ship.

I staggered on suddenly wobbly legs and whipped around toward Magdavellía. "*What was that?!*" I shouted.

"A small asterrock, most likely."

Another BOOM!

"And *that*??" I shrieked.

"Most likely a medium-size one."

And yet another BOOM!

This one was so violent that it shook the entire ship right down to its interplanetary guts and had our guts slamming back into our spines as it flung us clear across the room.

"And what about *THAT*?!" I asked, sprawled out on the floor beside Mags.

"*That* was a big one."

An instant later, through the window, streaks of something bright and silvery caught my eye, and I turned to look. In the distance, maybe five or so miles off the starboard side, and getting farther and smaller by the second, was what looked like fluffs of sparkly dandelion seeds floating into space. But I barely had time to say, "Hey, check that out," before another asteroid smashed into us, and the ship shuddered again, and the little door behind us slid open with a hiss.

I whirled in alarm, expecting to see the pair of strawberry-headed dudes standing in the doorway flanked by maybe an alien chef or two. But there was no one there.

No chefs.

No walking strawberries.

No interstellar life-forms of any kind, in fact.

And, I realized with another surge of relief, nothing and no one to keep us from escaping . . .

Maybe today was our lucky day.

CHAPTER TWENTY-SIX

·

LUCY IN THE SKY

As it turned out, today wasn't our lucky day. And as it turned out, most of the *really* lucky people—or, in this case, *aliens*—had already abandoned ship, and the four of us now made up exactly two-thirds of the *unlucky* passengers still aboard this doomed and badly damaged spaceship. Hooray us!

We found the remaining two back in the main control room: that fishy-looking lady with the gills and something like a squat, greenish, dome-headed little Martian dude.

"*Navigator!*" Magdavellía shouted like she owned the place, marching up behind the console where she sat. "Have all the other bandits fled?"

"Ye, the cowards! . . . Right along with their *fearless* captain!"

I remembered the dandelion fluffs I'd seen out in space. Escape pods—they had to be! "So how do we flee with them??" I screeched.

"Got some dark tides for you, rymling . . . This is currently the only space-worthy vessel within a thousand prauts." She held out a bag filled with clear, gummy ball–looking things. "Helium jelly snack?"

Honestly, I wasn't even a little interested, but Cheepee, probably preparing for an extended hibernation inside my pocket, peeked warily out, snagged a gummy ball between his fuzzy little hands, and quickly ducked back down.

Navigator, or whatever, gave him—and *me*—a curious look. "Why didn't you abandon ship with the rest of them?" Magdavellía asked.

"Because crashin' we most certainly *ain't*. I'm landing this giant space *pebble!*"

Less than twenty feet away, the little green Martian had begun gesturing anxiously at a display where the words ĘNJƎN MĘLFANGKSHĘN (which looked *suspiciously* like the words ENGINE MALFUNCTION) were flashing in bold yellow letters.

I watched his skinny green hand begin to creep cautiously toward a skinny red level in the middle of his console.

"Pal, you know we're a team and I love ya," said Navigator, "but you flip that release lever and I'm goin' to break every single one of yer thirty-five bony fingers and toes. *One by one.*"

The Martian's—or I guess, *Pal's*—hand immediately took off in the opposite direction of the lever as if the thing had all of a sudden sprouted *teeth*.

"Don't squid out on me now, Pal! We are *not* losing Lucy."

Totally confused, I glanced at Magdavellía. "Who's Lucy??"

"I'm guessing *that's* Lucy . . ."

I followed her eyes—

And gaped.

¡Santo cielo!

Through the viewport, I saw what was *very* obviously an asteroid. And a huge one, too—nearly the size of the MOON!

The ginormous hunk of cratered and speckled rock was as dark as space itself and all tangled up in some kind of stretchy, silvery netting that twinkled like faraway stars.

"You named that ginormous *space rock* LUCY??" I shouted, and Navigator's aqua blue–tinged lips split into a proud grin.

"Bet yers, I did . . . And she's all carbon cube, too!"

Off my frowning *huh-what?* look, Magdavellía said, "She means there's a diamond in that rock."

"*Correction!*" Navigator butted in, "Lucy *is* a diamond. Over six tons of intergalactic carbon compressed under *unimaginable* heat and pressure in the core of some faraway planet on the outer spiral arms of a long-forgotten solar system, resulting in exactly 30,398 *flawless* carats. Gorgeous, huh?"

There was a whine of twisting metal as the ginormous space rock, space diamond—space *whatever!*—began yanking us steadily off course.

An unpleasant shudder went through the entire room, and Magdavellía shouted, "It's too heavy! It's going to tear this vessel apart!"

The floor of the alien command bridge had begun to vibrate like an out-of-control massage chair. My home planet (yeah, I was feeling mucho homesick right about now) loomed in the viewscreen: big and blue and beautiful. And we were rocketing straight for it!

Suddenly the swaying little green spaceman did exactly what he looked like he was about to do and passed right out in his seat, slumping over as limply as a wet tube sock. His big green dome of a head clunked off a small red button, and somewhere an alarm began to blare.

Navigator whipped around in disbelief. "*Seriously,* Pal?!"

"What happened to him??" I shouted.

"He's a coward, that's *what!* Lost every last scrap of courage when he lost those"—she made little antenna-fingers above her head—"those *Martian head thingies . . .*"

"What??"

"Just wake 'im up, will you?"

"How?!"

"See that birth'nmark between 'is eyes?"

I did. It looked like something between a maze, a fingerprint, and an upside-down, slightly off-centered question mark.

"Poke it," instructed Navigator.

So I did, carefully, respectfully, and immediately jumped back. Call me a scaredy cat, but up until about fifteen minutes ago, I had exactly ZERO experience with extraterrestrial life. And so far, what experience I had hadn't been so good.

A moment later, the alien's paleish pinkish eyelids slid stickily open, and for a second he just blinked up at me with a sort of sleepy look.

"Hi," I said.

His tiny lime-green lips bent down in a frown.

"*Oh,*" I said. Then, turning to Magdavellía: "Do these things talk?"

"Not to or in the presence of beings they do not know," she explained.

Huh. An extraterrestrial don't-talk-to-strangers policy. Kind of neat.

An instant later the entire nose of the ship was suddenly engulfed in bright reddish flames, and for a heart-stopping second, I panicked, thinking we'd caught fire!

But then I noticed it wasn't just the ship—Lucy the space rock was burning up, too.

Which could only mean one thing: we were reentering Earth's atmosphere!

There was another whine of twisting steel as the asterdiamond continued pulling viciously on the front of the alien spacecraft. Yeah, this was definitely no bueno . . .

"We have to cut it loose!" shouted Magdavellía.

"Oh no we dun't!" Navigator—er, our suicidal captain—shouted back, pounding out a long and complicated combination into the panel of half-invisible buttons shimmering above her head. "I jest gotta get the rest of our engines firing and we'll be pearls!"

More whining, twisting sounds. More shuddering (both me and the ship).

Man, I wish Mikey was with us right about now! I bet she could fly this rock. With all the flight simulator games she played it would probably be a cakewalk for her!

Or, in this case, maybe a *spacewalk*.

Deus Ex, still wrapped around Magdavellía's arm, started beeping in a nervous sequence that sounded suspiciously like an SOS signal; meanwhile, Cheepee, who had climbed out of my pocket at some point, was now standing in the middle of the Martian's control console, trying with all the strength in his teeny squirrel-size body to flip the release lever. When he realized he just didn't have the muscle, he began screeching and waving tiny brown arms, trying to get our attention so we could do the heavy lifting for him.

"*Navigator,*" growled Mags, eyes locked anxiously on the flickering viewscreen. But Fish Sticks just kept on poking at invisible buttons. "One mintock, please . . ."

"*Navigator* . . ."

"Mintock, I need a mintock!"

A huge explosion—¡Dios mío!—rocked the ship and had me wobbling like my knees were made of Jell-O.

Bracing myself against the back of one of the pods, I shouted, "Magdavellía, we gotta do something!"

"Oh, *enough!*" she huffed. Then, balling her hands into fists, she half marched, half swayed over to the Martian's station, gripped the red release lever, and flipped it.

There was a bang and clanging, and whirling of saws, and a loud snipping sound, and Lucy, now free as, well, an *asteroid* in outer space, spun happily off into the clear blue sky, growing smaller and brighter until she was just a tiny burning speck almost too small to see.

Deus Ex stopped its beeping. Cheepee collapsed against the control console in exhausted relief. I heard the alien dude swallow, and, somewhere below us, a sound like a thousand boat propellers whirring to life.

"There!" cried Navigator. "See?? All engines are now *fully* operational! Lucy's no longer gonna be a struggle. Now, if you two would jest sit down and shut—" The words died on her lips as she turned to gaze with disbelief out the front of the ship. "PAL, WHAT 'APPENED TO LUCY???"

And all fifteen bony alien fingers swung accusingly up at Magdavellía. Then the Martian fainted again, woke up again, pointed at Magdavellía again, and promptly fainted again.

"It was either *us* or *the rock*," Mags replied calmly.

Navigator sank to her knees in despair, burying her face in her small scaly hands. "The rock! I choose the ROCK!"

"Uh, excuse me, but—WHAT ARE YOU DOING, CHICA?!" I shouted at her.

She gave this awful, terrible, deflated sigh. "Mourning Lucy . . ."

"Hey, if you don't start flying this ship, people are going to be mourning *US*!"

"Navigator, I will *not* repeat myself," said Magdavellía in a tone of simmering impatience. "OPEN YOUR EYES, TAKE THE FLIGHT CONTROLS, AND *LAND THIS SHIP!*"

She'd shouted that with all the pomp and authority of a queen (which was apparently her default personality), and even though I couldn't imagine a scenario where it would actually make this fishy lunatic do what she wanted her to do—somehow, it *did*.

Navigator's pale face rose slowly out of her hands. Then she dragged herself up and sat herself back down at her station and, with a look of fury burning in her stormy gray eyes, took the flight controls.

Finally she said, "From whence yeh hail, rymling?"

I was pretty sure she was talking to me, so I said, "Earth!"

"In that case, get ready to meet yer home planet up close and real persnel," she said, and Magdavellía and me quickly strapped ourselves into the closest set of state-of-the-art office chairs.

The alien asteroid harvester sliced through the clouds like an interplanetary missile. Earth's surface shimmered in the viewport, filling every inch of the glass. Unfortunately, none of it looked particularly soft . . .

"'OLD ON!" cried the Navigator, yanking back on a joystick-looking thingy, which (because why not?) snapped right off in her webbed hands.

I screamed.

Magdavellía screamed.

Navigator screamed.

Pal woke up, screamed, then quickly passed out again.

Squeezing my eyes shut, I braced for impact.

Then, with a hiss of rockets, a rattle of electronics, and the earsplitting shriek of hardened steel grinding against desert rock, the extraterrestrial cruiser banged and banked and finally slammed to Earth like the BFG crashing into bed after a hard day in the dream laboratory. I caught a glimpse of sand, then more sand, and then sandy hills as the ship bounced and tumbled, slid, and then went into a wild tailspin, before eventually— *mercifully*—coming to a jarring, grinding, screeching stop, half jacked up on its side and smoking all over.

I realized I hadn't blinked in about five straight minutes and made myself do so now.

I realized I hadn't been breathing either and also made myself do so.

"On behalf of United Intergalactic Airlines," I said weakly, "thanks for flying!"

CHAPTER TWENTY-SEVEN

TRANSMU—*HUH?*

From the second we climbed out of the busted spaceship, Magdavellía and Navigator were at each other's throats. Mags clearly wasn't her biggest fan ("How can a former soldier of Agartha, even one as vulgar and self-serving as *yourself,* deny her citizens assistance?!") and Navigator didn't really seem to give a rip ("With my tongue and with my lips," she said, strapping on a rucksack). So they argued ("I *command* you," shouted Magdavellía, "by the power of the EverRisen Sun, to take us to Rymworld!") and argued ("I'm not taking the likes of *you anywhere*—by the power of EverRisen Sun or by any *other* power!") and argued ("You violate Rymworldian law!") and argued some more ("You find me colluding with a skoöl of space *scum* aboard a *thrice* outlawed vessel, and you still somehow figure I give a *flipper* 'bout Rymworldian law??") until Navigator finished gathering her things, and she and her Martian friend set off under a scorching sky toward the shimmering desert horizon. Something told me that she was still pretty sour over the whole losing-a-diamond-the-size-of-one-of-Jupiter's-smaller-moons thing.

"You wanna just follow them?" I said, turning to Mags, who was sitting on a hump of hot orangey sand, examining that strange metal orb we'd found inside her bot. Probably checking it for damage or something.

"No," she snapped angrily. "No, I do *not*! The entire Rym now stands on the doorstep of doom, and that *morongus* is off chasing *rocks*!"

Beside her, Deus Ex, who was back in spider mode now, scuttling up and down the sand dunes, beeped and buzzed in apparent agreement, while everybody's favorite chipmunk chased after her with excited little chitters. This might've been the first time he'd ever stepped foot—er, *paw*—outside of Bermythica. Or maybe he was just happy to still be breathing. I know I sure was.

"Merfolk are a stiff-necked and *salty* people," grumbled Magdavellía.

"Wait. Is she, like, a *mermaid*?"

"I would've thought her gills would have given it away . . ."

"What I mean is, mermaids *exist*?"

"This surprises you? Haven't there been *countless* merfolk sightings in inworld? Rumor tells that their kind swim beneath the Ice Ring all the time."

"Well, yeah, people *claim* to have seen mermaids and stuff. But no one *actually* believes them." And I guess we had the Flat Earth Society to thank for that. Keeping all the coolest stuff from us inworlders. Bunch of buzzkills.

"Did you know that they are the only 'civilized' species (and I use the term *civilized* in its absolute *loosest* sense) whose governing bodies still sanction piracy? Piracy! Think of it!" Yeah, her blood was still boiling.

"But, if she's a *mermaid* what is she doing—*not* in water?"

"Because she's a *mudder*. Only half mermaid. You can tell by her gills. They don't reach all the way around to the back of her neck. And some mudders they keep, some they exile. I think it's safe to assume she's part of the latter group." Magdavellía gave her head a frustrated shake. "She's nothing more than a petty chancer, anyway. No, we go *north*. An onboard navigational chart showed that we crash-landed somewhere in northeast Egypt, not far from civilization. Is that way north, northeast?"

"It's the other way actually." I pointed.

"Well, then that's our heading."

Behind us the crumpled carcass of the once proud but "thrice out-lawed" alien asteroid ship simmered and hissed with dozens of small blue-green fires.

Every few seconds I heard another sizzling *zap!* as some badly damaged circuit first overloaded, then fried, and then exploded permanently out of order.

"I'll search the ship for sustenance," Magdavellía said, rising. "Hold this."

And she went to hand me the little lead-colored ball—

Only I hadn't been paying attention and it slipped right through my hands.

It hit the sand and started to roll. D

o

w

n

d

o

w

n

d

o

w

n it went, picking up speed until it banged off the side of the ruined ship, coming to a stop right in the middle of one of those small fires.

"Quick! We can't let it reach its melting point!" shouted Mags as we both took off down the dune after it. "Fetch something! A stick!"

"Uh, this is a *desert!*" I pointed out. "There are few somethings and even fewer sticks!" Fortunately, I spotted a nice stick substitute about a yard or so from where the orb was currently being charbroiled: it was half-buried in the sand, jutting out like a crooked finger. Probably a broken-off piece of the ship. Thinking fast, I snatched it up and had just started to reach for the ball with it when Magdavellía stopped my hand and shouted, "Wait. *Look!*"

"Look at *what,* chica?? It's gonna melt!"

"No, *LOOK . . .*"

So I did. And what did I see? Not only was the ball *not* melting, it was *changing* somehow . . . transforming right before our very eyes!

My jaw nearly smacked the sand.

"It looks like . . . *gold,*" I gasped. "*Solid* gold!"

CHAPTER TWENTY-EIGHT

THE ALCHEMIST'S BALL

My mind flashed back to one of my favorite old bedtime stories my aunt used to read me when I was little. To that silly goose—what was its name? Did it even *have* a name?—and the golden egg it had laid. I thought back to it because that's *exactly* what the orb now reminded me of: the goose's golden egg!

"I—I don't get it. So it trans . . . *formed*?"

"Close," Mags whispered excitedly, "it trans*muted*! It underwent a complete molecular change—on an atomic level!"

I started shaking my head, honestly mind-blown. "That's . . . *bananas*."

"What is it with you and that fruit?? Bananas have *nothing* to do with this. No, this . . . *this* is *alchemy*!"

"Alchemy??"

"Look at the glowing symbol!"

I hadn't even noticed it until right then, but there it was, glowing like lines of carved fire in the side of the ball. It looked like an upward pointing triangle.

"That's the ancient alchemist symbol for fire," explained Mags, her violet eyes glowing almost as vividly as the golden ball. "Which is also the same symbol they sometimes use to represent the sun and sometimes gold. The word *alchemy* is derived from the ancient Agarthian word *hem*, which, later, within the Ice Ring, became the Arabic word *khem*—the word for the so-called Primordial First Matter. Alchemists believe everything in the physical world came from this original matter and that because everything came from that something you can then, in effect, turn *anything* into something else. Thus, the theory behind the transmutation of metals."

Needless to say, I was fascinated. Seriously, if my school ever offered Alchemy 101 as an elective, I was gonna be all over it.

"Which means," she whispered with steadily growing excitement, "that *this* must be an *Alchemist's Ball!*"

"What's an Alchemist's Ball??"

"Well, for centuries—and in the not-so-distant past—alchemists were the targets of unprecedented persecution. Even in Rymworld. When you possess the knowledge to turn base metals into ones of immense value, you're a very real threat to collapse virtually any economy. So alchemists created these balls as a sort of portable safe to hide their most sacred objects as well as to pass secret messages among their many cults."

"You're saying that alchemists used to hide stuff in those things?"

"Yes."

"Important stuff?"

"The *most* important stuff . . ."

Now, I wasn't exactly a superstitious kind of guy, but I still crossed my mental fingers (and my mental toes) as I asked, "Stuff, like—the *Star of Lôst* maybe?"

"I'm hoping *exactly* like it!"

And she wasn't the only one.

"So how do we open it?" I asked, and watched her lips split into a dazzling smile.

"You've already figured that out."

I blinked. "I—I have?"

"Of course you have! It opens through a chemical reaction. The very *foundation* of alchemy! Earth, fire, wind, and water—the four classical elements. Revered by all alchemists." She thought for a second. "*Water . . .*"

"Huh?"

"We need water!"

Fortunately for us, earthlings weren't the only life-forms in the galaxy who hydrated themselves with that miraculous chemical combination of two hydrogen atoms and a single oxygen. We dragged a giant carbon fiber jug of—well, *space water* out of the ship's kitchen (it happened to be right next to the giant blender Abadacus had been preparing for us— yikes!) and the moment we'd dumped it over the ball, there was a loud hiss, and this great plume of white-hot steam billowed upward, blinding us and making us cough.

The stink and smoke had been sort of a surprise. But the even *bigger* surprise was what we saw when it all cleared!

The small lead ball, which had since become a small gold ball, was now a small silver ball. And the symbol on its side, which a moment ago had shown the alchemist symbol for fire, had changed. It was now a downward-pointing triangle.

"The alchemist symbol *for water*," whispered Magdavellía in a tone of hushed wonder. "It *worked!*"

On my shoulder, Cheepee was clapping his furry paws in delight and pointing at the ball, like, "Look at it! Amazing!" Apparently, his teeny-tiny brain could process stuff a lot faster than my big old human-size one, because all I managed was, "Uh, I don't get it . . ."

Magdavellía, meanwhile, was grinning like Gretel and her brother Hansel when they'd stumbled upon the gingerbread house. "See, fire caused the first transmutation, from lead to gold. So it only stood to reason that if we exposed the ball to the other three elements, it would result in three more transmutations. And then it should open!"

"Is that really how this thing works?"

"As far as I remember."

I mean, it did make a strange sort of sense. And it *had* worked. Twice. But we hadn't quite rounded home plate just yet.

"Well, now what?"

"Now earth!"

And so we dropped down onto our hands and knees and began to dig and dig until we'd hollowed out a narrow trench in the sand just deep enough to completely bury the amazing alchemist ball.

Then we pushed and packed and piled the sand back on until the trench was no longer a trench and the ball was no longer visible.

Magdavellía figured two minutes underground should do the trick. And the instant we'd dug it back up, I saw that the Alchemist's Ball had once again changed! This time a highly polished bronze—not gold and definitely not silver—winked brilliantly up at us out of its sandy trench.

And the symbol in its side now looked different, too. An upside-down triangle bisected by a horizontal line.

"Is that the alchemist symbol for earth?" I asked, and Magdavellía was all giggles and excited nodding.

"Now *air*!" and she began tossing the ball straight up into the sky, way, way up there. As if she was tossing pizza dough.

But unlike the other three times, no matter how high she tossed it, or how long it hung up there, nothing happened. Not immediately, and not even after several minutes.

Frowning, Mags wiped the hot sand off her flustered cheeks. "It . . . doesn't make *sense*. The last of the four elements is air. It just *is*. It's . . ." she trailed off.

"It's *what*?"

"Hmm."

"Hmm *what*??"

"*Perhaps.*"

"Perhaps *WHAT*???"

"What if air *isn't* air. . ."

"—But isn't air . . . *always* air?" That sounded a little silly, sure. But Mr. Miles, my favorite math teacher, always said that there weren't any stupid questions. So there.

"What I mean is, alchemists were the original chemists. They didn't experiment with plain old '*air*'—they experimented with *gases. Specific* gases. Radon, argon, krypton, for example. So what I'm trying to say is, what if it's a *gas* that unlocks it? That causes the final transmutation?"

"Uh, okay. But which one?"

"Well, alchemists have always favored the noble gases because of their chemical stability."

"There's a bunch, though. Like six."

"Exactly six."

"So which one?"

Her eyes shut briefly, and a moment later, two words sighed softly off her lips: "*Of course . . .*"

"*Of course?*" That didn't sound like any gas I'd ever heard of.

"The noblest of them all. The alchemists' *perfect* gas—*helium!*"

"Helium?"

"Yes! It exists as a single atom. Completely stable!"

Helium. Okay. I could go with that. But even if she *was* right, even if helium would somehow unlock this thing, how were we supposed to get our hands on any in the middle of the *Egyptian desert*??

And I had just opened my mouth to point out that unfortunate fact when the obvious answer smacked me square between the eyes— smacked Magdavellía, too!

"THE ALIEN GUMMY SNACKS!" we both shouted in pitch-perfect harmony.

Shooting a hand into my pocket, I whipped out the one Cheepee had scored in space—while the chipmunk raised a tiny angry fist, chittering in fierce protest—and then smashed it against the smooth metallic skin of the Alchemist's Ball.

A moment later, the familiar hiss and pop of a blossoming chemical reaction had me grinning.

Right before our eyes the ball began to dissolve, to disintegrate, to decompose until it was nothing more than a tiny mound of bluish-gray ash.

And smack-dab in the middle of that ashy mound now glittered some kind of stone: cube-shaped—*perfectly* cube-shaped—and sort of cunning looking. Its six flat faces were a deep bloodred, shot through with streaks of an even darker red that zigged and zagged like the course of some wild river. Tendrils of grayish mist curled dreamily around it. They made me think of ghostly fingers fanning out to protect something very ancient and very, very precious.

"Is that . . . *the Star*?" I whispered, almost afraid the stone might hear me and run away. I mean, it *could* have been a Star. Or at least a chunk of one. But it definitely didn't look anything like a compass capable of leading anyone through an unnavigable maze at the heart of some ancient temple.

"I—don't *think* so." Magdavellía reached slowly out to touch it. Then her hand instantly recoiled and she let out a choked gasp.

"Is it hot??"

Magdavellía didn't answer. In fact, she was silent for so long that I started to wonder if she'd heard me at all. Finally, she said, "We have to get this back to Rymworld. We . . . we must learn its secret."

"What *secret*?? It's a *rock*!"

"No, this is no ordinary rock. Notice its shape . . . It's a perfect cube. And the cube is a very important shape in the Rym. It represents Earth. What's more, it's one of the five Platonic Solids."

"So?"

"So?? The Solids are the five base shapes revealed to Plato himself. Some believe that *everything* is based off the Five."

"What do you mean *everything*?"

She said, "I mean *everything* . . ." And just the weight of the look she leveled on me could've broken Atlas's back. "Besides, do you seriously think my parents would go through all that trouble to hide a simple *rock*?"

She had a point.

"Okay, so what's the plan?"

Magdavellía thought for a moment. "We need to find a port."

"A *port*? Uh"—I gestured around at the shimmering universe of sand-iness stretching endlessly out as far as the eye could see—"in case you hadn't noticed . . ."

Magdavellía said nothing. So I said, "Whatta we need a port for, anyway?"

"Because that's how we get to Rymworld."

CHAPTER TWENTY-NINE

THE STOWAWAYS

Walking through the hot, sprawling desert was like being trapped in a giant hourglass. Time ran, and it ran and it ran, faster and faster, while we slowed and stumbled and occasionally slipped, and there was sand, sand, *everywhere* sand, so much so that it even seemed to be drizzling from the sky in annoying little streams.

Anyway, as we walked Magdavellía talked and I listened. And according to her, there were these fleets of undercover trading ships that moved secretly between our worlds. The ships were called crawlers, and according to her, they were operated by the families of some of the earliest inworldian sailors who had ventured out and shipwrecked in the Rym. Also according to her, you could find these ships at nearly any major port. In fact, she made it sound easy peasy. The only problem? Actually *reaching* one of those ports before *our faces* melted off. It must've been close to ten thousand degrees out here, and there wasn't a sliver of shade in sight.

Eventually, though—a lot of hours later—we came to a busy coastal city, and eventually—a lot of minutes after that—we found our way to its busy coastal port, where Magdavellía was pretty sure she'd spotted one of those secret cargo ships.

It took us about five minutes to figure out that we couldn't get past the security checkpoint and another five to sneak our way into the big port warehouse and into the largest shipping container marked for the crawler. Then inside of twenty minutes, we felt ourselves lifted off the ground and rolled out of the warehouse and out past the gate with the security checkpoint and finally into the belly of the ship.

From that point, we only had to wait to feel the earthquake of a massive diesel engine and hear the cry "Anchors up!" sweep loudly across the main deck, sweep like a chant, before finally lifting the crate's heavy wooden lid and climbing out.

I couldn't stop smiling as I gazed around the massive cargo bay at the endless stacks of boxes, at the barrels and vats and the thick burlap sacks hanging in nets. This was all *way* too cool! Almost surreal. I mean, here we were, deep in the heart of some secret trading ship bound for the edge of the world. It was as if we'd stepped into the pages of a wild pirate adventure—a couple of stowaways hiding in the cargo hold in search of hidden treasure. Only this was much cooler than any pirate adventure. Because it wasn't some old coins or a box of stolen loot waiting for us at the other end of our rainbow. It was a whole new world. An entire hidden civilization!

Rymworld, with its rainbowgem mines, its ancient alien technology, its sky fortresses, its oceans, its fabled forests teeming with mythical beasts. I'd honestly never been so psyched to see anything—or any*place*—in my entire life. I felt like a little kid on Christmas morning.

But even as hard as my blood pumped and my heart thumped at just the mere *thought* of what I might see, of where we might go, of what we might do—and who we might find when we got there—not ten minutes after having climbed out of the crate, I found myself sprawled on a mound of old netting in the corner with Cheepee curled up on my chest. And not ten minutes after that I was fast asleep.

CHAPTER THIRTY

THE FROŌSEN PASSAGE

My eyes blinked open in half darkness. I felt my arms and legs all tangled up in the salty-smelling nets, and as I wiggled myself free I saw Magdavellía standing near a porthole, peering out. Dizzy sunlight was slanting in through the open steel circle, painting her (and everything else) in a gauzy, otherworldly glow.

I sat up slowly, rubbing my sleepy eyes. "Hey, what are you doing?"

"Waiting for you!" she whispered excitedly. Then she snatched my hand and yanked me up and off my butt and toward a set of steps by the entrance.

The steps led up into a narrow hall that led to an even narrower door that opened upward and outward and onto the main deck.

And the moment we'd stepped through it, I froze. Partly because of the cold (it must've been a good thirty degrees colder than I'd expected), but mostly because of what I saw. And what I saw was a sky so white and so solid looking that it hardly seemed real.

Then I realized that it wasn't sky at all, but a *wall*. A GINORMOUS wall of ice!

It rose straight up before us like a massive tidal wave that had frozen solid, frozen into a single, spectacular sheet just as it reached its apex.

"Amazing, isn't it?" Magdavellía's breath puffed out white and misty between us. "Solid ice, through and through, and as wide as sight. Don't stand too close to the railing, though. And brace yourself for the—"

I didn't catch the rest of what she said, because right then there came a thunderous clinking, clanking, clanging sound and the deck moaned and the slowing ship groaned like a wounded woolly mammoth and the entire world lurched suddenly sideways.

We staggered on the ice-encrusted deck, holding on to each other as the clinking, clanking sounds intensified, growing louder and louder until every square inch of the deck was rumbling and jumping and bouncing and bucking beneath our feet like the world's angriest rodeo bull.

"WHAT'S GOING ON??" I shrieked.

"This is the Froōsen Passage," Magdavellía replied with an air of easy calmness that I really didn't appreciate.

"The Froōsen Passage???" I could hear the dry scrape of ice against the steel underbelly of the ship, and all of a sudden it didn't feel like we were sloshing through water anymore. No, it felt like we were grinding over some giant, frozen *plate*!

Gripping the railing, I stuck my head out over the edge, into the cold wind, and peered straight down. And surprise, surprise, I was *right*!

The ship wasn't floating on water.

In fact, I couldn't even *see* water!

We were now being dragged along solid snowy ground on what looked like a set of enormous subterranean tracks—tracks like gigantic metal teeth.

And those teeth, I noticed, were dragging us straight into the heart of that frozen mountain.

Steep cliffs loomed up, impossibly high, on either side. Huge chunks of snow and ice calved off their jagged peaks, splattering to the deck around us in crumbly blocks.

Deus Ex, who had followed us up to the deck, barely dodged one, buzzing angrily, while Cheepee (who had also tailed us) ran up the side of my leg and took cover inside my shirt pocket.

The next instant we were swallowed up in a frosty world of sharp-edged snow and enormous frozen blocks, and I had a terrifying vision of being buried alive beneath an avalanche of ice and rocks and I staggered backward on my heels screaming, "WHAT. IS. HAPPENING???"

Magdavellía tipped her head back in a burst of childish laughter. "Don't you remember your geography lessons? How inworld was surrounded by a giant ring of ice? Well, this is it . . . the Great Ice Ring. And the Froōsen Passage is one of only three ways through it." She gazed around the frosty tunnel with something like wonder in those shining gold-flecked eyes. "After the conclusion of the Hundred Sunsets' War, all of Rymworld came together to establish an eternal barrier between inworlders and Rymworlders. They brought with them the fabled earthrakers and mountainbreakers, which carried rock and ice from the heights of Fväll, and the ancient weather machines, which breathed their frigid breath upon the formless mass, unleashing raging blizzards for nearly a thousand sunsets until the ice and ground had first hardened, then fused, and then finally froze over, separating our two worlds forever. I believe you are the first inworlder since Admiral Richard Byrd to navigate the ice."

There was a soft splashing sound and the ship now bobbed and it bounced, and then we were back on water again.

For several moments I just stood there. Staring out at the vast and icy ocean burning in the fading light of sunset. And felt the steady rhythm of the sea around us, and of the ship upon it, and of the world underneath, and smelled the salt in the air, breathing it in slow and deep, until I could taste it—not just on my tongue, but inside me. In my bones.

"It's amazing," I whispered. "This entire planet . . . it's *amazing*."

I felt Magdavellía's warm fingers slip between mine, and pulling me forward, she whispered, "I know an even better view!"

CHAPTER THIRTY-ONE

•

HAPPY THOUGHTS

Mounds of skinny rope lay like loops of ancient, crustacean-encrusted spaghetti among the mess of nets and mooring gear. Magdavellía grabbed two, tied one end to the guardrail and the other around our waists, then climbed over the railing and out onto the tiny lip of deck that extended over the water. Watching her, I couldn't help thinking, *She's gone bananas!*

But Mags said, "I prefer pears, personally."

"Hey, stay out of my head!" I snapped.

"Then climb over already!"

"But someone's gonna catch us!"

"Not at dinnertime they're not. Now moves'it!"

I thought about arguing with her, but what was the point?

Below us, maybe three or four stories straight down, the freezing blue water churned and foamed in the wake of the ship's massive propellers. I tried not to look down.

"Relax," Magdavellía whispered, smiling into the cold breeze.

"I'm over the railing. Happy?"

"Now let go, like me."

"Let go of the railing?! Do you have a death wish I should know about?"

"Do you trust me?" Her breath was soft and warm against my ear.

Squinting against the sea spray, I turned to look at her, and saw that she was looking back at me, her face only inches from mine. In the fading reddish light of a frozen sunset, her eyes were the color of courage.

"Yeah, I trust you . . ." I managed, and watched her smiling lips smile a little wider.

"Then do it," she whispered. "And close your eyes."

So feeling a little bit childish (and a lotta bit reckless), I did. The cold, snow-tinged air gusted around me and my legs shook, and for a moment I felt myself sway, I felt myself totter.

"Now imagine you're floating," Magdavellía instructed. "Really picture it. See yourself rising up, up, *up* . . ."

I decided to play along—you know, just for the heck of it. But it wasn't a minute or so before I actually started to feel . . . *different.*

No joke, I felt incredibly light, incredibly airy. Like I was standing on nothing but empty, wide-open air.

"Yeah, I get it now," I said, grinning. "This is pretty fly . . . Almost feels like you're floating."

"It's flyer than you know. Open your eyes."

I almost didn't want to. The sensation was awesome. But eventually I did, and *when* I did, my breath stopped.

My heart stopped.

My entire *world* stopped.

And suddenly the weightless, floating-on-nothing feeling made sense. Made perfect and *terrifying* sense!

And that was because I *was* floating!

Literally. Maybe a hundred or so feet above and behind the rear of the ship like some deep-space astronaut tethered to a slowly drifting satellite.

The thirty-or-so-foot length of crusty rope tied around my waist gave a little jerk as it pulled taut against the railing, and I swung my head around to see Magdavellía floating right beside me, purple hair blowing in the breeze.

"Breathiful, isn't it?" Grinning, she gave me a little bump with her elbow, and the tiny impact sent me wobbling through the air, and I immediately began to panic. Which, unfortunately, seemed to wake gravity back up, and I immediately began to drop!

Out of the corner of my eye I saw Magdavellía's hand snap out. Her fingers closed tightly around my wrist and she pulled me slowly back up.

I didn't even think, just grabbed on to her like a terrified toddler grabbing on to its mommy. That seemed to help somehow. It made me feel light, stable, and then I was floating again.

"How are you doing this??" I exhaled, slowly letting go.

"It's not me. It's *you.*" Magdavellía gave me a proud sort of smile. "*You're* skywalking."

"But—how???"

Her slim shoulders went up and down in a shrug. "It's easier out here. Away from all the people noise. Here the magic can flow free . . ."

Free. That was the perfect word for it. Because way out here, a world away from any big city, away from all the buildings and buses, the house lights and streetlights—away from all that *busyness* pollution—I felt freer than I ever had before.

I felt free as a bird.

Free as the clouds.

Free as the sky and air and breathing.

Free as friendship.

All around us night was beginning to fall like sleep, slowly, slowly at first, and then all at once. Overhead, the skyfield of stars had sprouted its first white-hot seedlings.

"This is my favorite time," whispered Magdavellía, "when the day dims and the sun bows to the moon and everything just goes . . . *quiet.*" She drew a deep, cool breath. "When I was little, I used to love astronomy. The stars; the shapes and colors of the planets. But it wasn't until I got a bit older that I realized it was all so much more than just the extravagant beauty of nature. The constellations hold the secrets of the universe . . . Did you know that?"

She was looking at me so honestly now—so earnestly—that I didn't think she was teasing. "Um, I didn't, actually . . ."

Magdavellía nodded. "They are us, and we are them. We're stars. Every single one of us."

I gazed up at the twinkling canopy in quiet fascination. "You think so?"

"Oh, it's quite true. Human beings and stars share ninety-seven percent of the same kind of atoms. All the building blocks of life—carbon, hydrogen, nitrogen. Stuff as old and wise as the universe exists inside all of us."

I didn't know what to say to that. It was probably the coolest thing I'd ever heard.

Up ahead, beneath the endless expanse of slate-gray sky stretched an endless expanse of slate-gray sea; in that watery wilderness, I could see dozens and dozens of frozen floating islands, some as small as bricks, some as big as ships. They seemed to be going nowhere. And yet, I realized, they were exactly where they were supposed to be.

Nature was wiser than we gave it credit for—*so why not stars?* I thought.

For the first time in maybe my entire life I stared out at the open horizon without the slightest shiver of uneasiness.

No anxiety.

No panic attacks.

I wasn't terrified that I'd never see what was beyond, because I knew that I would see it. Nothing and no one would hold me back out here.

And that was an amazing feeling.

If only Aunt Celeste could see me now . . .

A moment later, I realized Magdavellía was staring at me again. And now I watched a slow smile spread up from her lips and into her eyes as she looped a strand of purplish hair behind one ear, and for some reason my insides started feeling all hot and fluttery, and my brain turned to mush.

She opened her mouth then to say something, as I opened my mouth to say something, too—but just as I did, and just as she did, there came a loud *clang!* and a wedge of yellow light spilled across the ship's pitch-dark deck.

An instant later a figure emerged from the rear door of the crawler's command bridge. And for a moment they were just a shadow standing among shadows. Then I realized that one of those shadows was looking our way.

"Don't get all jumpsie," laughed Magdavellía. "The sailors on this ship are simple merchants. They're no threat to us."

"But he's gonna *see* us!"

Only that wasn't exactly true. Truth was, he'd *already* seen us . . .

"YAE TWO!" roared the man from below. "COME DOEN FRUM THARE!"

Cheepee, whose apricot-shaped head had been peeking out of my pocket from the second we'd started floating, quickly ducked back down as Magdavellía said, "Perhaps it *is* time to go."

We were barely fast enough, though. The old seadog had nearly reached the rear of the ship by the time we'd finally reeled ourselves in and wiggled ourselves out of the rope belts.

"*Let's'it!*" Magdavellía snatched my hand, yanking me through a little door just beyond the nearest winch, while Deus, who'd been patiently waiting for us on the deck, got right with the program, skittering rapidly along after us on all eights.

Behind us, I could hear the sailor dude shouting, "STUUP! STUUP WHAUR YA STENNT!"

But we didn't stuup or stop or anything even remotely like that.

We did just the opposite, in fact.

We ran harder, faster.

Down a long hallway, down a longer flight of steps d o w n
                                    d
                                    o
                                    w
                                    n
                                    d o w n
                                        d
                                        o
                                        w
                                    into a
world of thick steamy air where angry flames leapt and roared inside the huge steel cages of furnaces, then up, up, up and through an armor-plated archway, Magdavellía's hand holding tightly on to mine, our fingers laced, glued together by sweat and panic, both of us laughing and stumbling and struggling to breathe as we threw fast little glances over our shoulders and tried not to trip or laugh too loudly or fall or bang our heads on the low ceilings.

Around the next corner, Magdavellía jerked me into a dark little room and shut the door noiselessly behind us.

A heartbeat later, there came the rapid *thump, thump, thump!* of heavy boots and an even heavier pair of legs as the sailor went pounding down the hall past us.

"He's so *fast!*" I whispered, half freaking out, half cracking up, and I heard Magdavellía clap a hand over her mouth to keep from breaking into stitches.

In the cool dark I watched her raise a finger to her smiling lips: "*Shhhh!*"

And, of course, we both burst into laughter again . . .

Honestly, I couldn't remember the last time I'd had this much fun. With anyone. *Ever.* And I didn't think things could get any better—was, like, *ninety-nine* percent sure they couldn't.

That is, until Deus shed some light on our current situation and I saw that the walls were filled with cubbyholes and that those cubbyholes were filled with *cakes.*

Carrot cake and cheesecake, flan cake and mooncake, tres leches cake and cupcakes, angel food cake and lemon cake and chocolate cake. And those were just the ones I recognized!

We're in some kind of walk-in refrigerator! I realized with a jolt of giddiness. And then I found myself staring around so hungrily that it actually *hurt.* (Yeah, I have a bit of what you might call a sweet tooth . . .)

"You know," whispered Magdavellía, "in Rymworld, we don't usually eat those with our eyes . . ."

"Are you saying we can *have* some? Like, I mean, are we *allowed*??"

"Antares, we aren't even *allowed* on this ship . . ." Then the corners of her mouth tugged up in a mischievous grin. "The real question is, do you prefer tres leches or chocolate?"

CHAPTER THIRTY-TWO

---•---

RYMWORLD

That night, as a silver moon rose above the dark rim of the world and the great crawler crawled soundlessly to dock, Magdavellía and I cracked open one of the huge portholes that stuck out of the ship's starboard side like a row of giant glass eyeballs and slipped silently off into the silent city.

The air was thick with shadow, heavy with mist. And as we made our way through a winding, twisting maze of backstreets and alleyways, past carved stony walls that spread out like hedges and opened up like treetops, Magdavellía began to tell me all about this strange and wonderful place.

The island itself was called Mü. It was the largest of the chain of large volcanic islands (La Siete Hermanas, or the Seven Sisters, as they were often called, because of how closely the islands resembled the Pleiades constellation) that lay exactly 156 miles off the eastern edge of the Great Ice Ring. Its citizenry (aka Lemurians) was a mix of nearly everything that Rymworld had to offer: humans and humanoids, yetis, fauns, dryads, trolls and moles (molemen and molewomen), merfolken (both the dry and the deep), as well as all kinds of faefolk (fairies) and all sorts of sentient—and *partially* sentient—extraterrestrial life-forms, all of whom had lived peacefully together for untold sunsets. The humans who had settled here were supposedly the direct descendants of the very first inworld explorers who'd braved the dangers and cold of the sea and homesteaded among the ancient lands of Rymworld. (This, of course, had taken place many years before the Hundred Sunsets' War, and most of these people had fought alongside the Rymworlders.) According to Magdavellía, like the were-kin to the south and the giants to the east (but *unlike* the merfolk who governed themselves by means of kratocracy—or, rule of the strongest), Mü's government was a coalition of citizen-rulers, and, like the eleven major territories (or Terrarealms) of Rymworld, were completely autonomous.

The moment we'd stepped foot on the island my mind flashed on the book my aunt had given me the day I'd gotten kidnapped—the book from her private collection.

The title had been *A Brief Metaphysical History of Mü*. And now I couldn't help but wonder if she knew about this place—if she'd known about Rymworld all along! Maybe she was even *from* here, as wild as that sounded.

Hey, my dad supposedly knew about one of the Rym's most closely guarded secrets, and it would certainly explain some of my aunt's "kookier" behavior. Maybe my mom and dad had accidentally discovered Rymworld while flying around mapping inworld. It was definitely possible, wasn't it?

Anyway, everything about this strange and mysterious place fascinated me. And as we hurried along, I told Magdavellía how it had always been a dream of mine to explore, to see what was out there, on the other side of things, and how this was basically a dream come true for me. Then I asked her to pinch me, and she said, "Why?" obviously not getting it.

Eventually, we came to a dead end between two enormous brick buildings. High overhead, something like huge sky lanterns glittered above the yellow-tiled roofs. The fish-shaped paper lamps danced and rippled in the cool breeze, casting a soft reddish glow over the building tops.

Magdavellía crouched in the corner, in the dark, her bright eyes fixed on some tiny design carved into a brick in the side of one of the buildings. An old family crest, maybe. Two crowns crossed by two swords floating above two gilded golden thrones.

"That is the secret Imperial Signet of Agartha," she whispered, as if reading my mind. (Or more likely, *actually* reading it.)

"I thought you said we were in *Mü* . . ."

"We *are*. But this seal traces back to one of the greatest kings in the Land of the EverRisen Sun. To Agartha's first mighty king, his lordship Agamundías."

"Great name," I said.

"Even greater king." Her fingertips danced lightly along the edge of the carving. Then—like she'd pressed a button or something—a brilliant green light shone out from its center, and an instant later, a section of the brick wall slid smoothly into a slot in the ground, revealing a dark tunnel. "And this is one of the many hidden passageways he had his personal architect secretly install throughout the city," she informed me with a proud grin.

About a dozen blind, crawling steps later, we pushed through a revolving door and into a ginormous bustling kitchen where an army of robot chefs in puffy white chef hats were hard at work slicing and dicing and salting and sweating and steaming and shaving and rolling and boiling and breading and broiling and blending and basting and baking, and they were all so busy and they were all so focused that not a single one turned its steel head in our direction or swung its electric green eyes around, and soon we were out of the kitchen and hurrying down an opulent hallway with ceilings high enough to fit a flock of fluffy clouds up near the endless rows of gigantic chandeliers. Everything in here was glass and marble and screamed *look but don't you dare touch!*

"What is this place??" I whispered.

"Hôtel Pleione."

I gaped. "This is a *hotel* . . . ?"

"Part hotel. Part newspaper publisher. The hotel takes up the upper fifteen floors of the building and is probably one of the oldest in the entire Rym. It has housed royalty and travelers alike for nearly a hundred thousand sunsets. The newspaper takes up the bottom seven and employs all those robot chefs you just saw to feed their army of journalists."

Interesting . . . "And what *exactly* are we doing in this part hotel, part newspaper publisher?"

"This is a safe place. I have friends here."

"So we're looking for a friend of yours?"

"Yes. Her name is Vermiya."

"She sounds important."

"She is. She's personal consigliere to the Empress of the Deep."

"Whoa. So there's an *Empress of the Deep?*"

"Uh-huh."

"That sounds so cool. And I've never even met a *regular* empress before."

"Well, keep your fingers crossed . . . you might just get your chance." As we turned another corner, Magdavellía added, "Oh, and when you meet Vermiya, try not to stare."

Confused, I shook my head. "Why would I stare?"

"Because people tend to stare when they see—"

"*Le'sacre Empario!*" shouted a voice behind us.

We turned, we both turned (actually all four of us did—Cheepee and Deus might've turned first, as a matter of fact), but it was only my mouth that nearly left a dent in the probably priceless marble floors.

At the other end of the hall, staring back this way, stood a lady. She was a lot taller than us, and a lot older too, and she wore a long, tiered dress made of a beautiful lacy fabric. Her eyes were molten black. Her hair was silvery white. But it wasn't her hair color or her eye color or her very medieval fashion sense that had me gaping, that had my eyes trying to jump out of my face. It was just . . . *her*. Because she was completely, utterly, *unmistakably* translucent.

Like, you could see right through her.

And I don't mean in the metaphorical sense. I mean in the very real, very *physical* sense—i.e., you could see the picture hanging on the wall behind her by looking through *her head*!

Translation: Magdavellía's friend Vermiya was *a ghost*.

CHAPTER THIRTY-THREE

THE PHANTOM OF PLEIONE

The ghost lady didn't really walk so much as glide, and she really didn't glide so much as she floated along, hovering lightly over the polished marble as she approached us.

"I thought I'd seen a *specter!*" she shouted, which I found more than a little ironic. Then she threw her barely there arms around Magdavellía in a great big hug, which I found more than a little disturbing. (Especially considering the fact that just thirty seconds ago I didn't believe ghosts even existed, much less that they were *huggers*.)

"I . . . please forgive my lack of etiquette, Cesarica." The phantom lady pulled away, assuming a rigid military stance. "But—where have you *been??*"

"I was kidnapped," replied Magdavellía like it was no biggie.

The specter's shimmering and mostly see-through mouth dropped open so widely that you'd think someone had just told her that Earth was actually round. "*Kidnapped?!* By WHO??? And HOW?!"

"You will soon hear me tell my tale, Vermiya. But first I need you to arrange travel for us back to Agartha. And as whiffsly as you can manage!"

"I—I'm afraid that's impossible . . ."

"Impossible? *Why?*"

"The state of the Rym has only deteriorated since your disappearance. War and unrest have spread like wildfire: ancient disputes have rekindled to the south, in the Sinking Isles and beyond; civil war to the east; disaster to the nordeth—the red-tailed yetis and merfolk clashing over recently discovered rainbowgem mines along the disputed Iguanian coastline. Governments teeter. Economies are being *crushed.* The Terrarealms have been forced to temporarily suspend all travel."

"Even Thunderport?"

"Yes. The Electric Curtain has been raised in an attempt to quell the fighting."

"So we cannot get a message down into Agartha?"

"No, not with the Curtain engaged." The phantom lady's face darkened. "Not since the fall of Thäll have I seen the Rym so set ablaze . . . You will not find a corner of peace on any map. In fact, I am beginning to fear that the rumors might be true, after all."

"Which rumors?"

"That the Mystic now plays puppet master over the entire Rym. Pulling the strings of war from just beyond the edges of our sight, in shadow."

"Have there been more troop sightings?" asked Magdavellía with a tension in her voice that was hard to ignore.

"The Wyld Byrds have reported nothing new. And yet, the Rym *trembles.*"

Yeah, I wasn't exactly up to date on my Rymworldian current events, but none of that sounded particularly promising.

The spirit bowed her head slightly as she said, "My best advice—if I may be so bold as to give it—is that you remain here for the time being. Pleione is still the safest place in all of greater Mü."

Magdavellía was silent for a moment, then she reached into her pocket and brought out a pouch containing the strange cube-shaped rock we'd discovered inside the Alchemist's Ball.

"See what you can learn about this," she whispered, and without another word ghostly fingers had taken the rock and made it vanish beneath folds of ghostly fabric. It was some serious Houdini-level stuff . . .

"In the meantime," said the phantom lady, cutting me a suspicious sideways look, "I shall prepare your rooms."

The "room" turned out to be the largest, most magnificent space I'd ever had the privilege of stepping foot in. It was so large and so magnificent, in fact, that words like *large* and *magnificent* didn't even come *close* to doing it justice.

Every square inch of the place—and everything *in* it—was adorned with precious metals, finely sculpted crystal, rare stones.

It faced west, open to the full radiant moon, and the effect of so much refracted light in a single, enclosed space was mesmerizing. I wished I had about fifty more eyes to take it all in. Only I didn't, and my head was already starting to swim a little from all the flashes and sparkles, winks and glints—so maybe that was a good thing.

"I'll show you to the guest room," said Vermiya, motioning for me to follow.

No big surprise, the guest room was almost as lavish as the main room, with its very own sitting area, massive ivy-covered balcony, and huge four-poster bed large enough to sleep a family of bigfoots.

The bathroom looked like it had been carved out of a single chunk of meteor rock, and according to Vermiya, it actually had been, and the type of rock was called pallasite.

After almost drowning myself in a shower that had more jets and nozzles and oddly shaped spray heads than your average water park, I dripped my way into the changing room, where my favorite phantom hotelier had laid out all the latest "Lemurian fashions" for me to try on.

By the time I was dry and dressed, I looked like a pirate trying to dress like a circus performer trying to dress like a genie who'd just been barfed on by a rainbow. I was a sight to behold.

But since it was all pretty comfortable and smelled really great, I convinced myself that I didn't look like a total dork (which wasn't easy) and eventually wandered back out into the living room, where I found Cheepee hanging out on a lavish ottoman and flipping through a newspaper—a house copy of the *Pleione Gazette*.

"Read anything interesting in there?" I asked, patting his brilliant little head as I passed by.

He chittered something at me and I made it about halfway to the circle of enormous fur-lined couches when I froze like a snowman in a polar vortex.

Opposite the main entrance, the long purplish curtains that hung like waterfalls had been drawn all the way back, while the massive glass doors beyond them had been thrown open to the fragrant, nighttime breeze. And spread out before me now, pulsing with light and life like some primordial cocoon on the verge of hatching an enormous neon butterfly, was the ancient city of Mü.

Now, I was pretty familiar with most of the great cities of the world. I'd read about them in books, had seen them in movies, on TV shows, in travel magazines—New York, Mumbai, Rio, Paris—and I know that's not the same thing as *actually* visiting those places, but nothing, not being there, not even all of them put together could have compared to the majesty, the sheer awesome *magnificence* that was Mü.

Standing there, I felt like some tiny winged insect that had flown up very high into the sky to gaze out over an enchanted forest—a secret place where the great trees had changed themselves into glass and steel and concrete, and stood like twisted sculptures against the twinkling night.

I could see actual trees, too—huge ones. Easily thirty or forty times the size of any redwood, and as majestic as the sea. Winding paths of flowers bloomed between them like freshly born meadows; to the east, an immense river, like the Loire in France or the Nile of Egypt, both bisected and illuminated the city with its electric greenish-purple glow.

In the distance, where the tail of the river curved gently out of view, I could just make out the black silhouette of pyramids, sharp and pointy, rising up like stark mountains. And beyond them, real mountains.

I was afraid to move. Afraid to breathe. Afraid that even the tiniest sound or the slightest movement might make it all suddenly vanish. Like the memory of a dream upon waking.

Only I didn't want to wake. Not right now. Because I'd spent practically my *entire life* dreaming about places like this—hoping that places like this *actually* existed. And finally, here I was . . .

Right then, one of my aunt's favorite sayings came back to me: nunca es tarde si la dicha es buena. In other words, some things are worth the wait. Even if the wait has felt like forever. And in this case, it couldn't have been any truer.

I was still standing there several minutes later, just sort of lost in my own wide-eyed wonder, when the sound of Magdavellía coming out of her room snapped me out of my thoughts.

"You gotta check this view out," I started to say, but as soon as I turned, every thought of views or buildings or even of Mü itself suddenly went tumbling out of my brain like planets falling out of orbit.

Up to that point, this city had been the most spectacular thing I'd ever seen.

That is, until I turned around and saw *her*.

CHAPTER THIRTY-FOUR

●

STARSTRUCK

For what felt like a very long time I just stood there, trying not to look directly at her.

Magdavellía wore a long shimmering gown, something between a quinceañera dress and a traditional Indian sari, and her hair was gathered up in a loose mass with glittering purplish ringlets, which dangled by her lips, her cheeks, her ears.

The dusty badges of escape were gone.

No more smudges of concrete on her nose.

No more crumbles of cinderblock in her hair.

In her own choice of clothes and in her own part of the world, she was more beautiful than ever. More beautiful than anything.

"If you think that's something," she said, looking bashfully down at her sandaled feet, "you should see the city during Illuminox, the Festival of Rebirth. It's a weeklong celebration commemorating the day Xalteriá, the first sovereign of Mü, and her fiercest friend, Agamundías, that great king of Agartha, came together with less than five hundred warriors between them to defeat the ancient sea beast, Kazazök, Swallower of

Islands, before it could wrap Mü up in its mighty tentacles and drag her down into the depths. On clear nights, you can look eastward and see the Wild Woods from where all the little children of Mü looked down upon the great battle."

She smiled at me, making my insides squirm in a way I didn't know insides were capable of squirming, and I had to quickly look away or my knees might've given out.

I gave talking a shot ("—You, uh . . . you look . . .") but trailed off as a thousand different words rushed into my mind all at once, and I realized, all at once, that every single one fell totally, miserably, utterly, *completely* short of describing the purple-haired girl who now stood before me.

I watched color rise into her cheeks as she whispered, "Thank you."

"I—I didn't say anything . . ." I whispered back.

"You didn't have to." Her kohl-lined eyes rose shyly to mine, and now my face was burning, realizing that she'd probably picked the words right out of my head.

A sudden knock at the door had me jumping—had us both whirling toward the sound.

"*Enté*," called Magdavellía firmly. The door didn't open, but that didn't stop Vermiya from passing right through the thick seven inches or so of solid oak as easily as Peter Pan might fly through an open window.

Her ghostly face was pinched with concern as she raised the pouch containing the mysterious cube-shaped rock. "Cesarica, how came you by such a thing . . . ?"

"Why does she keep calling you that?" I whispered.

"It's . . . a term of endearment," answered Mags. Then, to Vermiya: "What were you able to learn about it?"

"Much. Though I have not come across anything like it in all my sunsets. I do not believe it is of this world . . ."

Then she snapped fingers that looked as substantial as morning mist, and the sound of marching feet filled the room an instant before the door to the suite swung suddenly open and a never-ending procession of hôtel staff in bright-green tailcoats and white-and-gold-striped riding pants came filing in, carrying stacks of ivory-colored paper in their white-gloved hands. They set the stacks down on a massive jade table in the middle of the room, silently, orderly, then filed silently and orderly back out.

Vermiya gestured at the papers. "This is the sum of what the Seers were able to retrieve."

"What does she mean, *retrieve*?" I asked Magdavellía, so she explained.

"All things, both animate and inanimate, possess their own psychic energy. Some call that *aura*. And in that aura, one can make impressions—projected in the form of energy—in otherwise lifeless objects. It's what I thought I'd felt when I first touched the cube. The art of extracting such information is called psychometry." She began spreading the papers out until they covered every inch of the enormous crystal tabletop. The writing, though—at least to my eyes—looked like nothing more than a bunch of chicken scratch.

I didn't get it. "So—that's what was inside the cube? All that . . . *mess*?"

Vermiya the friendly ghost nodded. "It would appear so. The Seers could make nothing of it."

Wasn't hard to see why, either. I mean, what *was* there to make of it?

For a while the three of us just sort of stood there around the table in thoughtful silence, staring down at the dizzying jumble of scribbles and scratches, slashes and dashes.

There didn't seem to be any rhyme or reason to any of it.

In fact, I was just about to give up when I noticed something: a few of the marks (the thicker, bolder strokes) seemed to slope sharply across the papers at almost *identical* angles.

And without really stopping to consider the ridiculousness of it, I sort of began to line them up, sheet to sheet, like I was assembling a weird paper puzzle.

When I was finished, I was surprised to see that I'd actually made a shape. Something like an octahedron—only two-dimensional.

I also noticed that some of the little lines and dashes around the shape seemed to form neat little pictures of their own. Sort of like hanzi, the Chinese writing system. But older looking. Even more ancient.

"That's . . . *incredible*," Magdavellía breathed, shaking her head in disbelief.

I turned toward her. "What do you think those little symbols are?"

"I don't *think*. I *know*. It's elder Marcien."

"Marcien?"

Her razor-sharp eyes fixed on mine. "It's the language of the first astronauts."

CHAPTER THIRTY-FIVE

THE SHUBBA

Vermiya wholeheartedly agreed with Magdavellía. She said it was very obviously an archaic form of Marcien—supposedly the oldest known language in the entire universe. She also said that it was going to be impossible to learn its meaning *without* a Martian because the language was so old and hardly ever used anymore by anyone *except* for Martians. And that since most little green space people are drawn to space like mammoths to ice, it was going to be almost as impossible to find one down here on terra firma. What she *didn't* know, though, was about our little trip up to the stars, and about the alien asteroid ship, and—most importantly—about *Pal.*

Anyway, after telling her the whole wild story, Magdavellía gave her a pretty picture-perfect description of the Navigator lady and her alien side-kick, and told Vermiya to begin her search for the odd pair in the deserts of northeastern Egypt.

But now it was the phantom hôtelier's turn for surprises, and she pretty much knocked our socks off (or whatever you called these silly purple stockings I was wearing) by saying, "Not northeastern Egypt, but southwestern *Mü!*"

Apparently, Navigator was somewhat famous around these parts (or at least *in*famous), and apparently she'd just recently been busted trying to steal some big shot's boat—a hydroblimp, which was supposed to be one of the rarest, most expensive boats in all the Rym.

As you can imagine, Magdavellía and I were smiling kinda hard right about then. That is, until Vermiya returned a few mintocks later to inform us that, after looking further into the matter, she'd learned that the Martian was missing and that Navigator had been arrested by some local official called The Shubba. Vermiya had looked even paler than usual delivering the news, and Magdavellía looked absolutely sick to her stomach listening to it.

Which had me asking, "So who the heck is this Shubba?"

It turned out The Shubba was a moleman—a race of part-rat, part-human humanoids that live mostly in the vast subterranean burrows underneath the city. And as it turned out, he was the ex-head of the most violent and feared crime syndicate in all of Mü.

According to Magdavellía, after a few decades of lording over a vast criminal underworld, he had made a careful study of the business model of the Müvian justice system and realized that he could make more money by helping to enforce the law than he ever could by breaking it. He now owned and operated the largest collection of privately owned prisons in all of Rymworld. Yeah, I was not looking forward to meeting this individual . . .

"The Shubba is sentient *scum*," Magdavellía told me very early the following morning as we made our way through a maze of alleys and backstreets, heading south toward The Shubba's crown jewel, the Fossoriael Penitentiary. "It's believed that he's locked up nearly half of his relatives, two-thirds of his old syndicate, and even his own mother. But that's, of course, more rumor than fact."

"Well, *yeah* . . . I mean, who would lock up their own *mother*?"

"No, that one's actually been confirmed. But most authorities believe he's only arrested about a third or so of his past associates. Anyway, I figure if we both go in there together, we have a better chance of not spending the rest of our lives in shackles. However, I should warn you that The Shubba loathes humans, reviles inworlders, detests any mammal lacking a caudal appendage, and simply *abhors* children with reddish hair. So perhaps don't say much?"

CHAPTER
THIRTY-SIX

A DEADLY GAME
OF LEMURIAN CHESS

The Shubba's "royal pavilion" sat on the middlest room of the middlest floor of his notorious people pen. It was a large, almost lavish space with colorful carpets covering the floors and walls of silky curtains fluttering in the warm Lemurian breeze. Even though the room was fogged with incense smoke and the sweet smell of vanilla-scented candles, it was still one of the funkiest-smelling joints I'd ever had the *dis*-privilege of inhaling. And I was pretty sure most of that funk was coming from The Shubba himself.

The Shubba was an odd little fella. He was kinda tall for being so short, rather thin-legged for being so blubbery, and really sort of hairy for such a bald little man-thing.

When we walked in, he was reclining lazily on a fancy red sofa bed, his long, pale tail dangling over the side like a living hook, with a headless, three-armed robot feeding him handfuls of orange grapes and having to use all fifteen of its skinny metal fingers to keep up with The Shubba's ferocious appetite. His body looked like it would make a squishing sound if you squeezed it tightly enough, and his mouth looked like it would take a bite out of you if you tried.

"You two must have very excellent connections," he purred, glancing at us out of the corner of his beady eyes as he crushed another small grape between his large buck teeth. "I've been told it takes months to bribe a meeting with me." His gaze locked on Mags. "You look *extremely* familiar . . . Have I imprisoned you before?"

"I sincerely doubt that," she said flatly.

"Bah! Very well. And how may I ahssist you?"

"We're looking for someone," Magdavellía explained. "A prisoner of yours."

"I have *men*-y . . ." (And from the way he giggled at his own silly pun, you could clearly see what kind of jerk this dude really was.) "You will have to be a bit more specific."

"Her name is Navigator. She is of the merfolken."

Suddenly the jailer's fat, fleshy, flustered little face lit up, and he sat up, clapping his chubby hands together in a barely contained rush of excitement. "*Aha*! I know this one! Oh, the *comedy* of it all!"

On either end of his sofa bed, half hidden behind curtains of rippling red silks, two bodyguard types began to laugh deep, chuckling laughs.

"What's the problem?" asked Magdavellía. "Is she no longer here?"

"Oh, she is most *definitely* here!" replied The Shubba. Then, with a dark twist of his lips: "The question is—*for how much longer . . . ?*"

"What do you mean?"

"Come and see!"

We followed Mr. Stinks-a-Lot through a wall of hanging silks and out onto a wide, stone balcony overlooking some sort of arena.

At its center was this *ginormous* chessboard flanked by rows of soldiers carrying long iron shields and even longer iron spears.

Scattered about the board, standing on the black-and-white squares, were about twenty or thirty people in dirty, shabby clothes. Half wore helmets painted white, and half wore helmets painted black. And along the perimeter of the arena loomed huge iron pens, behind which thousands and thousands of even more shabbily dressed people shouted and whooped, rattling the rusty bars.

I hadn't noticed her at first, but there, smack-dab in the middle of it all, straddling a small wooden horse that could've easily passed for a little kid's plaything, was none other than Navigator. And exactly five squares to her left, looking half passed out on his trembling, skinny green legs, was the Martian—Pal.

"I've imprisoned, jailed, caged, and otherwise enshackled over six hundred thousand creatures in my life," confessed The Shubba. "And in all my years, of all the vagrants and vagabonds I have encountered, that *ocean parasite*—the one you seek"—he pointed straight at Navigator—"I hate *her* the most."

The mermaid happened to glance up then, and I saw her mouth form a perfect O of shock.

"What is the meaning of this?!" Magdavellía demanded, surveying the outrageous scene below.

The Shubba offered us an oily grin. "I play a weekly game of chess with Siimha, my favorite slumlord in all the Terrarealms. And we use the worst of my prisoners (and the worst of his occupants) as pieces in order to keep the number of bad seeds very, very low and the incentive for good behavior (and timely payment) very, very *high*."

From the opposite balcony came: "ARE WE STARTING AGAIN, SHUBBA? IT'S MY MOVE! PAWN EAT BISHOP!" and I looked up to see some ugly rat-like something reclining on a spread of fluffy pink pillows while being fanned with bundles of yellow banana leaves.

At the creature's command, a brawny soldier clad in bronze armor tossed a heavy spear to one of the prisoners standing near the middle of the board.

Catching it, the prisoner took a moment to adjust his helmet before whacking the guy one square in front of him clear across the head.

There was a sickening *thwack!* and the dude who'd just gotten the piñata treatment crumpled bonelessly to the floor.

Two other bronze-clad soldiers quickly dragged him off the board and into a shallow ditch, where several more shabbily dressed bodies lay unconscious.

"This is an *abomination!*" shouted Magdavellía.

"No, this is FUN!" cheered The Shubba, practically bouncing on the tips of his mousy toes.

"We would like to purchase those prisoners' freedom," Mags said impatiently. "The mermaid and the Martian. How does three hundred papal sound?"

"Like an opening offer. And *a low* one."

"Seven hundred."

"Ha! I would spit on an offer *three times* as high!"

"Ten times, then."

The slimy jailer hesitated. "Do you have the money on your person?"

"No, but you have my word."

He sighed, disappointedly. "Unfortunately, words are the *least* valuable form of currency in these parts . . . Besides, in merely three moves I am going to sacrifice that ocean *tick* to obliterate Siimha's kingside defenses!"

From below, I heard Navigator shout, "Eh, you two tryin' to negotiate my freedom, by any chance?"

"Trying!" I shouted back.

"Well, I *suggest* you negotiate a little faster . . . Tell 'im 'bout Lucy!"

The moleman frowned at me. "Who's *Lucy?*"

"A diamond," replied Magdavellía.

"A huge one!" I pitched in. "She found it in space!"

The Shubba's large, pointy ears perked up a bit. "And where is this *space diamond* now . . . ?"

"It's safe!" Navigator shouted up.

"Safe *where*?!" The Shubba shouted down.

"In a . . . *location yet t'be determined!*"

The jailer's questioning eyes shifted to Magdavellía. "So it is lost?"

"Yes, it's lost," she sighed.

"But I'm gonna find it!" Navigator said brightly.

The Shubba's frown, however, only deepened. "See, that's the thing I've learned about lost treasure: it tends to *stay* lost . . ." Now he leaned his bulging belly over the top of the stony balcony and shouted, "KNIGHT TO QUEEN BISHOP SIX!"

"WAIT!" screamed Navigator. "I'll give you ten percent of the FOR-TUNE it's worth!"

"But I require seventy-five percent!"

"WHAT?!"

"Seventy-five, or I feed you to my pet kraken!"

"Seventy-five? Ha! You'll NEVER get seventy-five percent of Lucy, you sniveling, inbred *rodent*! Go 'head and feed me to your stoopid *SQUID*! See if I give a scallop!"

"As you wish, sea scum!"

I felt my insides clench.

This "negotiation" was going nowhere bueno, and fast.

And I couldn't let our quest end this way.

Not here, and not like this!

Yeah, it had been amazing so far. More than amazing, actually. It was everything I'd ever dreamed of! But now my bad case of "explore-itis" had gotten even worse. I wanted more. I wanted to go on, I wanted to find my dad, I wanted to track down that lost and legendary compass, the Star of Lôst, and epically spoil whatever evil that so-called Mystic was cooking up. Not to mention, I wanted to spend more time with Magdavellía.

Do something! I shouted at myself.

So I did something. But I'll admit—it wasn't awfully bright.

Without thinking, my hands shot out and all ten of my fingers seized The Shubba's flabby upper arm. "C'mon, dude, don't be like this!" I pleaded with him.

In the same instant, the jailer's pair of oversize, over-muscled, and under-*brained* bodyguards rushed through the silky curtains, drawing twisted silver daggers from their belts.

The sound of sharp-edged steel grinding against scabbard echoed through the air like an explosion, and Deus, who had positioned herself protectively between Magdavellía and The Shubba, now began buzzing dangerously.

Magdavellía told her something in a language I did not understand, then whirling, she told the Shubba something in that same strange dialect, but, unlike Deus, who immediately settled down, the little jailer only seemed to be getting more and more worked up. His beady black pupils fixed intensely on me. "What did you call me?" he asked, his voice trembling with disbelief.

I gulped. This wasn't good. "—You mean, *dude?*"

"Please, stop talking," Magdavellía whispered.

"You know this word," The Shubba asked, as if astonished, "*dude?*"

"Uh . . . yeah?"

His face was a mask of shock. "I tell you no lie: I have not heard that word since I was a suckling babe in my mother's arms. It is the *most tender* expression in the lowspeek of my people!" His head snapped toward Magdavellía. "I like this one," he confided, pointing a clawed finger back at me. "I like him very much!" Which, by the way, had me letting out just about the BIGGEST sigh of relief *ever!* But now his gaze flicked darkly down to the arena pit where Navigator was still straddling that famous Trojan horse's mini-me. "Only I hate *that one* more . . . KNIGHT TAKE PAWN!"

"Wait!" cried Magdavellía. "What about this ring?"

"What *ring??*" huffed the moleman, turning slowly around—

And suddenly, his beady rat-like eyes narrowed. His too-wide mouth gaped.

Magdavellía was holding out her hand, displaying an exquisite ring. The massive square-cut gem set in three intertwining golden bands caught a thick column of Lemurian sunshine and sparkled with fiery brilliance in every color of the rainbow. And maybe even a few others, too . . .

Honestly, I'd never really been into jewelry, but that thing was so fresh that I suddenly had a pretty good idea of what Gollum felt like every time he looked with spellbound eyes upon the ring of power. And apparently The Shubba did, too, because the moleman was practically drooling on himself. Actually, scratch the "practically" part; the guy was *literally* drooling on himself.

A bead of shiny sweat formed in the dimple of his whiskery upper lip as he whispered, "Aye, *mí doe*—*where did you discover such a treasure . . . ?*" His greedy fingers reached out for it, slowly, quietly, and just as slowly, and just as quietly, Mags inched it back.

"Does it matter?" she asked coolly.

The Shubba's eyes shone as if entranced. "No, I don't suppose it does . . ."

"We have a deal, then? The prisoners for this ring?"

The moleman didn't answer her. Not at first, anyway. "That is a rainbowgem, is it not? Or so it is called in this part of the Rym. Though the Agarthians have another name for it—a name that they do not tell." His expression turned suspicious as his ratty gaze fixed sharply on Magdavellía. "*Are you certain we have not met before . . . ?*"

Mags's jaw tightened. "I'll offer it just once more, moleman."

For a moment the greedy little jailer stared longingly, lovingly at the sparkling gem and the little golden loops to which it had been fitted. Then he quickly snatched it out of her hand, shouting, "RELEASE THE PRISONERS!"

CHAPTER THIRTY-SEVEN

—— • ——

MARTIAN MAPS

Now that we'd found our Martian, I could hardly wait to discover the secret of the octahedron puzzle. Magdavellía, on the other hand, seemed more concerned with making sure that our secrets stayed as secret as possible for as *long* as possible.

Back at Pleione, she stuck Navigator in the fancy study, told her to wait there, then asked me to keep an eye on her. Both eyes. Then she took Pal, along with Deus Ex and Cheepee, out to the living room area where all the papers with the Martian scribbles were spread out.

The merwoman looked amused. "As you wish . . ."

But not five minutes later, the huge study doors swung open again and Magdavellía came marching triumphantly in.

"You were right!" she exclaimed, quickly rushing over to me. "It *is* an octahedron! *And* it's a map!"

Apparently, the scribbles we'd puzzled together to form a two-dimensional octahedron was actually a Martian skymap. And these skymaps, according to Magdavellía, mapped the currents of mystic energy that ran all over the world. What were known as ley and fey lines. Turns out, when Martian mapmakers map out planets, they don't bother with the usual topographical features like mountains and oceans and rivers. And that's because their technology allows them to settle pretty much anywhere; and so, like early hunter-gatherers gravitating toward bodies of fresh water, Martians, being psychic beings, gravitate toward the source of a planet's metaphysical power (i.e., ley and fey lines), knowing that these energies can be harnessed for a wide variety of purposes. I actually remembered watching a TV show about ley lines. I knew they had something to do with Earth mysteries and that they'd pretty much been discredited in inworld (thanks to the Flat Earth Society, obviously), but that was about it.

"Fairy paths, spirit ways—ley lines have been called many different things by many different people," explained Mags. "But the thing to remember is that they are like Earth's own fingerprints—and *especially* in spots where they cross with fey lines, which are simply ley lines that curve. Since no two groupings are exactly alike, they can be used to determine *precise* locations on the planet's surface. Problem was, we were thinking like *Earth* people when we should have been thinking like *space* people . . ."

From a nearby desk, looking freshly unrolled with the thick parchment curling tightly up at the corners, she brought over a different map. A fancy-looking one, with bright colors and everything.

"This is a map of the Nordeth, or the northern quadrant of the outer Rym, with ley and fey lines mapped."

Her fingers traced a circle around a cluster of islands near the top right-hand corner, and as they did, I felt my eyes bug.

But it wasn't because of the islands themselves. It was because of what was *underneath* them. The ley and fey lines. They seemed to come together to form the shape of a two-dimensional octahedron, just like the one we'd puzzled together!

Magdavellía turned a slow grin at me. "Notice any resemblance?"

"What is that place . . . ?"

"They're called the Platonic Isles. But notice the Isles *themselves*—the landmasses. They form the two-dimensional shape of *an icosahedron*."

It was true, too. I'd noticed that even before she'd brought it up.

"Now, I hadn't put it all together until a few minticks ago," she said, "but think about it . . . the Alchemist's Ball—the first clue we discovered—was a dodecahedron; the clue inside it, a cube; the skymap hidden inside the cube, the shape of an octahedron; and now the islands, an icosahedron. That's four of the five Platonic Solids. Not to mention the fact that the skymap itself is clearly pointing us to the Platonic Isles . . . I think it's all very obviously hinting at something."

And I was pretty sure I knew what she thought it was hinting at, too. "You're talking about the Star of Lôst?"

"I am."

"You think it's hidden somewhere on that island."

"I do. *And* I think the time has come to test my hypothesis." Then, with a smile in her voice and a sparkle in those violet eyes: "So tell me, Antares—have you ever wondered what lies at the very *edge* of the world?"

I smiled. "Only every day of my life."

CHAPTER THIRTY-EIGHT

— • —

A PERILOUS PASSAGE

(1)

"Surely you jest!" the merchica exploded a few mintocks later when we approached her with our plan. Over on the couches, Pal, Cheepee, and Deus were all sort of "recharging their batteries," but I doubt any of them could sleep through Aqua Woman's latest temper tantrum. "The Platonic Isles are not only arguablee the *least* explored region in all of Rymworld, they're quite *undebatablee* its most dangerous! No one ventures that close to the edge *that* far nordeth. Not even merfolk!"

Magdavellía was trying to keep it together, her eyes squeezed patiently shut. "You are the *only* navigator on Mü," she calmly explained. "We require your talents."

"What you both require is a *sanity* test!"

"What's your problem, huh?" I shot back. "You're a Navigator and you're passing up a chance to explore the unexplored? To see a part of the world that maybe *no one's* ever seen before?" It honestly didn't compute with me.

"And need I remind you," said Mags, "you are indebted to us. We saved your life."

"Yes! And now I am trying to save both of yours!" Navigator, turning away from her, gave a frustrated huff, her gills pulsing anxiously. "You have your mother's stubborn will! That much is *certain*."

Mags's gaze flicked momentarily in my direction, but she stayed silent.

"What's wrong?" asked the mermaid bandit, arching a scaly brow. "Thought I wouldn't recognize you . . . ?"

"You don't recognize me," Magdavellía replied in a completely cool tone of voice. "Because we've never met. And you didn't know my mother."

"Oh, but I *did* know your mother . . . I knew your father as well. And I know *you*. Which means I know what you're after—and more still, *whom* you oppose." She gave a sad smile. "I'm ashamed to admit that I almost didn't recognize you . . . Though you couldn't have been more than a fingerling the last time we met. Either way, when I saw what you traded for my freedom—well, let's just say that certain memories were brought to tide . . . Such treasures are rarely seen in this world. At least outside of the Agarthian Roial Court. In fact, the only mystery that remains at this table is the mystery of that poor boy, and why you have chosen to wrangle him into yer doomed service."

"She didn't wrangle me into anything," I said. "I'm here because I want to find my dad and because I want to help Magdavellía."

Those words slid like salt water off the merlady's scaly back. She leaned toward Mags, her eyes the color of a storm-tossed sea.

"I beg of you, my child, think this through . . . think it *through*! Even if you *were* to find the fabled Star, which you won't, and happened to discover the location of the island EverLôst, which you *can't*; and let's just assume that *all* the legends are true and that you come upon the Cavern of Limitless Wealth, or perhaps even the Fount of Youth—what are either of those to you? Or let's say better yet that you discover the Throne of Earthly Power; well, as you very well know, there is no power on this earth that can bring back the dead. So where exactly does this path of yers lead? Where does it end?" Her expression fell, and the scales along the backs of her arms darkened to a deep sea green. "Yer in a race that you cannot win. The Star you seek—if it even exists—has likely already bin found, for the Mystic's dark heart has long hungered for it. The Forgotten Order has bin dug out of its ancient tombs. A faceless evil once again stirs in the hearts of Rymworlders. It is not merely rumor. Like the wind is to the sea, so is this Mystic to nearly all that is wicked upon the Rym. A phantom lord seated high upon an impregnable perch, and beyond the reach of any. Yet it wars not alone. Under its spell are legions: the red-tailed yetis of the nordeth; frogmen of the Smarshums; molemen and ratmen and weremen, sailors and soldiers and traitors. To speak nothing of the marshes that surround the Isles . . ." Her stormy gaze sharpened on Magdavellía as she said, "Do you know the *treachery* of those seas? Are you acquainted with the *horrors* that lurk beneath its ever-roaring waves . . . ? The very waters you sail on are possessed of a dark will that only seeks to *sink* and *shipwreck*. We'll never make it," she said forebodingly. "The swamps will feast on our flesh . . ."

You'd think a warning like that would've made any reasonable person think twice. Heck, it almost made *me* think twice. But obviously Magdavellía wasn't reasonable, because she didn't even blink.

"Was I not raised on the Sinking Islands?" she said. "Did I not swim in the Vanishing Sea, and hear the olden tales of Thundera and of the elder Mountain Gods? I know the dangers of the nordethern Rym as well as anyone. And I've witnessed firsthand the wrath of that monster of which you speak. But I also know this: evil cannot be run away from . . . The world simply is not big enough."

"It's bigger than you think," grumbled Navigator—and for several seconds, no one spoke. At last the mermaid said, "No matter what I say, you won't choose caution, will you? You won't choose prudence. No, for your mother's iron blood pulses through your veins like thunder. So what I do now I do because I must. And I do it because yer parents would have wanted me to. This I do for *them*."

Then a serious look came over her face, and she dipped her gilled neck and she bent down to a knee and she said, in a singsong voice:

If I am to die in the sea
then let it be fer the glory of Agartha
let it be fer the glory of Thee.

And slowly—very slowly—I watched Magdavellía's eyes fill with a proud sort of look. "Welcome back, Navigator." And a moment later: "What will you require to get us to the Isles?"

"Safelee? Sixty sailors and two fullee-armed War Gattaleons."

"And more dangerously?"

"Has there been a shortage of soldiers or military vessels in Agartha since my departure?"

"No, just a severe difficulty in reaching them."

"I can smuggle you in. Give me ten sunsets."

"I have no doubt. But that's ten sunsets too many. Time is now merely an obstacle, but I fear it may soon become our doom."

The mermaid thoughtfully blinked glittery lids as if she was working out a tough algebra problem. "How many soldiers will make our company?"

"None."

"*None?!* Cesarica, there's an entire BRIGADE of robo-soldiers posing as robo-CHEFS hardly twelve stories beneath our feet!"

But Magdavellía's expression did not change. "The Mystic's spies fester like maggots in Mü," she explained. "I will not be the one to lead that evil to the Star if it has not already discovered it. We go alone. And we go *quietly.*"

"Without mariners or a proper ship, this is a *most* unadvisable journey . . ."

"Then I'm afraid we must embark upon it without your advice."

"*Trenches!* I'm not a mage, you realize that, yes? We *are* going to require a ship. And the *only* non-military vessel that I'd trust to take you into those waters is of my people—merfolken craft."

"You speak of a hydroblimp?"

"Ye, true skemmas, built by *true* seaventureers. Its steel gathered from the mountain volcanoes of the deep and its masts fashioned from the timber of the ancient pÿnes. Light, yet stronger than alchemist iron. And as it was designed with all the cunning of my people, and like the sea serpents of old, it will keep us out of view of unfriendly eyes." She let out a tired sigh. "Unfortunately, we'll not be finding one in Mü . . . There mayhap only be twenty left in the entire Rym."

Magdavellía's mouth twitched, and I saw the first rays of an ironic smile dawning on the edges of her lips. "As it happens," she said, "I just might know someone who owns one."

"*Who*??" asked Navigator. Then, realizing *who*: "No. No, *no, no* . . . You can't be serious. But I——*NO! Magdavellía, my answer is NO!*"

"Ahhh, *yes*," purred The Shubba, grinning from greasy whisker to whisker as the three of us walked uneasily back into his pavilion later that day. (We'd decided to leave Pal back at the hotel because just the thought of a return trip to Shubba's prison had made him pass out on the spot—twice.) "I was wondering how long it would be before you decided to return her . . ."

"They're not here to *return me*, you mouth-breathin' *rat*——"

"*Navigator!*" snapped Magdavellía. "I'll handle negotiations, thank you . . ." She turned back to the little jailer. "We're in need of a ship. A merfolken craft, to be exact."

And Mr. Short, Squishy, and Stinky propped himself up on his side, suddenly curious. "You mean my hydroblimp?"

"Yes."

"So you speak of my *favorite* ship of all five-hundred-and-ninety-two that I own?"

"I suppose so, yes."

"The same boat, mind you, that that *ocean parasite* standing next to you only a sunset ago attempted to thieve from my collection?"

"I believe that is correct."

"And I'm assuming that your plan is to sail to some far-flung place with that walking *nematode* as captain?"

"Correct again."

"Well, I must say, your forthcomingness *astounds* me . . . Truly. But my answer is simple: Never. NEVER, I saysay!"

"There it is!" shouted Navigator, flinging her webbed hands up angrily. "Can we please go now?"

"—UNLESS," The Shubba shouted over her, "I were to receive a PROPER cut . . ."

Magdavellía looked lost. "A proper cut of *what*?"

"You think me a FOOL, girly??? I know what you're after. And my price is *forty percent*—forty percent of *LUCY!*"

Confused, I frowned. "Lucy? What does that hunk of space rock have to do with—"

"Not even in yer *filthiest* dreams, ya *filth!*" roared the mermaid.

"Navigator!" snapped Magdavellía; this time the mermaid turned to look at her with something like an idea forming in the depths of her storm-gray eyes.

Then the merlady turned back to the jailer, saying, "Ten percent, and consider yerself of *extreme* fortune."

The Shubba crushed a grape between his big front teeth. They fascinated me, those teeth. They almost looked like miniature Domino tiles. "Twenty-five is my floor."

"And fourteen is my ceilin'."

"Twenty-four."

"Fifteen."

"*Praccharna!*" cried the moleman, and those annoying bodyguard dipsticks of his emerged from behind hanging silks, drawing daggers again.

"*Navigator!* What are you doing?!" shouted Magdavellía.

"Yeah, I think it's time you chilled out a bit," I agreed.

"Never! He can kill us if he wants," said the mermaid in a voice that was more bluff than boldness (at least I *hoped* it was), "but fifteen is as high as I go!"

The Shubba was quiet for a moment, thinking. Deep thoughts it looked like, too. Finally, he shouted, "Fifteen it is!" and turning to his bodyguards, "Prepare my things for voyage!"

And, well, I guess that was *one way* of getting a ship . . .

CHAPTER THIRTY-NINE

—•—

HEAVENLY WISDOM

I'd never seen another boat quite like her in my entire life. The merfolken-made boat, or hydroblimp (which The Shubba had named *La Princhepessa*), was more sleek gray fish than ship, with hammered steel sides that resembled scales and a spine of silvery sails that stuck straight up like a mighty fin. She was a little bigger than a yacht, a little smaller than a private cruise liner, and a whole heck of a lot cooler than both. And she was fast, too! In fact, just an hour or so after we'd taken her out of Poresma de' Po (a private high-security port on the eastern coast of Mü), we'd already sailed nearly fifty miles and had hit open ocean, where the only movement was the steady roar of the sea and slam and slap of the ship's iron prow as it crashed through the icy water again and again, sending up great frothy sprays.

Truth was, it felt like I'd suddenly become a character from one of my favorite books—Captain Nemo, maybe. Hanging out on a ship like this, sailing through wild and uncharted oceans in search of some half-forgotten relic with the fate of the known (and *unknown*) world hanging

in the balance. But wasn't this the kind of exploring and adventuring I'd always been so hungry for? Honestly? It was.

The ocean seemed to grow vaster somehow, and quieter, too, as we sailed on—rymward—toward the very edge of the world. Just the thought gave me goose bumps.

I wondered what my aunt would think if she could see me now. I wondered what my aunt was doing—how she was. If she'd been missing me as badly as I'd been missing her.

I'll see her again, I promised myself. *I will*. And just the thought was enough to make me smile.

Staring out at the coppery faraway horizon, I suddenly realized that I hadn't had one of my panic attacks in weeks. Maybe even months. And that made me smile, too.

2

Soon the day gave way to night and the sunlight to starlight; Magda-vellía and I found a nice spot up near the prow where we sat down to stare up at the skyfield of stars as they blinked, one by one, and then all at once to life.

With my face turned into the fresh ocean breeze, I leaned back against the railing and listened with interest while Mags told the story of the stars, as it had been told all over Rymworld for hundreds of generations. She pointed out the planets and constellations, paying special attention to the Scorpius constellation, whose brightest star had a pretty cool (and pretty familiar) name.

When she finished, we drifted into silence for a while, while the ship drifted silently along, both of us gazing out at the dark sky stretching above, and darker sea swelling below.

I could have happily sat there forever. And we might've, too, had a small, polite voice not startled us out of our thoughts.

"If your sight was strong enough," it said, "you could pierce the veil of time and space and see my planet dancing among her sisters."

I looked around in surprise. Pal was standing next to me, motionless, unblinking—those strange Martian eyes, so large and melon-like, staring longingly up at the stars. Or maybe even beyond them.

And, I realized, he'd used . . . *words.*

Which had pretty much left *me* speechless. It was the first time I'd ever heard him speak.

Now, I gotta admit: I'd always wanted to talk to an alien about space and stuff (I mean, who *wouldn't?*), and since I figured this might be my once-in-a-lifetime opportunity, I just said the first thing that popped into my head.

"Hey, so can you phone home from way down here?" I said. It was a joke. Obviously. But apparently—or *ironically*, I guess—the Earth-stranded Martian had never watched that movie.

Lime-green lips pulled down into a small frown. "A standard radio wave transmitted from a terrestrial radio tower or orbiting satellite, when projected into deep space and confronted with the radiational interference of stars and the cosmic noise of pulsars and quasars, would not even reach the outer spiral branches of the Laniakea supercluster." His voice was soft, but bright and clear like the twinkling of the stars he gazed so longingly at.

"*Oh*," I said, making myself sound even smarter. (Suddenly, I wished I'd paid more attention in science class.)

"He probably thinks you hail from *Mars*," teased Magdavellía, grinning at me as Pal turned to grin at her—gradually at first, until his thin lips were pulled all the way back, tight against his bony cheeks, and you could see the hollow purple cave of his mouth.

"He *isn't*?" I said, looking uncertainly between them. "I mean, you aren't?" *Mars? Martian?* It just seemed to fit.

Laughing, Mags smoothed a strand of hair behind one ear. "No . . . he isn't."

"My home," explained the Martian, "is a small exoplanet not completely unlike your own. It orbits a circumstellar habitable region within a ring of seven million red dwarfs in the heart of what you might know as Perseus–Pisces." His long, bulbous finger, tipped with every shade of blue, pointed vaguely east—toward Venus, I guessed. "Not far. Though I wouldn't dare such a journey now . . . No, I wouldn't *dare* it."

I thought I knew why, too. And without realizing how rude it sounded (at least not until it was too late), I said, "So it's true that you lost your courage?"

Fortunately, though, Pal didn't seem to take any offense. He only nodded—a tiny, sad movement.

"But like . . . *how*?" I'd just never heard of anyone up-and-up losing their courage before. Well, except maybe the Cowardly Lion from Oz.

"I lost my antennae in battle," the alien answered solemnly. Then, off my confused look: "We Martians believe that our courage is cellularly compacted into the mitochondrial filaments of the cellular structures within our antennae. They are the only part of our anatomy that grows throughout our entire lifespans. To lose them—for any reason—is the greatest of disgraces."

There was a short silence. At last Magdavellía said, "In Agartha, we don't believe that. We don't believe anyone is born with, or naturally possesses, any amount of courage at all. We believe that courage is one of the primordial forces of the universe. That it is always around us—everywhere—so that in a time of need, anyone can avail themselves of its particular kind of strength. We call it the Cup of Courage; that is from whence comes the old song—"

And then (if you can believe it) she actually started to sing:

Oh ye, oh ye, drink ye cowards!
Drink ye fools!
Drink up, drink up, drink up!
Take thy cup!
and dip thy cup!
and drink the courage up!

She shrugged. "It's an old song. But its truth is eternal. In fact, I believe that simply the will to muster one's courage is a little act of courage all on its own."

Pal said nothing, only stared wistfully at the night sky, so busy with its ceaseless twinkling.

"I've always wondered what a Martian sees when they look up at the stars from way down here," whispered Mags. "—Would you tell us?"

The Martian's kind, wrinkleless face remained expressionless, his voice barely audible now over the swoosh and slap of the waves:

"I hear the silent songs of the Cepheids, and can still feel their icy-blue fire on my skin. But they are all so far away now, and so it is like meeting an old friend after many sunsets. You see them as they were, not as they are. And so it is with stars."

His tiny ovoid-shaped mouth closed and his large ovoid-shaped head bowed slightly, and since he didn't look like he was planning on saying anything else, I said, "So what's the coolest thing you've ever seen up there? In space, I mean."

But the Martian was quiet for so long that I didn't think he was going to answer. When he finally did, he spoke slowly at first, and almost in a sad way.

"I've watched supernovas bloom with petals of soundless light. I've beheld a triple sunrise on the iron planet of Fè. I've witnessed the birth of star clusters so gaseous and dense that they will one day give birth to universes of their own. But of everything I have seen, of all I have ever known or been told, your home, *Earth,* is by far the most interesting . . . Your planet is a miracle in a universe of miracles. And it has long been a source of great intrigue among my people. For eons, our greatest minds have contemplated your comings and goings, and I speak of a time long before the Great Construction."

"The Great Construction?"

"When we helped your earliest civilizations build the ancient wonders of your world. The monoliths. The great pyramids."

"Huh. So that *was* you people . . ."

"We have always pondered Earth and her earthlings. How you are the only life-forms within twenty-five thousand light-years of one another and yet are always at war. We Martians have never been able to comprehend this most terrestrial of predilections. Empathy is our great gift. As a species we'd rather perish from hunger or calamity than to steal from or harm another Martian. And that is because we see what you earthlings simply cannot.

"There is a saying among my kind: *Man was created with a fatal flaw: his brain is too big for his body and his heart too small.* Human beings contain seventy-eight organs. We Martians only eight. And our brains are not separate from our hearts. They are a single organ, which is to say that all the thoughts, impulses, and desires that enter our minds must first pass through our hearts before they ever reach our lips or our hands. This is why we have never fought against our own, and why we never will."

His dark, pupil-less eyes drifted softly spaceward, becoming lost there. "We believe that our ancestors who have passed from this dimension live on forever as the stars you see above, but we also believe that those stars reveal much about humankind. Stars are in a constant state of imbalance, always warring against themselves. The gravity of a star's mass is forever pulling it inward, trying to cause its collapse. And if there was nothing to stop it, that is exactly what would occur. But another force keeps the star from destroying itself, and this force is known as *light*. I believe you see this force on your planet from time to time, when kindness is shown to a stranger, when the hungry are fed, or the poor clothed, or the sick comforted. When individuals realize that there is no such thing as *I* but only *us*. This inner light is what keeps humanity from collapsing like a star, and like a star, keeps your people shining on in this miraculous universe . . ." A single green finger stretched skyward, as if it was trying to touch the celestial canopy. "Many stars, many planets, but only one universe." Now that same finger pointed slowly around at the three of us. "Many life-forms on this planet, but only *one* living organism. All life is interconnected, whether known or unknown. Even us *here*."

I realized that the super-cool birthmark in the center of his forehead had begun to pulse and glow like a neon vein. But I didn't get what was happening.

"He wants us to see something," whispered Magdavellía, "to see through *his* eyes . . ." Only I didn't get that, either. So I asked, "How??" and then she showed me.

She stretched the little pink fingertip of her index finger toward the Martian's long, flat, bluish one—as I did, too—and the moment all of our fingers came together, and at the very point they came together, the starry darkness around us was shattered by an explosion of blinding light.

CHAPTER FORTY

A NAVIGATOR'S BETRAYAL

In that flash, I saw it all—

A high and lonely mountain, cold with ice and deceit. The place where the Martian had lost his courage but found a friend.

(*no escape no breath and the smell of dying*)

A lie whispered.

Innocent blood spilled.

(*running red like a river running red over the earth and the earth red with it crying out for revenge*)

My heart seized with a fear that wasn't mine.

My throat closed with a sort of hazy, faraway, disconnected panic.

I shivered. I gasped. In the distance, someone screamed (it might've been me). And then I felt myself begin to tumble o
u
t
o
f
t
h
e
v
i
s
i
o
n
a
s
i
f
t
u
m
b
l
i
n
g
out
of
the sky.

Blinking back to reality, I looked dazedly up. Looked dazedly at Mags. Her eyes, wide and full of shock, were staring back into mine.

She knew.

And I knew she knew.

Because I'd seen it, too.

It had been an ambush.

Her parents.

Betrayed.

Betrayed and murdered.

By traitors.

Invaders.

And led by none other than a Navigator.

"*Magdavellía*," I breathed.

But it was too late. She was already on her feet, already tearing off toward the ship's command bridge.

I caught up to her just as she barged through the heavy steel door, charging toward the mermaid and screaming, "You treasonous APEAN-SNAKE! How could you?! How?! *HOW?!*"

In a blink, her nimble fingers had slipped a silvery dagger from her belt. Moonlight glinted wickedly off its razor edge as Navigator fumbled backward in panic, knocking over maps and compasses and shouting, "Just listn'na me, will you? I asked Pal to show you that, all right? It was MY idea!"

"Your idea to reveal your own treachery?! In that case, *brilliantly* done!"

Cheepee, up on the center console, was chittering nervously and holding out his itty-bitty paws, as if begging Mags to stop.

"Magdavellía, you're gonna hurt her!" I yelled.

"That's the idea!" In a rage, she raised the deadly dagger, probably preparing to relieve the merlady of the burden of her head.

But Navigator roared, "I WANTED YOU TO KNOW THE TRUTH, ALL RIGHT?!" And—somehow, someway—it stopped Mags.

Letting out a disgusted sigh, the mermaid shook her head, her eyes dropping to her webbed feet as she said, "Ye, yer parents *were* betrayed. But not by *me* . . . At least not *jest* by me. As I am sure you kno, there are many in the Wise Assembly who 'ave been seduced by mystic teachings and mystic philosophies, and many who were, if not openlee, then *secretlee* loyal to that monster. And together, and fer no more reason than political gain, these vipers conspired to lead the entire Imperial Caravan into what can only be described as a *blood trap.*"

The same emotion that had darkened her eyes now trembled in her voice. "I was ordered to lead the company to a high place, Mount Xérera, where the Mystic would be waiting. Your parents, as you know, were that monster's most vocal opposition, and I was told that they had refused a summit with the Mystic again and again, but that in this way a meeting would be forced upon them and war perhaps avoided. A lie, of course. And Mount Xérera itself stands upon the fabled Ley of Lights, a place of immense mystical energy, which would naturally render our navigational instruments useless, putting me in full charge of leading the caravan. At the time, that mountain had been home to a small Martian settlement. The Mystic, of course, wiped them out before we arrived, and I found Pal dying on the frozen slopes after our caravan was ambushed. The Mystic's forces let me live, because I was the one who had led us into the trap."

Silence.

At last Magdavellía murmured, "*But why . . . ?*"

"Because as a natural law power corrupts, and those with it only seek more. Because we are all fragile, fearful creatures. And because I was a fool." Her gaze, full of pain and ancient regrets, became distant. "When I realized how I'd failed yer parents—how I'd failed *my kingdom*—I didn't merely leave the Servÿce, or Agartha, or even Rymworld. I left this *planet.* And do you know what I found upon my return? *My purpose.* Which is why I agreed to take you into the nordeth, and why I will continue to do everything in my power to help you avenge them." She hung her head again. "This isn't a new war, my child . . . It has long been fought. This world is already lost, and I cannot save it. Neither can you. I wish I could tell you differently, I do. Yet, while I live, yer parents' blood will forever remain a stain upon my hands. And if my absolution is to be found at the point of yer sword, then I say don't just cut me with it, drive it thru my *heart*."

And now she held her webbed hands out at her sides in total surrender as tears welled in her eyes and a single tear traced a silent path down her scaly cheek.

For several minticks, the tip of Mags's blade trembled only inches from Navigator's chest.

Then, all of a sudden, she let it tumble from her grasp and wiped her face with trembling hands, and then she turned and, without another word, vanished past me and into the misty darkness.

Magdavellía was hiding out near the back of the ship when I caught up with her. I didn't know what to say, or if there was anything to say. So I just sat down next to her, thinking about how brave her parents had been. Thinking that now I knew where she got it from.

And obviously reading my mind, she whispered, "I'm not brave like them, Antares. Or as strong."

Around us the wind whipped and the pound and crash of waves sent sprays of chilly seawater drizzling over the moonlit deck. Far away, to the east, there came the shrill cry of seabirds.

"Did you feel its power . . . ?" Magdavellía asked me after a few seconds. "So dark and desperate, like a ravenous sea."

She was talking about the Mystic, and that was a pretty dead-on description of what I'd felt in the Martian's vision. I hadn't actually *seen* the monster, but oh, I'd *felt* it. In fact, just the memory was enough to send a fresh shiver of fear through me.

"I've never sensed a mind like that," she confessed. "Even my mother, whose mind had oft been heralded as the Juggernaut of Jeboém and whose mindgifts had been rumored to rival even the talents of Martians, could not compare to this."

"But your mother didn't fear the Mystic," I said. And I wasn't just saying that—it's what I'd felt in the vision (and probably because Pal had felt it).

"No, she didn't. Neither did my father. But you beheld their fate." Tears trickled down her trembling cheeks. "I fear the Rym is about to fall, and still more, I fear that there isn't a single thing we can do to stop it."

True hopelessness, if you've ever felt it, feels a lot like drowning, and a lot like a cold sea. And I could feel it rising all around me now, colder than even the real sea.

"If only this evil had befallen the world in another age," whispered Mags, "during another reign. Yes, even Agamundías's reign . . . That great king of yore could have stood against any enemy. But Agartha isn't strong enough now, Antares . . . *I'm* not strong enough."

Another thing about hopelessness: it tends to feed off other people's hopelessness. And mine was beginning to feed off hers, making it hard for me to breathe, when wise words suddenly sparked up in my heart like a match struck in a dark cave:

"True strength isn't best measured by success," I said, "but by one's willingness to fail."

Now Magdavellía's face lifted, slowly, and her lips slowly parted to say, "Who told you that?"

"Someone who believed in us. Someone who believed in *you*. Just like I do. You're so much stronger than you give yourself credit for," I whispered. "And so much braver. I mean, I think you're the shizness . . ."

Honestly, I hadn't even meant to use that word. I was just trying to say that she was awesome or whatever. And I wasn't really expecting her to respond because, in my mind, there was no way she would even know what that meant. So you can imagine my surprise when a laugh bubbled right up out of her, and she looked at me through smiling, teary eyes.

"*What?* Why would you say something like that??" she asked me.

"Oh, it doesn't mean anything *bad* or whatever. In inworld it means, like, *you're the best.*"

Magdavellía grinned. "In Rymworld it means *a cheesy baguette.*"

And now we both burst out laughing. It was a pretty funny coincidence.

Just then, from across the deck there came a crackling sound—scratchy, scratchy—and then a squeal of violins as music flowed over the deck of *La Princhepessa* in a gentle wave.

It was coming from up near the bridge where The Shubba and his bodyguards had set up some kind of antique record-player thingy on a rolling table.

I noticed Magdavellía was listening—listening and smiling.

"You know that song?" I asked, and she gave a little nod.

"It's called 'Za Höppaz.' It means 'The Hope.' It is the great anthem of Rymworld. It was written by the renowned Rymworldian composer Heivet, at the culmination of the Hundred Sunsets' War."

"Sounds a little like bolero," I said, which is this style of old-school Latin music. Sort of like a slow-tempo blend of tango, waltz, and rumba. Kind of romantic sounding.

"It's a very beautiful song," Magdavellía said quietly. "And it's a very beautiful dance."

"How does it go?"

"Oh, I don't know the steps. In Agartha, no one except for children and stage performers dance."

"Like, you're not allowed?"

"It's not *decree*. But it's considered . . . *undignified*."

A moment later, my heart did a little somersault in my chest as I decided what I'd do, and so I stood up and smiled down at her and held my hand out so close to hers that it shook a little.

"Show me," I said.

CHAPTER FORTY-ONE

THE FIRST DANCE

The cold wind blew strands of purplish hair across Magdavellía's face as she shook her head in an embarrassed way. "Show you what?"

"How to dance to 'Za Höppaz.'"

"I told you—I don't know how."

My mouth curved into a wobbly smile as I helped her to her feet. "That makes two of us . . ."

And so, without knowing the spacing or the timing or even the steps, we walked out into the misty night air, holding hands, and then, holding on to each other, began to dance.

We were shadows moving among shadows and sometimes hardly moving at all. For a long time, there was only the sound of her laugh, and her hands, her smiling eyes, and the mist furling and unfurling around us, clinging to our arms and legs like strips of ghostly fabric.

We laughed and spun, and spun and laughed, twirling and twirling and twirling until the world was beautiful again, and I was dizzy.

I found myself wishing that time would lock us in an eternal hourglass and just drizzle over us forever.

But unfortunately, before the song was even over, Magdavellía stopped swaying and her feet stopped moving and her mouth opened and closed several times like she was searching for lost words.

"What is it?" I whispered, searching her eyes for the words her lips could not find.

Then, like she had to force herself to speak: "I—I had a terrible premonition . . ."

"A premonition? About what?"

"This. All of this. I saw it the night before we met in Bermythica. I *dreamt* it. That's why I was so—so *prickly* toward you at first . . ."

An uneasy feeling swirled through my belly as I watched it swirl through her violet eyes. "What'd you see?"

"I saw *me*. Dead."

"*Dead?*"

"Toward the end of the vision, yes. In some strange, stony labyrinth. But see, that's the *bizarre* part . . . You can't have a premonition of your own death, because you can't *see* yourself die when, metaphysically speaking, you're already *dead*. It's simply not possible . . ."

In the silence, she studied me, as if trying to read my muddled thoughts.

"So—what do you think it means?" I asked.

"I don't know. But I fear we are running a race that's already been lost." She hesitated, looking grim. "Some believe that monster—*the Mystic*—is a wraith. That it never sleeps. That it will never stop searching."

"Then *we* won't sleep," I said. "And we won't ever stop searching, either." Her eyes, as anxious as they looked, and as scared, still shone with some inner unbreakable strength, and that strength made me feel brave somehow. Or at least *braver*. The world didn't really scare me as much when I was staring into those eyes. Neither did the Mystic.

"I'll go with you to the very end of the world," I whispered, and felt my heart flutter as her lips curved into a soft smile.

"That's not saying an awful lot, though . . ."

I blinked. "What do you mean?"

"Well, the end—or, the *edge*—of the world is probably less than twenty miles away by now," she explained, and I just started laughing. I couldn't help it. It was *sooo* like me to totally bomb a line like that. She was probably right, too. We couldn't have been far.

"Okay," I said, "so I'll go with you to the *opposite* end of the world. How's that?"

Now the dimples in her cheeks deepened and her eyes seemed to sparkle and dance.

"Now *that's* a very bold statement, indeed." A sweet, sad smile suddenly bent her lips. "They would have written songs about you, you know . . . Antares the adventuring spherer, come from beyond the ice to save Rymworld. Little rymlings everywhere would have heard your tale."

"Maybe they still will."

"Maybe. But the hour is dark, and all our hope seems as but a handful of seeds cast upon thorny ground. I'm sorry you came here at a time like this. I wish you could have seen this paradise as I saw it, in springtime and in peace. But I fear our time is nearly up, and I wish . . . I wish we had more of it—*more time*."

Slowly, slowly I watched her eyes dim and I saw their light fade until her smile was gone again, replaced by that worried, wondering look.

Magdavellía's fingers squeezed mine. "How can we save it?" she whispered. "What's the secret? How can we stop what's to come and change what will be? How do we save the world?"

I opened my mouth to answer her question (though I didn't really have an answer), but just as I did, I thought I saw another question—in her eyes this time. A very different question. Only I was so scared to answer the question her eyes were asking and didn't really have an answer for the one her lips had whispered, so I said nothing and did nothing, and soon the moment was passing, and she was fading away, though she hadn't really moved, and I was fading into myself, shrinking that awful shrink of fear, and suddenly I was scared of everything again, of the entire world.

Right then, a terrible shudder went through the ship. Yellow life preservers tumbled from the nearby railing, and the music flowing from The Shubba's old record player came to a screeching (*vvvveerrreeeerrrvept!*) halt.

I saw the squishy moleman come scrambling out of the bridge in a panic. He rushed over to the portside railing on quick little feet, followed closely by his bodyguards. The taller of the two swung something like a giant leaf skimmer over the side of the ship and came up with a saggy clump of glistening green algae.

All three of them gaped.

"This not *sea* water!" roared The Shubba. "This is *BOG* water!" He looked as terrified as he was furious. "CONSULT YOUR MAPS, NAVIGATOR! FOR YOU HAVE LED US ASTRAY! TO DEATH'S DOOR, I SAYSAY!"

CHAPTER FORTY-TWO

•

THE IRON BOG

"What's going on?" Magdavellía demanded to know as we hurried over.

"That salt-drunk FISH has led us into the mouth of oblivion! Into the very TEETH of the *Iron Bog*!" The Shubba gestured wildly around. "BEHOLD!"

I saw that we had entered a sort of inlet: kind of narrow, kind of quiet, kind of overgrown with thick roots and masses of swampy marshland. A thin bluish-yellow mist was rising from the thick yellowish-blue water, raising an eerie greenish veil over everything.

Through it—half hidden by it—loomed a forest like an army of silent sentinels. It grew in groves along the muddy banks and in stands along the steaming sands. Miles and miles of tall, tangled trees spread out over miles and miles of bubbling, boiling, burping bog.

Standing there, staring into its shadowy places, I could see glimmers and glints, flashes and winks; at first, I thought it was the bright full moon reflecting off water droplets on the leaves. But as we sailed a little deeper and the mist parted a little farther, I realized that it wasn't water reflecting the moonlight, but the trees *themselves* . . .

Because the trees that grew wild in this bog weren't trees of bark and branches and leaves, but trees of bronze and silver and iron.

I gasped. "Are those things actually made of—"

"Metal?" asked The Shubba, guessing my question. "Well, it certainly isn't called the *Iron Bog* out of *irony!*"

¡Que chido! "That's . . . freakin' *awesome!*" I cried.

"AWESOME???" His gelatinous jowls jiggled like humps of hairy Jell-O. "HAVE YOU NEVER HEARD THE STORIES?!"

"What stories??"

"Bog monster stories," answered Magdavellía.

"Bog *demons!*" corrected the moleman, nearly coming out of his knee-high leather boots. "Perèmalfaits! Dilygads! Swampbogeys! The *Eyeless Ones* who lurk deep within the *murk* . . ."

He'd said that last part with all the terror and tremble of someone telling a scary story, and I couldn't help feeling an uneasy shiver down my spine.

"They're called fryghteters," explained Mags. "Those who believe that the monsters exist classify them, taxonomically, as *insensatises.* Eyeless, earless, noseless. They lack nearly all the basic senses. They cannot see or hear or smell anything except for—"

"—Except for *FEAR!*" screeched the little jailer.

I heard myself swallow. "Seriously?"

She nodded. "It's how they hunt. They're dreadly creatures . . ."

That, I *really* didn't like the sound of. And mostly because I was already sort of terrified of these things.

"And how—how are we gonna avoid them?" I asked, hoping (really crossing my fingers here) that one of these geniuses had come up with some kind of plan.

"Via an elegant solution," called Navigator, strolling casually out of the command bridge.

"Of what do you babble?!" demanded the jailer.

"Blindfolds, telescreens, and radios. If we see no scary and hear no scary, then there'll be no reason for us to feel all scaredy. And with us not fearing, there'll be no way for any fryghteter—perèmalfait, dilygad, swampbogey, or *whateva* ya wanna call 'em—to know we're a' passin' thru."

CHAPTER FORTY-THREE

TVS AND MONSTERS

Navigator's plan was nuts. I mean, it was waaay out there. But it did sort of make sense. And to be perfectly honest, I was just glad that at least someone *had* a plan.

By the time we were done plugging things in and turning things on and dragging chairs around the deck and cutting strips of fabric from an old foresail so we could turn them into blindfolds, it was close to midnight and the entire swamp was deathly quiet.

As I sat there, blindfolded, listening to what sounded like an old radio broadcast from the 1950s (for some reason those ancient signals were the only ones our antennas could pick up out here), I imagined I could hear, over the speaker feedback, croaking frogs and creaking branches and the high, tinny music of a thousand and one cicadas.

But that was, of course, all in my head, because this was the Iron Bog and these were metallic trees, sharp and deadly, and their leaves did not rustle, nor did their sawlike branches offer any perch.

Beside me, The Shubba was laughing so loudly—and so *annoyingly*—

that pretty soon I couldn't even hear what the radios or TVs were saying. (Apparently, the guy was a sucker for stand-up comedy.)

"This is too much!" he was crying, all slapping knees and stomping feet. "This Johnny Carson is just too FUNNY!"

And beside *him*, his two bodyguards weren't being any less annoying. In fact, I had just turned to tell them all to shut the Rym up for a mintock (though I would've settled for just a few min*ticks*) when every single electronic device on the deck of *La Princhepessa* suddenly clicked off.

"Ei, what app'n?!" cried the moleman.

Then I yanked off my blindfold and saw "what." One of his two peanut-brained bodyguards had kicked the big plastic power strip (the one we'd plugged pretty much every single TV and radio into), pulling it loose from the outlet.

"Clumsy *rat*!" shouted Navigator.

"I did nothing!" the little jailer shot back.

"Everyone stay calm!" Magdavellía commanded. "Pal, plug us back in. And everyone put your blindfolds ba—"

But before she could finish, from deep within the iron trees came a low, hissing rattle. The sound seemed to crawl eerily over the swamp, and over the ship, and then down the nape of my neck, making every little bit of skin it touched prickle with fear.

Pal froze.

Magdavellía froze.

I froze.

In my pocket, even *Cheepee* froze.

"What was that?" someone rasped.

"It's just bog noise," said Magdavellía.

More hissing. More rattles.

Louder this time.

And close.

Too close.

With suddenly shaky hands, I gripped the back of my chair and slowly—very slowly—turned toward the sound in time to see wet, slimy, plant-like fingers reaching out of the swirling mist. A gush of muddy water flowed out from between the "fingers" as they gripped the starboard railing and pulled. A pair of dripping enormous shoulders—also slime-slicked and plant-like—rose up next, followed by a head with a face that was more wilted, withered flower than face.

Row upon row of tiny, razor-sharp teeth glinted under every sagging petal and above every slimy sepal. It was a horror to behold!

But even more horrifying, when I blinked again, they were *every*where . . . Dozens—no *hundreds*, of those lumbering, lurching, plant-faced monsters!

And we were surrounded.

Completely.

"Any bright ideas?" whispered Navigator.

"Yes!" The Shubba shrieked. "Feed them the children first!"

Just then there came a series of quick beeps, loud and clear in the swampy air.

I looked down and saw that Deus Ex (who had positioned herself protectively between Magdavellía and the nearest fryghteter) was now buzzing and flashing in every color of the rainbow.

Mags barely had time to shout "EVERYONE DOWN!" before Deus—like a spring-loaded trap—leapt high into the air while the rest of us dropped down to the deck.

There was a deafening crackle, followed by a flash of blazing blue that momentarily whited-out my vision, and next thing I knew a thousand and one swampbogeys were instantly reduced to a boiling, hissing puddle of greenish liquefied plant guts, which rolled slowly over the deck of *La Princhepessa* like a foamy sea wave. The gooey green innards oozed into the narrow cracks between the floorboards, spontaneously sprouting clumps of tiny white flowers as it spread slowly past our shocked and staring faces.

And for a moment there was perfect calm.

No more hissing.

No more claws.

No more swamp monsters.

"*DEUS EX!*" I shouted, turning huge grateful eyes on the little super bot. "Whatta *MACHINA!* —How'd she do that??"

"The real question," said Navigator tightly as we all pushed slowly up to our feet, "is how *many* times can she do that . . . ?"

And that's when I heard the low, hissing rattles again, and smelled that awful vegetably stink, and saw fingers like gnarled mossy branches wrapping themselves tightly around every single rail in sight. *Every. Single. One.*

That's when I knew we were in trouble.

CHAPTER FORTY-FOUR

THE FLIGHT FROM FRIGHT

"To the bridge!" roared Navigator. "RUN!"

So that's exactly what we did. We raced through the swirling, misty world chased by growls and hisses, snarls and near misses: talons like rusty hooks swept through the dark, swiping at our arms, our faces. Shapes loomed in the mist, growing larger, nearer.

We'd made it almost halfway to the command bridge when a tremendous ear-splitting, heart-stopping, brain-busting *BOOM!* shook the world.

I turned, in what felt like slow motion, and saw that The Shubba had fired something like a handheld pirate's cannon at a swarm of fryghteters. The smooth, melon-shaped iron ball that had exploded from the business end of the broad silver barrel whistled through the air, plowing a path of exploding plant guts as it smashed through one fryghteter, then another, and then three more, before slamming into the base of the ship's center mast with about ten times the force necessary to shatter it. Deadly, splintery chunks of wood flew in every direction.

The mast tilted, tottered, then began to fall as Magdavellía and I raced underneath its rapidly expanding shadow, leaping into the command bridge just as it crashed thunderously to the deck, and then *through* the deck, flinging us off our feet.

Navigator leapt in through the door next, carrying a totally unconscious Pal, and followed closely by a huffing, puffing, and completely sweat-drenched Shubba.

"SEAL THE HATCH!" cried the panicking moleman. "SEAL IT, SEAL IT, SEAL IT!"

"WHAT ABOUT YOUR MEN??" shouted Navigator.

"WHAT ABOUT THEM?!" And shoving Navigator aside, he yanked the door shut with a resounding clang, then cranked the door-wheel until I heard several huge locks clank into place. "NOW GET US OUT OF HERE, NAVIGATOR!"

The mermaid's scaly fist smashed a flashing green button on the wall near the ship's wheel. Then things got—well, a little *weird*.

On one of the small screens embedded in the wall, I watched as a huge, deflated balloon-like thingy attached to the roof of the command bridge began to swell and swell and swell until it sort of resembled a giant white-button mushroom. Then I heard a series of small explosions—and felt them, too, vibrating up through the floors beneath my feet—and the next instant, the bridge was changing . . . transforming right before our very eyes into some kind of *blimp*!

And just like that, the name hydroblimp started to make perfect sense.

With a hiss of rockets, the command bridge detached itself from the deck of *La Princhepessa* and rose smoothly, effortlessly into the misty night while way down below the rest of the ship began to sink slowly into the foaming, murky waters.

In a moment, she was gone. And so were all the fryghteters—every single swamp monster swallowed back up by the very swamp that had given birth to them.

And the bog was deathly still again.

CHAPTER FORTY-FIVE

—— • ——

ESCAPE FROM THE IRON BOG

(1)

What was left of *La Princhepessa* sailed through the thick, steamy air of the bog almost as gracefully as the rest of her had once sailed its sticky, muddy waters.

All around us, tendrils of grayish mist curled and uncurled like the tentacles of some ghostly octopus. The metal leaves of the metal trees stabbed out of the darkness at terrifying angles, deadly as daggers, their branches bent and bowed and gleaming faintly in coppers, in silvers, in golds. I could hear them scraping along the sides of the blimp like bear claws along tree trunks.

"Can't you fly above the branches??" I shouted at Navigator as she slid into a chair, gripping a pair of joystick-like controls.

"You can't fly above the Bog's canopy," she explained, pressing and clicking buttons. "The air is a toxic, acidic stew. We wouldn't last a mintock."

With a flip of a switch, the blimp's headlights—a pair of huge, bug-eyed lamps—burst to life, lighting up a shadowy world of hanging vines and deadly edges.

Trees crowded everywhere, forming a maze of iron roots below and a ceiling of iron leaves above.

Dios mío . . .

After less than a hundred yards the Iron Bog dead-ended, with only a tiny gap visible between the trees and only a tiny sliver of sky visible beyond.

"¡CUIDADO!" I screamed. "LOOK OUT!"

"Whaddaya mean, *LOOK OUT?!*" Navigator screamed back. "That IS our way out!"

The next few seconds were a terrifying blur of screeching, scratching, grunching, punctuated by flurries of bluish sparks as we surged *into* the gap in the metal trees and—somehow, someway—*out* the other side, out of the Bog, flying jerkily, erratically (like an injured honeybee) through wide-open sky toward the edge of the world.

Which, by the way, had just come stunningly into view . . .

CHAPTER FORTY-SIX

•

AT RYM'S EDGE

In the first waking glimmers of morning, maybe a thousand yards northeast, I spotted a shimmering island chain in the shape of a two-dimensional icosahedron.

It looked like some jungle paradise floating out in the middle of nowhere and on the edge of everything. It was breathiful.

The Isles! I realized, feeling a rush of wonder and excitement. *The Platonic Isles!*

"Let's'it . . . LET'S'IT!" Navigator was shouting as every meter, every readout, every single gauge on the flight controls began screaming at her, flashing red warning lights and blaring so loudly you could hardly hear the belching, popping sounds of the blimp's badly wounded engines. "Prepare for an expedited landing!" she cried, strapping herself in.

"*An expedited landing??*" shrieked the moleman. "Are we going to CRASH?!"

At the word *crash*, Pal, who'd momentarily regained consciousness, promptly passed out again.

Navigator watched him topple over like a felled tree. "I wouldn't say *crash*, exactlee . . . More like collide violentlee with the ground upon our most welcomed yet *un*prepared arrival."

The Shubba made a face like he didn't mind the sound of that—then, finally getting it: "THAT'S THE *SAME* THING!"

There was a loud *ba-ba-bang!* and a clunking sound, and the next moment, the blimp was rocketing through the sky, gaining speed almost as quickly as it was losing altitude.

One second, the island was two hundred yards out, then it was fifty, then twenty, then three. I wish I could say that the landing was as spectacular as the view, but it just wasn't.

The ground came up like a karate-chop of solid earth, smashing into the bottom of the gondola with enough force to launch us viciously against the ceiling as the blimp went into a wild rolling tumble.

By the time it finally stopped and we'd all managed to crawl, wincing, out through the shattered windshield (the main door had been crushed shut), morning was dawning, bright and yellow, and I could hear birds singing cheerily in the trees.

"I neva—NEVA—getting on any venturecraft with you *EVA AGAIN!*" roared The Shubba, baring his yellowing teeth at Pal. "You Martians are a curse! A curse, I saysay!"

"All right, all right . . . Everyone jess calm your clams," said Navigator, tapping lightly on the shield of a compass. "What's wrong with this thing . . . ?"

"Mine's not working, either," said Magdavellía. Inside the crystal dial, I could see the needle spinning crazy, erratic circles like it couldn't make up its mind which way was north.

Suddenly I started to feel really weird. Dizzy, and a little off balance. I closed my eyes for a mintick, waiting for the awful sensation to pass.

"This is my fault . . ." grumbled The Shubba. He stood staring sadly at the smoking, smoldering ruins of the blimp, which had once been the command bridge of a mighty mercraft. "I shoulda neva let any of you *fiends* on my beautiful *Princess* . . . Now look upon her!"

"I'm sure she's still salvageable," said the mermaid aviator, but not five seconds later, the engine near the blimp's rudder suddenly exploded, bursting into a mini fireball and setting the whole crumpled thing ablaze.

The jailer's beady eyes squeezed painfully shut. "Never speak to me again, *fish*."

A moment later, behind me, I heard Mags whisper, "H—*how* . . . ?" and turned to see her staring with wide, shocked eyes at a juicy-looking striped fruit that hung heavily from a nearby branch.

"What happened?" I asked.

"That ermelon . . . It was *a baby* a second ago."

"What are you talking about?"

Mags spun the oddly shaped fruit delicately between her fingers. "Ermelons are one of the slowest-growing fruits on the entire *planet*— Something's not right about this place . . ."

"I neva—NEVA—getting on any venturecraft with you EVA AGAIN!" roared The Shubba, baring his yellowing teeth at Pal. "You Martians are a curse! A curse, I saysay!"

"All right, all right . . . Everyone jess calm your clams," said Navigator, tapping lightly on the shield of a compass. "—What's wrong with this thing . . . ?"

"Mine's not wo—" Magdavellía broke off.

Her mouth slowly closed, and her eyes slowly widened as they rose even more slowly to mine.

"Yours isn't working, either," I said, feeling the icy fingers of fresh fear skitter tingling down my spine. "That's what you were about to say, right?"

"That's exactly what I was about to say. *Except*—"

"Except you feel like you've already *said* it."

"I *have* already said it . . ." she whispered, and right as she spoke those words that weird dizziness came over me again.

Then, as one, and without another word, we all turned to gape at the blimp, which—inexplicably—was no longer on fire. Or, at least not yet . . .

There was a loud *pop!* as the engine near the blimp's rudder suddenly exploded (again), bursting into a mini fireball (again) and setting the whole crumpled thing ablaze (*again*).

"Déjà vu," murmured the moleman, as if in a trance.

"*Not* déjà vu," corrected Navigator. "Time just . . . *looped*."

Yeah, that was it. Time *had* looped! Rewinding itself about a minute or so and then just starting all over again.

But . . . *how?*

"Time *can't* loop," Magdavellía said with a firm shake of her head. "It's a river. It flows only in a *single* direction—"

"Typically, yes," answered a half-familiar voice. "But one must also bear in mind that time is the most *unpredictable* river of all . . ." Then, from inside the wall of trees that grew high and wild around us, emerged a man: tall and slim, dressed in a dark leather jacket with a pair of pilot goggles hanging around his neck among a tangle of compasses and pocket watches.

His grin flashed white in a shaft of early-morning sunshine, and that was all I needed to see—

"*Dad?*" I whispered.

CHAPTER FORTY-SEVEN

•

A LONG-AWAITED HELLO

"*Antares*," he answered, reaching out toward me. And next thing I knew, I was in his arms and he was holding me, telling me how much he'd missed me, and how far he'd traveled, and there was a tremble in his voice, and in his hug, and the world had turned all bright and blurry, and I could feel my happiness rolling down my cheeks as I whispered, "*Where've you been . . . ?*"

He squeezed me. "*Waiting . . . forever waiting.*"

"Waiting for what??" I breathed.

And as he squeezed me even tighter he said, "*This moment.*"

I don't know how long we stayed like that, just holding on to each other, but it didn't feel nearly long enough before I heard Navigator say, "Grafias?" and my dad pulled slowly away.

For several minticks, his eyes refused to leave mine. Then his gaze shifted to Navigator and he smiled. "Hello, old merfriend."

The mermaid sounded—and *looked*—completely shocked. But it was a happy kind of shock. "I—I thought you were . . . *lost.*"

"Old explorers never get lost," my dad said with a sly grin. "We simply discover a new way home."

Laughing, they clasped each other by the forearms in what I guessed must've been the way they shook hands out here.

"But I dun't unnerstan," said Navigator. "How did you know we were comin' here?"

"Information is still Mü's most valuable export, is it not?" remarked my dad. Then he tossed a small leather pouch at The Shubba, who, catching it (and giving it a little jingle) gave his tail a little wiggle.

"And I her *leading* exporter!" proclaimed the mole man.

"Yes, but time is short." My dad's voice was tight, anxious. "I have— well, *friends* close by . . . They're procuring a boat. We must leave this island. *Immediately.*"

"No, we cannot *leave,*" said Magdavellía. "The Star of Lôst is here. Somewhere. We have to find it!"

"Don't worry. It's coming with us."

Mags gasped. *"You've found the Star??"*

"No, *you* have, my Empress."

And now I gasped.

"Empress??" Confused, I looked between them, shaking my head.

"Aha!" cried The Shubba. "I knew I recognized her Highness! I knew it! —Oh!" and he immediately bent at the waist, bowing his fuzzy face close to the pointy tips of his leather boots.

Magdavellía's eyes briefly met mine before turning shyly down toward her feet.

"Mags, what are they talking about?" I whispered.

But my dad's calloused fingers closed tightly around my upper arm. "Now is not the time for the unveiling of secrets . . . We are *all* in mortal danger."

Navigator frowned. "What kind'e danger?"

"I suppose he means me," said a new voice.

CHAPTER FORTY-EIGHT

•

AN UNEXPECTED REUNION

Everyone turned toward the voice, including Cheepee, who had climbed onto my dad's shoulder like they were old friends and was now chittering anxiously.

The trees began to quiver. And then a figure—hooded and with eyes like burning emeralds—strode powerfully out from between the glistening leaves.

They wore a long, dark robe decorated with silvery triangles and all-seeing eyes, and when an arm pushed back the heavy hood, I saw it was a lady—fair-haired and fair-skinned, and very, very beautiful.

With a skitter of spindly metal legs, Deus quickly positioned herself between Magdavellía and the woman like an eight-legged bodyguard and then began beeping and flashing just like she'd done before melting the horde of fryghteters.

My pulse spiked. But before I had a chance to duck, the most surprising thing happened. The lady sighed, waving a careless hand, and all the lights inside the little spiderbot's many eyes suddenly blinked off a moment before her many legs folded up like a table—*She'd shut Deus down*, I realized with a shock. *And she'd done it with nothing more than a wave of her hand!*

A heartbeat later, the ground seemed to tremble under our feet as a platoon of soldiers came marching through the trees in perfect military synchrony—human soldiers in futuristic-looking camo, and huge lumbering beasts with fur as white as snow and legs as thick as tree trunks.

I stared at them with my mouth hanging somewhere around my ankles, hardly noticing the smaller troops, itty-bitty little dudes, no more than four feet tall and possibly winged (faefolk, maybe?), until it finally dawned on me what the big guys were.

Yetis.

Those were *bigfoots!*

One of the yetis was dragging three struggling prisoners along by the end of a thick rope. All three were bound and gagged, and when I saw their faces, I had to do a double take. No, a *triple* take! Because they were just about the last three people I'd expected to see: Mr. Now, Mr. Minutes, and Mr. Hoursback!

"Next time you attempt to steal one of my boats, Grafias," said the woman, "I suggest entrusting the task to men with more of an acumen for thievery than yourself . . ."

"Stay back, Aella," warned my dad, sounding nervous, angry, and scared all at once.

"*What are you doing here . . . ?*" I heard Navigator breathe.

"Waiting for all of you, of course," replied the woman in an almost friendly tone, "just like *him.*"

"You knew we were coming, too??"

"Everything in Rymworld is for sale." She smiled coolly. "Particularly alliances and secrets. And in some cases, *both.*"

With frightening quickness, she pitched a small snakeskin sack sideways at the shrimpy jailer, who snatched it out of the air with significantly less spunk than the last one.

Navigator's translucent lips curled in disgust as she turned to glare at the moleman. "Is there anyone you *'aven't* sold our whereabouts to?!"

As they began bickering back and forth, I realized that the lady was watching me—carefully studying my face like an astronomer might study a newly discovered constellation. Then her lips pressed into a small smile and she said, "Hello, Antares."

And just like that—like a kick straight to the *gut*—I recognized her. Or rather, I recognized *her voice* . . .

She was the mysterious lady on the phone!

Goose bumps popped up all over my body like a second skin as I whispered, "Who are you . . . ?"

"Stay away from him, Aella," my dad growled.

"Dad, who is she?" I said, and watched a secretive smile stretch slowly across her beautiful brutal face.

"Tell him, Grafias . . . Answer your son."

But for several minticks my dad just stood there, looking helpless and very small. At last he said, "She is—well, she's *your mother* . . ."

CHAPTER FORTY-NINE

THE MYSTIC

Had a lightning bolt struck between my big toes at that very second, I couldn't have been any more surprised—any more *stunned*—than I was at the sound of those three most unlikely of words.

For a moment I couldn't move.

For a moment I couldn't *breathe*.

"The Mystic is yer mother??" Navigator burst out, half in shock, half in terror.

"She's the Mystic??" gasped Magdavellía. In that instant all the color seemed to drain from her face. And in the next, she lunged at her with a wild snarl.

"Cesarica, *no!*" cried Navigator, lifting her off her feet while she kicked and struggled and screamed, prying desperately at the webbed fingers restraining her. "She'll snatch the life out of you without a mintick's thought—not a mintick's!"

But Magdavellía wouldn't stop. She just kept kicking and screaming and clawing at the mermaid's hands until all her anger, all her rage, finally dissolved into a fit of helpless, hopeless tears.

With my heart in my throat, I turned back toward the lady—no, not just some *lady* . . . my mom. *My mother.* She was so young-looking, too. So beautiful.

But she was *also* apparently not so nice.

"You—you're *the Mystic* . . . ?" I whispered.

And when she sweetly replied, "I am," and even more sweetly, "And *you* are my son," I felt myself smile (without really wanting to) and frown (without really trying to).

Now she spoke to, but did not turn to, Navigator. "A great kindness you have shown the girl, soldier . . . Like her parents, she has proved incredibly meddlesome. But *un*like her parents, she has delivered me the Star, safe and sound, and for that, I will spare her."

"What're yeh talking about??" Navigator snapped (though it wasn't *quite* a snap; you could tell she didn't want to risk making her angry). "She hasn't delivered *anything* to you."

"Oh, but she has. Tell them, Grafias." A cunning grin now tugged at the corners of the Mystic's—I mean, *my mom's* lips. My dad, on the other hand, appeared utterly defeated.

"She has delivered her the Star," he said miserably. "Because Antares *is* the Star . . ."

CHAPTER FIFTY

·

THE STAR OF LÔST

"Whherappt?" screamed Pal.

"Waht??" screamed the jailer.

"What?!" screamed Navigator.

"What???" screamed Magdavellía.

And the string of questions that followed came just as fast and just as loud:

"How can the boy be *the Star*??"

"How can the Star be *a person*??"

"How can the Star not be a compass and the compass now be a person??" (That last one was The Shubba, and I'm sure it had made more sense in his head.)

The mermaid navigator gripped my dad's arm fiercely. "Grafias, how does that make any sense?"

My dad sighed like someone who'd just been asked to solve the world's most complicated math problem. "Because the Star of Lôst was never a *sacred object*. It was merely *assumed* to be by those who didn't know any better . . ."

At that point, everyone just sort of stood there staring at me like I was some rare, never-before-seen turtle in a zoo exhibit. It was honestly pretty embarrassing.

Then the jailer shouted, "We can verify the truth of this immediately! The Tetrinox. It was rumored to have taken place several months ago. That is the most famous prophecy regarding the Star, is it not? You all are the Star hunters—you tell *me*! What was the sign?"

"A meteor shower," answered my dad. "It was believed that it would reveal the exact location of the Star."

And when Navigator asked, "So where did the meteors make earthfall?" it was my turn to answer.

"*Miami.*"

The mermaid's gills turned pale pink with surprise. "How do you know?"

"Because," I said as the full weight of it settled over me—settled like a ton of stony-irons—"they hit *my* house."

After that, no one spoke for a long time. It was like the silence after a huge explosion—hollow and absolute.

Finally my dad said, "The Star is, for lack of a better term, simply a mathematical inevitability—a human being with a highly developed, even gifted, sense of direction." He turned to me, his expression hard but his eyes soft. "In a thousand years, everyone will possess your gift. But right now, you are the future . . ."

At first, I refused to let myself believe it. I thought back to everything I'd ever heard about the Star:

—how it hadn't been forged by human hands.

—how there wasn't another like it.

—how it could help navigate the way through that ancient temple, to power, wisdom, riches untold, even life eternal.

And I realized that nothing about any of that—not a *single* thing—actually disqualified it from being a person!

Then I thought back to how all my life I'd always had a really great sense of direction. How even in Bermythica, where traditional instruments of navigation were sort of unreliable due to the powerful magnetic field around the triangle, I never really lost my bearings. *So maybe it was possible, then . . .*

Maybe it was *actually* true.

"Had the Flat Earth Society been true believers," said my dad, "they would have been ever vigilant; they would have been watching for the great sign in the heavens and would have found you immediately. But they were slow of heart, and so they did not see exactly where the meteor shower made earthfall, as did I—as did your mother. They were forced to calculate a perimeter; then, left with no other choice, they descended upon that inworldian suburb with everything they had, taking any child that fell within the age range pretold by various other Pythagorean prophecies."

I thought back to the strange storm that descended on Miami. To the screaming, shouting voices of kids I'd heard back in the Hurricane Prison on Bermythica.

That's why The Society had kidnapped them, I suddenly realized. They'd been trying to make sure that the Star didn't slip through their fingers.

Trying to make sure that *I* didn't slip through their fingers.

And it had worked, too. At least the whole finding/capturing me part.

"But I don't understand," said Magdavellía. "If he's the Star, why would my parents' clues have led me *here*, to this place?"

"Because your parents had long since given up their search for the Star of Lôst," my mom answered her. "They understood that locating the Star based on their limited knowledge might prove impossible, but finding EverLôst itself would be *vastly* easier."

Navigator's voice trembled as she said, "*This* is EverLôst . . . ?"

I saw the jailer make the sign of the nine-pointed nonagon over his lips like he was casting a protective spell while Pal began to sway on his bare green feet.

"Emperatta Delomina and King Magmūs's strategy was quite simple," explained my mom. "They sought to discover this place and position troops here in order to prevent me from entering the temple, whether I acquired the Star or not. A shrewd tactic. And one that necessitated their removal."

At those words, Magdavellía lunged at her again, and again Navigator wrestled her back while she kicked and struggled and screamed.

My mom, meanwhile, had turned her fierce attention back to me. Her mental strength was incredible; I could feel it like a physical force every time she looked at me.

"You have no idea how long I've been trying to find you, my son . . . But many are the obstacles which have beset my path. Not the least of which being your father—who, I might add, was already quite the nuisance when there was only *one* of him."

"What . . . do you mean?" I whispered.

But this time it was my dad who explained. He looked sadly at the downcast faces of the three prisoners—Mr. Now, Mr. Minutes, and Mr. Hoursback—then at the smiling face of my mom, and said, "Antares, I'd like you to meet . . . *me*."

I blinked. "I—I don't get it . . ."

Honestly, I didn't. Sure, they all *did* look ridiculously alike. They were all about the same height. They all had the same dark eyes. The same strong cheekbones. Even the same upturned and freckled nose. The only real difference, I guess you could say, was their ages. In fact, looking at them like this, side by side, you'd almost get the impression that they *were* all the same person, just in time lapse. But that was, of course, *impossible* . . .

"Antares, you asked me where I'd been and I'm going to try to answer that to the best of my understanding. And the best of my understanding is this: For the last three thousand sunsets, I've been falling . . . falling through *time*."

CHAPTER FIFTY-ONE

THE FALLING MAN

When I only stared, blinking and completely speechless, my dad said, "The concept is a difficult one to grasp, I know. But there is no other way of expressing it. I've been falling, Antares . . . falling through the years and decades and centuries like a man falling from the sky. It began slowly, at first. I'd spend as long as many months in a particular time. But the longer I fell, the faster I fell, and soon I had only moments in a particular year before I was falling again, plummeting through a meta-physical universe full of yesterdays and half-remembered memories." His dark eyes searched mine for a moment. "It was only your face, held like a burning beacon in my mind, that kept me from losing my sense of reality . . . my sense of everything."

I shook my head, hardly even knowing what to say to that. "How—how did you stop falling . . . ?"

"I honestly don't remember that part. Which makes me question if I ever *did*." Off my confused look he added, "Truth is, I don't understand it all myself. But some weeks ago, I opened my eyes and I was just *here* again, as if time had somehow looped around and deposited me back into my original timeline. The fact is I don't even know if I'm the real *me* or just another projection. Like them."

He glanced at Mr. Minutes, Mr. Now, and Mr. Hoursback as I said, "They're . . . *projections* of you?"

"It's easier for me to explain than for you to understand, because I experienced it—I *felt* it—but try to imagine time as a physical force, as tangible and dynamic as light. Now imagine time *as* light. Say, the light from a movie projector, exploding out across what we know as this material universe. Now imagine something—an object of some kind—falling between the visible universe and the force of time being projected over and through it. Since time—or, in this case, light—is *behind* that object, it would cast a shadow, and depending on the physical makeup of the thing, it might even cast *multiple* shadows or—"

"—projections," I said, sort of getting the gist of it, and his lips pressed together in a small smile.

Looking up at the three prisoners again, at my dad (or *dads*, I guess), I couldn't help thinking how upside down I'd had everything. How just a little while ago, when this whole wild thing had started, I'd trusted the lady on the phone, thinking she was good when she was actually bad, and how I'd run away from the three weirdos (Mr. Minutes, Mr. Now, and Mr. Hoursback) thinking that they were bad when they were actually *good*. It seriously twisted my neurons.

"They *are* me," said my dad, "but projected across space-time from different points in my life—different ages—and knowing only what I knew then. Nothing more. They're all reflections of me, or maybe me of them, or maybe all of us of the real me." He gave me a look of quiet pity. "I know this is a lot, but all you really need to know—all *I* really know—is that I am your father and I love you and I would fall through time for all eternity if that meant I got to spend just *one more* second with you."

And as he reached out to touch my face, I saw, on the inside of his wrist, a familiar tattoo: the triple triangles with an all-seeing eye.

It was the exact same tattoo—and in the *exact same spot*—as Zamangar's.

My mind flashed on the old sage. On the way he sometimes looked at me. How he'd smiled just before he'd sacrificed himself for us. How willingly he'd done it. How selflessly.

Had he known?

Had he somehow figured it all out?

Something told me he had. And the thought made me smile.

"What is it?" asked my dad.

"I, uh, think there's at least one more of you . . ." I said, and now he began to smile, too.

"I had a feeling there might be."

"This is all quite touching," hissed a new voice. And now a small, strange-looking little man stepped out from behind a pair of huge, snowy-furred yeti. His pointy face, fuzzy cheeks, and whiskery upper lip looked more human than rat, but he looked way more like a rat than any human I'd ever seen (The Shubba included). "However, I believe we have more pressing matters . . ."

His pupil-less eyes flicked to my mom, who gave a silent nod.

"Take them all," she said, signaling to the soldiers. "But bring the boy to me."

CHAPTER FIFTY-TWO

CONVERSATIONS WITH A MYSTIC

The yeti soldiers led us into the trees and to a campsite under the canopy where rows of large, camouflaged tents sat in the shade. Then one shoved me into the first tent in the row and onto a hard metal chair among a mess of tables and maps and strange brass instruments.

A moment later, the yeti disappeared out the back as a voice spoke up from the entrance.

"You have no idea how many times I've dreamt of this moment," it said softly. I turned. My mom was standing just inside the flaps, watching me with a sweet sort of look. "I held it so long in my heart that the dream became a nightmare, a haunting reminder of what could never be. Yet, here you are, alive and well, and I am awake again."

She sat down next to me. Her expression was gentle. Her fingertips brushed hair out of my face while fresh tears brimmed in her eyes and ran down her own face. And even with all the horrible stuff I'd heard about her—all the horrible stuff I'd *seen*—I couldn't help but feel sorry for her.

"My son, my sweet angelito, how have you been?"

"Okay, I guess . . ."

"I've been working tirelessly to bring us together, but alas, you slipped through my fingers again and again—both in inworld and when I besieged Bermythica to rescue you."

When I didn't say anything, she leaned closer. "I can feel your concern for your companions. But I promise that no harm will come to them, for your sake."

Then she squeezed my hand, her touch incredibly soft, incredibly tender, and I couldn't help but squeeze back. I mean, how many times had I dreamed of this? Or at least of *something* like this? How many times had I imagined her walking in through the front door of my house, or into my room, and smiling at me, and wrapping me up in her arms, and whispering that she loved me, telling me that she'd never leave me again, and that everything was all going to be okay? Honestly, I'd lost count. And now, as she turned my hand over on her lap, a small tattoo on the inside of her left wrist caught my eye:

It was the triangles and all-seeing eye design.

Just like Zamangar.

Just like my dad.

"It is the mark of the Pythagoreans," she said, feeling my thoughts. "The ancient order which I am now privileged to lead. And yes, your father was once one of us. But time and fear have stolen his sight."

Now I understood why Magdavellía's mother, Emperatta Delomina, had left her Pythagoras's famous quote as the first clue. She'd been hinting about the Mystic. About this whole Pythagorean cult.

"There is so much I want to tell you. So much you need to know. But alas, time is our great enemy. At least for the moment . . ." She wiped her eyes. "Now, I'm sure that by now you've already heard all about what a terrible person I am and how terrible my plans are and what a terrible calamity it would be for this world if any of those terrible plans were ever to come to their ultimate and terrifying fruition. Am I close?"

"Pretty much," I admitted.

"But who you haven't heard from is me, from my own lips, my own heart, what I've lived, what I've seen, how I've hurt and all that hurt has taught me." Her voice shook as she spoke. It was so strong, yet so incredibly fragile. "You have a sister . . ." she whispered. "Did you know that?"

"—I do?"

"She's a year older than you, but you both looked *exactly* alike when you were babies. So precious, so *pure.*"

"Is she—*here?*"

"Not yet. See, your sister's life was stolen from her before she'd ever taken her first steps. Before she'd even uttered her first word." Her voice seemed to catch, but she continued. "She was killed by an errant bombing raid toward the end of the Lemurian civil war. It was an age-old territorial dispute perpetuated by the Flat Earth Society in order to maintain regional equilibrium, and like most wars on this Earth, it had lasted for centuries. They were fighting over a well of water. A *well.* When only twenty miles north lies the largest natural aquifer on the planet. Because the truth was, they weren't really fighting over water. They weren't slaughtering each other over thirst or hunger or need. No, their only thirst was for power. And more of it—always more. Gutless leaders inciting useless wars to hypnotize and entertain a powerless and stupefied populace in order to cement their pôlitikal power and increase, if only infinitesimally, their chances at maintaining that power. These hollow souls recruit our sons and daughters to battle over imaginary lines drawn on imaginary maps and squabble over infinite resources in a world as abundant and unlimited as our imaginations. And in the end, what are the people left with? Only death and disaster and empty promises of a different and somehow better tomorrow."

A thundercloud darker than the one that had settled over Miami that fateful day now settled over her face—though whether it was from sadness or rage, I couldn't tell.

"Holding the lifeless body of your sister in my arms was, as you can imagine, one of the most painful experiences of my life . . . But as I grew older, wiser, I realized that I was not so unique in my tragedy. How many mothers have lost children to senseless wars? And to injustice? And how many more lives have perished at the dark whims of nature—natural disasters, plagues, pestilences? I realized that evil had infiltrated this world like a poison cloud, invisible, yet filling all and killing everything it touched.

"I grieved at the oppression I saw all around me, at the tragedy happening every moment of every day in every corner of this planet, whether a result of the fallibility of nature or the fragility and cruelty of the human heart. And in my anger, I, along with your father—whose eyes were once truly open—sought to remedy this most earthly dilemma—a cure for the mechanisms of evil, if you would. So we resurrected the ancient Order—the Pythagorean Order—and with the help of some of the most cunning minds that have ever lived, we turned inworld into our laboratory. We began by toppling governments, corporations, destabilizing regions, fomenting various revolutions, but no matter the circumstances or the pôlitiks of those in power, nothing truly changed. The oppressor still oppressed, the powerful grew still more powerful, and nature still raged and roared. The innocent perished and no one looked twice upon their plight.

"Thus we determined to find another way, assuming in the gullibility of our youth that one had to exist. And as the fates would have it, there did. See, wealth can be overwhelmed by power, power usurped by knowledge, knowledge corrupted by greed. But how to break this circle of iniquity, which invariably leads back to the root of all evil? That was the question. And the answer: We required something stronger than all these ancient vices. And that something we discovered *here*, in the most ancient place on Earth . . ."

The entrance to the tent shivered as the hulking form of a yeti poked its immense snow-white head inside: "We are ready, High Priestess."

My mom acknowledged it with a small nod, but her bright eyes did not leave mine. "Did you see the great temple out there, sitting on the edge of the world . . . ?"

I shook my head.

"You will," she said. "Some say that within it pulses the very heartbeat of the universe. You wouldn't have heard its legends because your father robbed us both of your childhood, but all over Rymworld even the littlest of children hear its tales and tremble. Its secret history has been whispered into hungry ears before bedtime and around dinner tables for countless generations: how death lurks round every wrong turn, how ancient destruction waits patiently underfoot. Yet, for any brave enough to navigate its unnavigable labyrinth, there awaits in reward life, wealth, wisdom, and power *unimaginable*."

"So, what *exactly* is inside the temple . . . ?" I whispered.

"The very source of everything I have just spoken of. For who can live longer than he who cannot die? Who is wiser than him who has existed from the beginning? Who is richer than he who has had eternity to build their fortune? Who is more powerful than him who knows what is to come before it has happened? Life. Wisdom. Riches. Power. After all these things does man seek. But inside that temple lies the authority over the only *truly* precious and scarce resource in the entire universe . . . *time*."

CHAPTER FIFTY-THREE

—•—

THE TEMPLE OF THE STUDENT

"You—you mean, like . . . *time travel*?" I asked.

"Yes, but even better: time *manipulation*." Her eyes gleamed with an indescribable intensity. "The ability not only to move through time but to step *outside* it—to see it as it truly is, with all its infinite permutations. And the ability to alter an *infinite* series of events, causing an *infinite* number of ripples through its flow without ever having to physically occupy any space at any time-point in metaphysical reality. Just imagine being able to see all future evils, all at once, like a gardener witnessing the growth of brown rot, and then like that gardener, being able to snip away these evils before they are ever realized. This is my vision. A world without pain or loss, a world where none dies before their time, where no one goes hungry, and where nature no longer kills or destroys. A world without tyrannical kings and uncaring queens."

Even as she spoke, I could feel her in my head. In my thoughts. Searching. Probing. Rummaging through them like someone might rummage through a kitchen cabinet. Her mind was otherworldly.

"What's wrong?" she whispered after a moment. And since I was pretty sure there wasn't any hiding it anyway, I told her.

"If your plans are so good and if everything you want is so noble, then how come you go around doing the same thing you condemn people and nature for? I mean, you *killed* them . . . Magdavellía's parents. You're a murderer, too."

"On the contrary," she said without the slightest hint of offense. "To have let them live would have made me guilty of a far greater wrong. If you knew you could save the world and everyone in it, and only two single souls stood between you and total salvation, wouldn't allowing those people to live corrupt true morality?"

It was an interesting question. And not one I thought I could answer right away. So instead I asked her another question.

"Okay, but what about everyone else who might not agree with your vision? What about them? Are you just gonna kill them, too?"

"Blood has always been the price for freedom. Bloodshed the foundation of revolution." She cupped her hands around my face so that her eyes could stare directly into mine. "There is so much to accomplish, Antares . . . So much that we can accomplish *together*, if we simply show the courage to do all that is required. A great destiny has been laid at your feet, my child. You are as important to the future of this world as anyone."

"So it's really true, then? About me being the Star?"

Her lips curved tenderly. "Fate has willed it, don't you see? It has given me the very tool necessary to change the course of history. Born to me a son, the sweetest of gifts in the bitter darkness of this world. Together we will rid ourselves of all lies and those who seek to keep this world bound and blind. Together we will rid this planet of the blight of the Flat Earth Society and free humankind from itself." Her expression was soft, her eyes earnest. "Will you help me, Antares . . . ? Will you help me liberate this world?"

Shaking my head, I stared down at my dirty, mud-caked shoes. So much of what she said sounded true. Sounded *good*, even. But a lot of it sounded just plain *wrong*, too. "I—I don't know," I said. "I don't think so."

"Why not?"

"Because I need time to—to *think*. To try to understand everything you're saying."

"Eventually there will be a time for reflection, but now is not that time. A daunting task lies ahead of us. Gather your courage, my precious son, and do not let it go until all is finally accomplished."

Still shaking my head, I said, "I . . . can't. I—it just doesn't *feel* right."

And for the first time during our talk—for the first time in my entire *life*—I saw my mother frown.

"I cannot let you say no," she whispered firmly. "Because I cannot let you fail your destiny. I *won't*."

"You can't make me."

"No, but I *can* make it much worse for *them*." Her head turned, and I followed her gaze out the tent and to the middle of the clearing, where I could see our odd little company—all of them, all bound up, my dad and Magdavellía trying to steady the swaying, half-passed-out form of Pal. "Please do not force my hand, Antares. Their deaths are not what I want."

"You promised you wouldn't hurt them."

"And I *won't*. As long as you don't make me."

"That isn't fair . . ."

"Life isn't fair! But if you've been listening, I am planning on changing that . . ." Then she took my hand and led me out of the tent, and together we walked to the edge of the meadow where the tall trees formed a solid green wall.

"Fourteen years ago, your father stole you away from me," she said. "He realized, even before I did, that you were in fact the Star of Lôst. He deduced this, of course, from the sacred writings. And so he faked your death, changed your name, and sent you into hiding in inworld with another traitor, his sister. He may have stolen you away, robbed us both of your childhood, but we will take it back. We will take back *every second* . . . and more."

She led me deeper into the trees, over fallen mossy trunks and beneath wet, fragrant leaves, until the jungle finally opened up, and suddenly I froze.

Only at first, I wasn't even quite sure *why* I'd frozen, because at first, I couldn't really make any sense of what I was looking at—my half-stunned brain was completely incapable of translating the information my eyes were reeling in. And even when I'd finally decided that I *wasn't* hallucinating, that I was *actually* seeing what I thought I was seeing, it was still—well, hard to *see* . . .

It was like looking at a TV screen stuck between two channels—one, a majestic, sprawling courtyard paved with white stone and bordered by towering monuments; the other, a forgotten wasteland overgrown with trees and overrun with roots like sleeping snakes.

The entire place appeared to be trapped between some point way back in the past and another way out in the future, flickering between magnificence and ruin, perfection and destruction, beauty and decay. In fact, there was only one thing in the entire courtyard that wasn't flickering between past and future: something like a great temple with soaring whitewashed walls overgrown with ivy and massive ruby-red columns made of light—yet *solid* somehow.

There it sat, on the far edge of the island, on the very edge of everything, unchanging in a world of constant change.

And just like that, it hit me.

The shape of the temple.

It was a tetrahedron.

Which made it now the *fifth* Platonic Solid we'd come across!

First, the Alchemist's Ball, a dodecahedron; then the strange rock, a cube; next, the map of ley and fey lines, an octahedron; then the Platonic Isles, an icosahedron; and finally, *this*.

Magdavellía had been right. The shapes *had been* hinting at something. And that something was *this* temple!

I mean, it made sense, didn't it? Here we were, at the end of the clues, and we'd found the final shape.

We'd solved it. We'd solved the mystery of the Alchemist's Ball!

Only (and I couldn't really explain why) I felt as though the shapes were hiding yet *another* secret . . . an even bigger one.

"Stunning, isn't it?" whispered my mom. "It was there, deep in the belly of that ancient place that your father, in his infinite arrogance, did plot my demise. Had he been bold enough to have brought you along to guide him, he might very well have succeeded, and all would be lost. But he feared that I was lying in wait—which, admittedly, I was—so he attempted to navigate the maze alone. But the labyrinth is *cunning*, and with its many traps and endlessly branching halls it did ensnare him, and so he began to fall. Perhaps the real him is still falling through time, I do not know. But what I *do* know is that unlike him, I have *you*. And unlike him, I will not fail."

She gazed out at the ruined and beautiful courtyard. "The temple you see in the midst of the city has long been known as Et Tiempeus Estudiate, or the Temple of the Student—Plato himself being the foremost student of Pythagoras. It is one of the reasons why this entire region is known as the Isles of Plato, named after the beloved Rymworldian philosopher. However, *this* particular island has had many names—Loría, Lôst, Ever-Lôst—but it is known in the lower tongues, the tongues of inworlders, as *Atlantis*."

CHAPTER FIFTY-FOUR

• ●

THE LOST WORLD

"*Atlantis?!*" I heard myself gasp. "Did you just say we're in *Atlantis*?"

"Have you heard of it?"

Had I heard of it? Who *hadn't* heard of it? Atlantis was probably the most famous lost island in the history of lost islands! Heck, there were even TV shows about real-life archaeologists who'd devoted their entire lives to finding this place. "Yeah, I've heard of it . . ."

"Not the city lost in the sea as some fairy tales tell," she said, "but the city lost in *time.*"

And you could see it, too. Time continuously pushing and pulling on this place, like the rise and fall of the tide.

"You see, the inhabitants of Atlantis, when faced with their time of testing—a series of megaquakes just after their great war against the ancient Athenians—did not grasp hold of the gift which had so graciously been bestowed upon them. And so their city now lies in ruin, neither past nor present, a flickering memory forever without beginning and forever without end. And yet, if we make a study of their tragedy, from within the ruins of their own temple we will find the power to save all creation."

I felt her eyes on me again. "And you *will* help me, Antares . . . As the legends say, you will lead me to the very heart of the temple and into its mystic river, and together we will grasp onto time itself and I will build my throne upon those everrushing waters and all things beneath the sun will finally exist in perfect paradise."

Less than five mintocks later, we were all gathered before the great Atlantean temple—our little company, maybe thirty soldiers, and around half as many hooded figures in long, silky robes similar to my mother's (priests, one of the yetis had called them). Everyone except for Mr. Minutes, Mr. Now, and Mr. Hoursback. My dad noticed, too.

"What did you do with them?" he growled at my mom as a yeti sawed through his restraints with a huge machete.

"They're all quite safe," she assured him in a voice of cold indifference. "I suggest you worry about yourself."

"I *am* worrying about myself . . ."

Beside me, the rat-faced priest snorted. I noticed he was holding some kind of huge, clock-like compass attached to a pair of big batteries—almost like car batteries.

They hung from woven sacks that dangled off the backs of two other priests—very short ones—whose faces I could not see.

"Hate to be the one to tell you," said Navigator, eyeing the strange contraption, "but that's not going to be much use to you in there."

Ratman snarled. "Aren't you a little far from your *salt stinks*, mermaid . . . ?"

At the same moment an enormous gray-eyed yeti stepped between them, glaring down at Navigator from its incredible height. Its voice was a booming, hissing growl that seemed to leap out from between its fanged teeth. "Converse not with Pythagorean priests, *fish*."

I looked around for Cheepee and Deus Ex but didn't see them anywhere.

Beyond the soaring pillars of the temple, other soldiers had begun lighting thick steel-and-tinder torches by snapping their fingers near the flammable ends. They passed most of the torches to the priests, and now a dark, reddish smoke choked the air. It smelled like fireworks.

Behind us and to the east, the morning sun was warm on our backs, but before us the darkness within the temple was as cold as death on our faces.

CHAPTER FIFTY-FIVE

•

ENTER THE MAZE

The priests led the way. They moved as one, crowded tightly together, each holding glittering, silver compasses whose needles were spinning madly. And the farther in we walked, the faster the needles spun.

Soon we came to a section of the temple where the glyphs and strange symbols carved into the walls began to join together, forming even stranger shapes.

The Shubba, all wondering eyes and gaping whiskery mouth, staggered up to it, hands out to touch. "Is this trulee the Mural of Shapes . . . ?"

"It is," answered my dad. "Revealed to the first Plato by the Ancients and inscribed into stone by the greatest mathematicians in all the Rym. Some believe it is the great riddle of creation."

I turned to Pal, who was standing next to me. "What does it say?" I whispered.

But it was my mom who answered. "This not even a Martian can interpret," she replied. "Some call it Et Thearato à Allt—or, the Theory of Everything—and it is believed to have been carved before the sunsets of the first king. Long ago when the world was still young and language did not yet exist—only numbers. If the legends are to be believed, then what you see here is the very blueprint of the universe . . . It must be read diagonally and from right to left, but the underlying theory is that the two known dimensions—the physical and the metaphysical—were constructed with mathematical shapes. Our world (the physical world) was formed from basic three-dimensional shapes—cubes, cones, prisms, spheres—while the higher plane was formed from the more complex four-dimensional shapes such as the glome, the tesseract, the pentatope, and the hyperplane. It is believed that the two dimensions are separated by a great chasm, and many believe that this chasm is time itself. Those who believe this *also* believe that time possesses its very own *secret* shape. However, up until today, no one has yet to uncover that secret. And without understanding the shape of a thing, you can never hope to truly understand it. Hence, why time has always been the most mystifying of all the natural forces. But perhaps not for much longer . . ."

The passage twisted between cold corridors of stone and through vast and empty spaces where the darkness nearly swallowed up the torchlight, and along winding walls and hollow halls and past slippery steps as the path branched off again and again. I tried to follow the compass in my gut, but it wasn't easy. This place really *was* a maze. And an old one. It looked lost and forgotten and utterly ancient. Older than the pyramids, older than the Pyrenees. As old as time itself.

Eventually I began to notice little streams. They ran lightly along the ground, and along the walls, sometimes dipping under them, and in some places climbing over them.

My first guess was that it had to be water. But the rivulets were too bright, too silvery, too *syrupy*, with whispers of soft colors moving like breath just below the surface.

And as we passed a particularly bright one, some kind of bird—a dove, maybe—suddenly burst out of the shallow water as if bursting out of a bottomless ocean.

It went darting through the air, quick as a thought, and in the span of a heartbeat I watched it go through its entire life cycle: one moment, a baby bird, the next full-grown, and the next nothing but gray, fluttering bones.

And then it was gone, plunging beak-first into another stream.

For a long time, no one moved. When we finally started walking again, no one said a word.

CHAPTER FIFTY-SIX

— • —

THE VANISHING PASSAGE

(1)

As we marched on through the dark, the massive walls that crowded the passageway began to retreat far t h e r a n d f a r t h e r into the shadows while the shadows themselves seemed to grow closerandcloser; and soon the only part of the maze that was visible was the narrow stony bridge beneath our feet.

Currents of freezing-cold air howled up from the chasm below and swirled our clothes and our hair and made the reddish flames of the torches hiss in protest.

About halfway across the bridge, it split into three even more narrow, even more crumbly-looking bridges.

"Which way, Antares?" whispered my mom.

I closed my eyes, trying to feel for true north, but the compass needle in my stomach had begun to spin in crazy circles, just like the rest of the compasses.

"I—I'm not sure . . ." I admitted.

"Not sure is *not* a direction," hissed the rat-faced priest, his hood flapping noisily about his whiskery mouth, revealing only the sharp, yellow gleam of his teeth. "Focus, *boy*!"

I tried, and as I tried, I felt the faintest of tugs straight ahead. "Middle," I said. "I think it is mid—"

A rumbling, grinding, splitting sound echoed through the shadows. The bridge shuddered. Cracks appeared in the stones ahead and behind us, spiraling outward toward the edges.

"It's collapsing!" cried one of the priests.

"RUN!" my dad roared.

So that's exactly what we all did.

Slabs of withering stone split and splintered, dissolving underneath our feet as we raced through the dark. The cold air turned to fire in my throat. My feet flew across the crumbling stone. Up ahead the torches of the priests bounced and bobbed like flaming buoys. I chased them even while a hungry, hollow sound like the opening of some gigantic, stony mouth rumbled in the shadows, and then we reached the other side, scrambling through a curtain of sticky cobwebs just as what was left of the bridge suddenly fell away, plunging into the chasm below.

Several moments later, a soldier approached the edge of the chasm with cautious steps, peering uneasily down. "We're trapped!" he cried.

"Not trapped," answered my mom. "*Behold!*"

Over the chasm, back the way we'd come, I saw something impossible. Chunks of stone and bits of crumbly rock were beginning to float up out of the chasm in reverse. They tumbled backward through the air, spiraling against any logical influence of gravity, and began fitting themselves together, forming huge concrete pillars. The pillars settled over nothing and upon nothing as more bits and crumbles floated out of the darkness to join them. They fused and merged at the points where they'd crumbled and cracked, erasing every fracture, every fissure, and forming solid pieces of bridge again.

Within a matter of mintocks—maybe two, *max*—a brand-new bridge stretched across the chasm, gleaming gray in the torchlight.

"*It decays and is born again . . .*" murmured one of the priests.

"Like all things," answered my mother.

CHAPTER FIFTY-SEVEN

— • —

THE HEART OF THE LABYRINTH

The whisper of madly spinning compass needles was the only sound as we marched on, deeper and deeper into this maze of turning, twisting halls and endlessly forking passageways.

We were now in a more ancient part of the maze. The ground wasn't quite dirt, it wasn't quite clay, it wasn't quite stone. The streams were deeper here, they flowed stronger here, and I could see that the shapes and colors moving just below their surface were actually places—*faces!*

People moving in fields and in towns, through faraway landscapes. Places I hardly recognized. People laughing and talking and dancing. But the weirdest part? I thought I could *hear* them . . . It sounded like they were calling out to me. Inviting me to come closer, to look, to see, to—

Strong hands gripped my shoulders. They spun me roughly around, and I saw my dad standing over me, his expression grim.

"Time is a seducer," he whispered. "Do not stare into the little rivers or it will sweep you away . . ."

2

Round and round the maze wound as we plunged deeper and deeper underground. Every now and again, we'd come across complete human skeletons in the walls. Their bony hands reaching, their hollow, empty eyes staring dead ahead. They seemed to have been swallowed alive by the stone—swallowed while still moving. They were not a pleasant sight.

Soon the passage split off again: two choices. And as was quickly becoming their annoying little habit, one of the priests rasped, "Which way?"

And so I closed my eyes again, to feel for it, when—

(*Dun't let'em reach the source—not yet.*)

Navigator.

It was Navigator's voice!

She'd spoken directly into my mind.

And her words had carried with them something else—something like an intuition: she was planning a surprise attack. No, they *all* were . . . Magdavellía, my dad, and her!

But they weren't ready.

Not yet.

They needed time or the opportunity or maybe both. And since I could help with at least one of those, I concentrated, felt something like a tug off to my right, and said, "Left . . . The way is left."

3

My plan was simple. Just take everyone on a wild goose chase and buy the three some time. Which, considering the fact that we were all wandering around a mind-bogglingly massive gloomy labyrinth, shouldn't have been too difficult. Except it *was*, because my every wrong move was plain as day for everyone to see.

The first time I chose wrong we barely made it twenty yards before the ground turned all soft and gray, like quicksand, and three priests were suddenly swallowed up, torches and all!

The second time, we stumbled right into some kind of trap: someone stepped on a loose stone in the floor, which triggered an avalanche of dirt and rocks, and several more priests (and a bunch of soldiers) were buried alive.

The third, I wasn't even sure what happened. The shadows became so thick that they swallowed every scrap of torchlight, and the next moment, there was a lot of screaming and tearing sounds, and when we'd all run back the way we came, several more soldiers were missing.

It was just like my mom had said: *every wrong turn equaled death.* And I was beginning to think that if I just kept this up long enough there wouldn't even be a need for a sneak attack, because there wouldn't be any bad guys left.

Unfortunately, the rat-faced priest was already onto me . . .

"That's the *third* wrong choice in a row!" he hissed, whirling toward my mom. "Look at my instrument. Look at the *needle!*"

"It's not settling," she observed.

"No, but it has never once pointed in *that* direction—not once! Which means it cannot *possibly* be true north. The boy is lying to us . . . *Fools* he is playing us for!"

"How would you know, *rat?*" snapped my dad. "That compass of yours is *worthless* in here!"

"On the contrary! I designed this as a *learning* instrument . . . Thus, at every turn in the maze where the boy chose correctly (and I know this because there were no penalties for that choice), I inputted it into my compass, so that it has been gradually calibrating and has, in fact, already predicted his previous five *correct* choices in a row. However, the last three *incorrect* ones, it did not agree with." He gave a particularly ratty, particularly fiendish grin. "It seems the truth is quite the reverse: it is, in fact, *technology* that is on the verge of rendering human talent *worthless* . . ."

"Antares?" whispered my mother, and I heard myself swallow.

"Yeah?"

"Are you purposefully leading us astray?"

"I—*what? No.*" I could feel her rooting around in my head now. In my thoughts. And concentrating, I tried blocking her out. But it was pointless. I would've had a better chance trying to arm-wrestle a *grizzly bear.*

"You force my hand," she said after a moment. "Move his companions to the head of the company."

And immediately the soldiers began shoving Magdavellía, my dad, Navigator, Pal, and The Shubba toward the front. They all struggled and shouted and shoved back (well, besides Pal, who was nearly passed out), but there was only so much struggling and shoving you could do against twelve-foot-tall yetis.

My mom's fierce eyes locked on me. "Remember," she warned in an intense whisper, "to stray off the path is death. You wouldn't lead your friends to their deaths, would you?"

CHAPTER FIFTY-EIGHT

RATMAN'S FOLLY

The answer to that was, of course, *no*. Which meant that leading us the wrong way was no longer an option. Which meant that all I could do now was stall. Basically, just take my sweet time picking a path. And that meant game over. Because even with all my delays, all my pauses and all my playacting, I could feel us moving ever closer to the source. And soon we came to yet another choice in the maze.

The path to our right seemed to run on forever, stony and cold like the rest of this place. The one on the left narrowed as it went, choked with saw-grass and glowing green fungi, and the gnarled trunks of oily black trees.

I closed my eyes, feeling for true north again, and felt its pull—easily, too easily now—and said (even though I really, *really* didn't want to), "Right. The way is right."

But the words had barely left my mouth before the rat priest shrieked, "WRONG!"

And everyone froze.

Everyone turned.

Everyone stared.

"The boy lies!" he hissed, his whiskers quivering with rage. "My compass shows it is *that* way! Not right, but *LEFT*!"

I watched my mom's eyes slip slowly shut. She looked . . . *disappointed.* "Left," she said at last, and the soldiers began shoving us all in that direction.

"Mom, no!" I shouted. "His compass is *WRONG*! It's the other way! Read my mind. Do whatever! I'm telling the truth!"

My mom hesitated.

The rat priest noticed.

"You don't *believe him*, do you, Aella? My Priestess, we all know the legends . . . The source is *verdant*, overflowing with life. *Behold!* The maze itself now points the way!"

When my mother still hesitated, the ratman lost all patience. "Very well. Then I shall *prove* him a liar!"

And he began marching with the two tiny priests scuttling along behind him, hauling the big, heavy batteries on their tiny, bent backs.

They made it maybe thirty yards down the tree-choked passage before the rodent priest abruptly shouted, "Behold! No danger here! The boy lies . . . And he might very well be convincing himself of the wrong choice so as to make reading his mind useless!"

My mom was silent for a moment. Then she said, "Go."

"Mom, no—*please!* That's not true!" I screamed. "It's *not!*" But the soldiers were already pushing, already shoving us all that way.

"We mustn't allow the boy to distract us any longer," I heard the humanoid rat say. "We now stand on the *precipice* of history. Simultaneously on the edge of yesterday and on the foothills of tomorrow!"

Then he proudly proclaimed, "The boy's talents are now obsolete. My instrument is all we need!"

And those were the last words that ever came out of his whiskery, rat-like mouth, because right then, just as he took his very next step, the cynical rat vanished, as if he'd stepped right off the edge of a cliff.

A murmur of shock and surprise passed over the remaining priests as several soldiers rushed to the spot where he'd disappeared.

"A pit!" one cried.

"And nearly invisible!" cried another. "Hidden in shadow!"

My mom, meanwhile, stood absolutely silent as my dad came silently up beside her, grinning. "Apparently, his compass still had a bit to learn . . ." he remarked.

CHAPTER FIFTY-NINE

—— • ——

A STAR AMONG STARS

The other passage—the one that *didn't* lead into some bottomless pit—ran on, straight as an arrow, for almost three hundred yards. It didn't curve or bend or twist, and about halfway down, I began to feel Navigator in my head again, telling me to stall.

So when we came to the next place where the maze split, I just stood there staring up at the huge ivy-carpeted walls and shaking my head like I was totally and completely lost.

"What's wrong?" asked my mom.

"—I'm not sure which way," was what I said, but the truth, of course, was exactly the opposite. I knew the way. I could feel it as clearly as ever.

"Antares, concentrate . . ."

"I *am*. But—"

"*Concentrate* . . ."

And after another mintock she said, "Well?"

I started shaking my head again, doing my best acting job. "I—I don't know." But I didn't think I was winning any Oscars with this performance.

My mom's eyes again slipped shut. She obviously didn't buy it. "Why do you insist on lying to me, Antares?"

"I'm not."

"Why are you making this more difficult than it has to be?"

"I'm *not*." Then, feeling suddenly cornered, desperate, I said—pleaded, really: "Mom, let's just forget about all this, okay? It's too dangerous. Let's get outta here. Let's—*let's just go home and be a family again* . . ." If it sounded like I was begging, it's because I was. Begging was all I had left.

"I would love nothing more," she said in a tender way, gently stroking my cheek with the back of one pale hand, and I could feel in her voice that she meant it, too. "But this world has been poisoned, and only we hold the antidote. Now, show me the way, Antares."

"I don't know, okay? *I. Don't. Know.*" And this time I squeezed my mind shut, rolling it up, tight, tight—like a fist, before she could get in.

A disappointed sigh escaped my mother's lips. "Understand that you brought this upon yourself . . ."

In a flash, the fingers of her right hand snapped open and, in her palm, like magic or illusion, appeared a dagger of glittering golden light.

Then it became a blur, too fast to see, as she flung it through the air.

An instant later, Magdavellía's eyes flew open as it struck her through the heart like a lightning bolt. She swayed for a moment, and her mouth closed and her skin paled, and then her legs suddenly gave out and she collapsed.

"NO!" my dad cried, catching her. Gently, carefully, he eased her to the hard, dusty ground, and I was there in a heartbeat, holding Mags's hand. Squeezing it.

Her wide, unfrightened eyes were staring up at me, unblinking. "I'm sorry," she whispered, and already I could feel the coldness creeping into her skin.

I searched her face. "Sorry? What could you possibly be sorry for?"

"Lying to you. I should have told you who I was. But"—she winced against some invisible pain, and I winced with her—"but I so desperately wanted to . . . *forget*."

"Forget what?"

"Everything."

"Why?"

"Because I never wanted to be empress," she confessed. Then, trembling and paling even as I held her: "There's nothing special about me, Antares . . . I might share my parents' blood but not their heart, and certainly not their skill. I could never lead such a great people. And especially not at such an hour, with all the Rym come to the edge of doom. —*Forgive me*."

"There's nothing to forgive," I said, squeezing her hand again. "And you're so *wrong* . . . There *is* something special about you. Maybe you can't see it or maybe you don't wanna see it, but I've seen it every second of every day since the moment you came crawling out of that hole in my cell." She flinched, giving a watery laugh, and I said, "You're the smartest, bravest, kindest person I've ever met. *Ever*. And you'd make the greatest empress the Rym has ever *seen*. I know you would."

Her eyes were fluttering now, barely open, but as her fingers squeezed mine, I saw they were still my favorite color: the color of courage.

Pressing my hot, sweaty cheek against her cold, dry one, I whispered, "Please don't go, Mags . . . *Please*." But even as my words drifted through space between us, I could've sworn I felt her soul drift past them and away.

"Aella, *WHY???*" raged my dad.

And the Mystic—I couldn't think of her as my mom, no, not anymore—said, "Because her parents were a nuisance, and she seems an unfortunate victim of morphic resonance."

Shaking my head, only shock holding back my tears, I stared numbly down at Magdavellía. She wasn't bleeding, but she didn't seem to be breathing, either.

The phantom dagger had vanished, but there was a slit in the shape of a blade in her top and a scar in the shape of the slit in her skin.

"What'd she stab her with??" I breathed.

"A psionic dagger," answered my dad. "A blade of the mind. More deadly than any steel."

"What??"

"The most powerful psychics can conjure metaphysical weapons," he told me. "They can kill with thoughts," he explained. "And your mother is probably the most powerful psychic on this *planet*."

"Pal! Pal, get over here already!" cried Navigator.

The Martian bent over the dying empress. His long, flat fingers spread above the scar in her skin and the palm of his skinny green hand began to glow bright blue.

"Is she going to be okay?" I said, swallowing, breathing, everything around me wobbling and spinning.

Suddenly, a cold chill ran through me as I remembered Magdavellía's words—her premonition. The one she'd revealed back on *La Princhepessa*. How she'd seen herself die in some ancient, stony labyrinth. But—

But she'd also said that it didn't make any sense.

That you couldn't see yourself die if you were already dead.

So maybe that meant that she *wasn't* going to die!

That she was going to be okay!

I turned toward Pal with a sudden rush of hopefulness. "She's gonna be okay, right? I mean, she's gonna make it, right??"

But the Martian ignored me, and when he ignored me, I erupted, "I SAID, SHE'S GONNA BE ALL RIGHT, RIGHT?!"

Finally, Pal's large, dome-shaped head slowly lifted. Those large melon-like eyes found mine, and he whispered a single word, only two measly letters, but they shattered everything, my entire world.

"No."

I felt like I was falling even though I was sitting, drowning even though I was breathing. Tears I could hardly feel tumbled hotly down my cheeks. And then I heard my dad and Navigator begin to cry, too.

"*Magdavellía* . . ." I squeezed her hand again. And again. And again. And again. But this time, she didn't squeeze back.

Pal's slim shoulders had fallen. His voice was small—incredibly small—and filled with incredible sadness. "She now rests in the Heaventree . . . A star among stars forever."

I felt like I was falling again.

Nothing about this moment seemed real.

A second later, I realized Aella was standing over me. The many gems on her many rings sparkled as her fingers reached out for mine. "Come now, Antares . . . Show me the way."

And I just exploded, shoving her hand away. Shoving *her* away. "GET AWAY FROM ME! *YOU MONSTER!*"

But she caught my wrist, her grip intensely strong. "Don't you understand, my child? Death haunts all living things. But we can *change* that . . . You must only lead me to the source."

"*I hate you*," I growled, staring up at those poison green eyes. "You're pure evil . . ."

The Mystic gave me a quiet look of pity. "No," she said softly. "I am simply inevitability."

CHAPTER SIXTY

THE THRONE OF TIME

I walked on in a daze, hardly slowing when the maze split, hardly stopping to think when I started down another hall, around another turn, through another passageway—

Antares . . .

. . . *listen to me*

Antares . . .

. . . *too close*

—and kept walking with only that pull in my stomach and my heavy feet dragging me on and on—

(Magdavellía was gone Magdavellía was gone She was gone She was gone gone Magdavellía was gone She was gone forever)

． ． ． *listen*

Antares . . .

． ． ． *far enough*

—and on and on and on.

Antares . . .

． ． ． *listen*

． ． ． *listen to me*

． ． ． ANTARES!!

Bright lights battered my eyes. I blinked, gazing painfully around. We had entered a vast, dazzling space. Some kind of subterranean cave.

Here the maze ended, and here, at its deepest part, was a secret garden. A sparkling oasis sprung up in the dark heart of the labyrinth.

The air was clear and cool and pure, and the walls and floors and ceilings were lush with vegetation. But this was no ordinary garden. The thick flower beds that grew out of the ground in bushels and in bunches were every shade of the number five, and all around us I could smell the sharp scent of geometry hanging in the air like the scent of jasmine on a rainy day.

"*The Throne Room of Eternity . . .*" murmured the Mystic as if fallen into a foggy trance. "Sought for over nine *thousand* years by all wise enough to seek it. Yet, we are the first, perhaps since its very builders, to step foot inside this place."

A mintick later, nearly all the priests—and all at once—cried, "High Priestess, *behold! The Source!*"

On the opposite side of the chamber was what appeared to be the shore of a vast and beautiful ocean. An intense silvery glow radiated from its watery depths—so strong that it dimmed the blazing flame of the torches. But it wasn't like LED light, and it wasn't like fluorescent light. It was a dazzling, lovely light. A cool light—but somehow warm and inviting. It shimmered and it shone, it sparkled and it glowed, and after all the darkness and staring into shadows, I couldn't look steadily at it.

Near the shore water bubbled and waves broke constantly, flowing into smaller streams and creeks, then plunging into gaps and cracks and crevasses, which disappeared into the deep places of the earth.

And now, for the first time, the Mystic's voice trembled when she spoke. "The Wellspring of Knowledge, the Fount of Youth, the Throne of Earthly Power and Wealth: the very *River of Time* . . ." Her burning green eyes shifted slowly to me. "The light you see is leylight, the illumination produced by ley and fey lines. And there—in that very river—is the central point from which all the mystic currents of the Earth flow forth." She paused, as if to bask in the moment. "Can you feel the weight of eons pressing down upon us?"

What I noticed next was almost incomprehensible. Beyond the shore was not a wall of glittery stone, as I'd thought on first glance. Instead there was nothing. Nothing at all.

No walls.

No borders.

No more maze.

Just a vast, limitless expanse of nothingness. Empty, starry space. The edge of the temple, if not of the world, stretching on and on, far beyond what any eye could ever dream to see. And a great unseen wind blew constantly from that direction, frigid and somehow alien.

"We must hurry," whispered the High Priestess. "For we do not know what may lurk on the edge of eternity."

With a swipe of his monstrous claws, a yeti soldier ripped open a large duffel bag, producing wet suits, bubble masks, and two pairs of water shoes.

"*Dress*," he commanded in a growling, beastly voice, handing me one of each, and I didn't care enough not to.

Another soldier tied one end of a thin silvery rope around the Mystic's wrist and the other tightly around mine. "So we don't lose each other in the water," she explained.

I didn't respond. I didn't care. But as I stood there, feeling nothing and staring down at nothing in particular, I heard, not in the ears of my head, but in the ears of my heart:

Do NOT take her into the source . . .

You must go alone.

Antares, do you hear me? You. ALONE!

I was just barely aware enough to realize that it was my father's voice. And just barely aware enough to think back, *How?*

Then I got my answer.

With perfect synchrony (and astonishing quickness), my dad whirled. They *both* whirled—him and Navigator—striking a pair of soldiers in the stomach before whirling again, flinging out their hands and disarming three more soldiers (yetis) from almost twenty yards away. The guards' long silver spears clattered heavily to the ground, then one leapt up, as if pulled by an invisible string, right into my dad's waiting hands.

He jabbed the air with the spear, two quick stabs. And light—a brilliant blue light—exploded from its razor tip. The next moment, two more soldiers collapsed on the grass-carpeted ground, smoking and twitching.

In a flash my dad spun again, leveling the spear on the Mystic. He'd caught her off guard. Totally. Completely. "Goodbye, my love," he whispered, and with another brilliant flash of the spear—

—I heard, not in the ears of my head, but in the ears of my heart:

Do NOT take her into the source . . .

You must go alone.

Antares, do you hear me . . . ? You. ALONE!

I was just barely aware enough to realize that it was my father's voice. And just barely aware enough to—

Wait.

No!

Time had looped.

Again!

Just like it had when we'd first crashed on the island!

It had looped back around and now—

Now, she *knew* . . .

Panicking, my dad and Navigator did what they'd already done, spinning, whirling—but this time, it didn't work.

Because this time up went the Mystic's left hand and then back went the mermaid, flung viciously into the rock wall.

I heard a sickening *crack!*, and even before she'd hit the ground, something like an electric sword crackled to life in the Mystic's other hand, stretching eight, nine, ten yards across the throne room.

With the sizzling, electric tip of her psychic sword she drove my dad back, back, back against the rocky wall. Then her lips thinned into a humorless smile as she whispered, "This close to the source, time becomes quite unpredictable. Goodbye, my love."

She was strong. Too strong.

And way too fast. There was nothing I could do.

She swung her sword.

A cry erupted from my dad's lips.

Then he was gone.

My dad was gone.

So was Navigator.

So was Magdavellía.

And so was any hope of stopping the Mystic.

CHAPTER SIXTY-ONE

—— • ——

A RIPPLE IN TIME

The remaining priests, huddled closely around the water's edge, hadn't noticed the fighting. They were all too busy babbling amongst themselves, and to themselves, and waving the fiery heads of their torches over the silvery waters in something like a trance.

For a moment I watched them through tear-blind eyes—watched as The Shubba tried to blend into their group—then turned to the Mystic as the weight of her gaze fell on me.

"It seems that out of your entire company only the rat and the alien showed *true* intellect," she said coolly, haughtily, "and for that they shall be rewarded . . . So tell me, Martian, what is it that you desire most?"

Pal, meanwhile, hadn't so much as blinked from the second we'd entered this place. And he was still just standing there, trembling on his skinny green legs, probably on the verge of passing out. But somehow he managed, "M—m—my *courage*, High Priestess."

And the Mystic grinned in a pleased sort of way. "Ah, yes. Your *antennas*. And I shall make it so . . . I shall make it so."

She'd just bent to pick up the other bubble mask when I heard Pal say (in a voice so small I'd almost thought I'd imagined it), "No. *You don't have to.*"

"And why is that?" asked the Mystic, a confused frown wrinkling her forehead.

The Martian's lips did not move, but all the same I heard: "*Because simply the will to muster one's courage is a little act of courage all on its own.*"

I froze. Those were Magdavellía's words. The *exact* words she'd said back on *La Princhepessa*.

And now I saw the remaining stumps of the Martian's antennas begin to wiggle on the bald green dome of his head. They looked like two baby worms trying to squirm out of the earth.

And now I understood.

Our eyes met—earthling and spaceling, terrestrial and extraterrestrial—and I whispered, "Drink deeply of the cup of courage, my friend."

The Martian nodded. Yeah, we both would drink.

For Magdavellía, I thought.

And for my tribe, he thought back.

Suddenly the machete strapped to the leg of the nearest yeti leapt out of its leather cover. It came whistling through the air, end over end, and stopped an inch from my face.

Snatching it, I whipped the weapon down in a shallow arc to slice the silvery cord tying me to the Mystic.

At the same instant, an invisible but tremendous wall of energy rose up between us—rose up like a tidal wave! And a second later, I heard Pal think:

Now, Antares—go!

The Mystic stiffened, panic narrowing her dark eyes to even darker slits. "Antares, no—"

But it was too late. I was already running, already pushing my way past the circle of babbling priests and crashing through the surface of the (alwaysflowing neverflowing) waters.

But it wasn't really anything like jumping into a river. It wasn't like jumping into a pond or a pool or a lake or even the ocean. It wasn't like jumping into water at all, in fact. It was more like being born. Transitioning—in an instant—from darkness to light, blindness to sight, death to life. I could now feel time . . . I could *feel* yesterday, and right now, and tomorrow, and the next day, and on and on until the end of everything, and I wasn't swimming so much as floating or floating so much as drifting or walking or breathing or standing still or falling, but I could feel myself flowing toward the source of it all, toward true north, its pull as clear and strong as ever, calling out to me like some sweet half-remembered song, and so I swam and I ran and I flew toward its tug, momentarily glimpsing the edge of the world out there in the infinite beyond, the very edge of everything where it all fell away to nothingness and where nothing at all waited in the vast, ever-expanding emptiness (except, of course, for space itself; and light; and let's not forget that eternal force that holds all things together), and I felt myself drawn up into its flow, up, up, up, then up some more, and then I was outside it—outside time—

No longer bound by it—by the seconds, the minutes, the hours—(and suddenly I knew its shape—it was *every* shape! All of them folded and twisted into one: the shape of time!) and I found myself flipping through the years and centuries and millennia like you might flip through an old yearbook

Time was just a fragile thing that I could hold in the small of my hands

When do I go?

When do I choose?

And a voice from Somewhere, Somewhen, Someplace said, *Go to the moment you could not live on without ever having lived again*
And then I knew
And then I was reaching
And then I touched—

CHAPTER SIXTY-TWO

●

TIME AND AGAIN

—and then I was here again.

In her arms again and she was in mine again and I was smiling into her eyes and she was smiling into mine again.

Heivet's anthem was playing in the background. Scratchy, scratchy on the old record player.

And I could feel the sting and salt of the cold seaborne air on my face again.

(Here again.)

And the moon was smiling down on all of us again, on everything again.

(Here again.)

And Magdavellía squeezed my hand again.

"How can we save it?" she asked me again. "How can we stop what's to come and change what will be? How do we save the world?"

And I opened my mouth again, to say what I'd said before again—

Only this time, and for the first time, so very different than last time, what I said was, **"What if I told you I knew how?"**

Because this time, unlike the last time, I did know the answer. And this time, unlike last time, and without fear or fret or fright or shame—

I started by saving my own.

I kissed her.

EPILOGUE

RYMWORLD
TODAY
WAR IS AVERTED!
celebration sweeps the rim

LUCY
WORLD'S
LARGEST
DIAMOND
SOLD
at Auction

MÜ TIMES
ANTARES the ADVENTURING
SPHERER SAVES RYMWORLD

PLEIONG GAZETTE
THE EMPRESS OF AGARTHA
FULFILLS HER PARENTS QUEST
— FOILS THE MYSTIC! —

ACKNOWLEDGMENTS

———————•———————

A huge, heartfelt thank-you to my brilliant editor, Maggie Lehrman. You are truly a joy to work with. Your energy and passion for your craft have made this whole experience one I will forever cherish. I can't put into words how grateful I am for all the time you devoted to Antares, Magdavellía, and the rest of the gang. Thank you for loving their story from your first read. You are a writer's dream editor!

To my publisher, Andrew Smith. Thank you for believing in *The Shape of Time* and for publishing such beautiful books!

To Chelsea Hunter, for designing a jacket so stunning that it is immediately going up on my wall for display! You're amazing—thank you!

To Erin Slonaker, eagle-eyed copy editor extraordinaire. Your attention to detail is awe-inspiring and I am so grateful for all of your hard work.

To Samuel Rodriguez, for one of the coolest covers EVER! I'm still blown away!

To Julia Iredale, whose whimsical illustrations perfectly captured the spirit of this book. You rock!

My deepest gratitude to my agent Rena Rossner.

And to the rest of the amazing Abrams family—THANK YOU!!!

ABOUT THE AUTHOR

———•———

RYAN CALEJO is an award-winning author born and raised in sunny South Florida. His critically acclaimed Charlie Hernández series has been featured in half a dozen state reading lists and earned starred reviews from *Booklist* and *Kirkus Reviews*, was a Texas Bluebonnet Master List selection, and won an International Latino Book Award, a Sunshine State Young Readers Award, and a Florida Book Award (Gold Medal). He lives in Miami, Florida.